"You w
told me

"And you left!" Liv shouted back. "You should have just asked me to marry you in the first place!"

"How could I? I didn't know about her!"

Hunter watched Liv's expression cave. He saw the tears gather in her eyes, shining and wet.

"Exactly," she said, clipping off the syllables.

She put the car in gear. Hunter moved around in front of it to stop her from driving off. She wouldn't actually run over him. At least, he didn't think so.

"'Exactly'?" he demanded. "What does that mean?"

Liv stuck her head out the window. "Why did you need to know about the baby, Hunter, to want to stay with me?"

She gunned the engine. He leaped aside just in time to avoid being flattened. He watched her car smoke up the road.

He scrubbed a palm over his mouth, still tasting her. Still wanting her.

He realized he could hate her for that alone.

Dear Reader,

It's always cause for celebration when Sharon Sala writes a new book, so prepare to cheer for *The Way to Yesterday*. How many times have you wished for a chance to go back in time and get a second chance at something? Heroine Mary O'Rourke gets that chance, and you'll find yourself caught up in her story as she tries to make things right with the only man she'll ever love.

ROMANCING THE CROWN continues with Lyn Stone's *A Royal Murder*. The suspense—and passion—never flag in this exciting continuity series. Catherine Mann has only just begun her Intimate Moments career, but already she's created a page-turning military miniseries in WINGMEN WARRIORS. *Grayson's Surrender* is the first of three "don't miss" books. Look for the next, *Taking Cover*, in November.

The rest of the month unites two talented veterans— Beverly Bird, with *All the Way,* and Shelley Cooper, with *Laura and the Lawman*—with exciting newcomer Cindy Dees, who debuts with *Behind Enemy Lines*. Enjoy them all—and join us again next month, when we once again bring you an irresistible mix of excitement and romance in six new titles by the best authors in the business.

Leslie J. Wainger
Executive Senior Editor

Please address questions and book requests to:
Silhouette Reader Service
U.S.: 3010 Walden Ave., P.O. Box 1325, Buffalo, NY 14269
Canadian: P.O. Box 609, Fort Erie, Ont. L2A 5X3

All the Way
BEVERLY BIRD

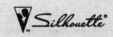

INTIMATE MOMENTS™

Published by Silhouette Books

America's Publisher of Contemporary Romance

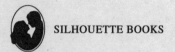 **SILHOUETTE BOOKS**

ISBN 0-373-27243-X

ALL THE WAY

Copyright © 2002 by Beverly Bird

Books by Beverly Bird

Silhouette Intimate Moments   Silhouette Romance

Emeralds in the Dark #3   *Ten Ways To Win Her Man* #1550
The Fires of Winter #23
Ride the Wind #139
A Solitary Man #172
A Man Without Love #630
A Man Without a Haven #641
A Man Without a Wife #652
Undercover Cowboy #711
The Marrying Kind #732
Compromising Positions #777
†*Loving Mariah* #790
†*Marrying Jake* #802
†*Saving Susannah* #814
It Had To Be You #970
I'll Be Seeing You #1030
Out of Nowhere #1090
In the Line of Fire #1138
All the Way #1173

Silhouette Desire

The Best Reasons #190
Fool's Gold #209
All the Marbles #227
To Love a Stranger #411

*Wounded Warriors
†The Wedding Ring

BEVERLY BIRD

has lived in several places in the United States, but she is currently back where her roots began on an island in New Jersey. Her time is devoted to her family and her writing. She is the author of numerous romance novels, both contemporary and historical. Beverly loves to hear from readers. You can write to her at P.O. Box 350, Brigantine, NJ 08203.

For Justin,
Jeff Gordon's good luck charm and greatest fan (mine, too!)

Prologue

Saturday, September 3
Millsboro, Delaware

The murmur of the diners' voices was muted and pleasant, the air redolent with hints of garlic and bread baking in the open-hearth kitchen. Olivia Slade Guenther was content, enjoying herself and the time with her daughter, then *he* walked into the restaurant.

His gaze rolled idly over them, then it jerked back to pin them into their flamingo-pink, not-quite-leather booth. Liv felt shock fly through her—icy and hot all at once, searing her nerve endings, then numbing them. Panic gripped her and she thought of running.

It was out of the question. For one thing, Vicky was still digging into her buttermilk-fried chicken, and she was chattering in judgmental tones about the pink rococo ceiling over their heads. And he was between them and the door.

Besides, Liv was damned if she'd let him see her sweat. She gathered air into her lungs and fell back on one of the many lessons she had learned at her Navajo grandmother's knee. *You are what you think you are.*

"I'm tough as nails," she muttered aloud.

"What?" Her daughter looked up at her, still chewing.

"Eat your dinner."

Vicky swallowed, frowned. "I was."

"Then concentrate on it."

"Mom, it's just chicken—and it's not even as good as Aunt Kiki's. How much can I think about it?"

There was that, Liv thought. Vicky was often too smart for her own good—not to mention her mother's.

Hunter Hawk-Cole was three feet away now, approaching them.

"Don't say a word," Liv hissed under her breath.

"How come?"

"Because I said so." Liv groaned aloud. They were the very words she had promised herself she would never say to a child of hers should she be blessed enough to have one. Then she opened her mouth and they fell out, shattering like fine china on the restaurant table. Less than a minute after he had walked back into her life, Hunter was once again challenging everything she knew about herself.

He stopped beside their table. One glance at Vicky and his midnight-blue eyes narrowed with speculation. No matter that Vicky was small for her age, that she could easily have passed for seven or even six. No matter that Hunter had every reason to believe she was Johnny Guenther's daughter. Liv knew he'd figured it out that quickly—Vicky was his own.

Her heart started pistoning. Tough as nails indeed.

"Of all the gin joints in all the world..." Hunter's voice trailed off. "Well, Liv. What were the odds of us running into each other again on the East Coast?"

His voice had always reminded her of smoke. It had a way of sliding over her skin, of heating it to the point where she'd no longer needed promises. Liv grabbed her wineglass and downed half of its contents. "I was hoping for slim to none."

"Then you've turned into a gambler after all."

His words went through her like a knife that had been passed through flame. Liv was saved from answering by a group of Hunter's fans.

As soon as they recognized him, diners popped up from the surrounding tables like hyacinths in a May garden. They crowded him, holding out menus, napkins, a few prepurchased race-day programs. He signed each of them without a smile, accessible enough but keeping that look about him that she'd noticed on television. It said there was something inside him that no one would ever touch again.

She knew what had changed him—or at least what he'd probably like her to think it was. *Not you, Liv. You're the only person who ever knew when I was gone.* There had been anger and betrayal in his eyes when he had spoken those words to her, eight and a half years ago over a scarred oaken bar. But in the end, he'd gone.

When Hunter handed a menu back to a diner who was surely going to have to pay for it, silence proved to be too much for Vicky. She swallowed the last bite of her chicken. "What are you, famous or something?"

"Or something." Hunter finally grinned for Vicky's benefit. The curve of his mouth melted everything inside Liv as though the past eight and a half years hadn't happened.

"Are you a movie star?" Vicky asked.

Hunter rested his palms on the polished surface of the table to lean closer to her. Liv felt something shrivel inside her as the man and child went nose to identical nose—then there were those same blue eyes, the same onyx hair, that stubborn thrust of both their jaws.

Vicky did not look like Liv. And she didn't look like Johnny Guenther at all. At least, Liv didn't think so. She had never forgotten a plane or an angle of Hunter's face, but she had a hard time recalling Johnny's features.

"Nope," he told Vicky. "I drive cars."

"That's not special."

"It is when you do it very, very fast."

She thought about it. "My mom never does that."

His eyes angled off her, to Liv. "Still methodical about getting where you're going, Liv?"

"I'm exactly where I want to be, thanks." Her nerves were beginning to feel like cut crystal, painfully fragile under her skin.

"Divorced?" His dark-blue eyes fixed on her ringless left hand.

Liv let go of her wineglass as though a snake had suddenly appeared inside it. She dropped her hand to her lap, under the table.

"And touchy about it," he concluded.

"Now that all the social niceties have been exchanged," she replied, "you can feel free to go." Her throat felt too tight for the words.

He shot a brow up as though considering it, then he shook his head. "I don't see that happening this time around."

It was a promise and a threat. Liv had never known him to hesitate to make good on either one.

He straightened from their table, and she watched him stroll to one that had apparently been reserved for his party at the back of the restaurant. Those incredible blue eyes raked her one more time before he was seated. Liv took Vicky's hand quickly.

"Come on, honey. Let's go."

"But I want dessert! That bread pudding—" Vicky broke off when Liv practically lifted her from the booth.

"We'll stop at an ice cream stand on the way back to the motel," Liv promised.

Vicky wrinkled her nose. "Oh, yuck, Mom. Please."

"For once—just for once—couldn't you be a normal child?" But it wouldn't happen, Liv thought helplessly, it could never happen, because her daughter had been born into a lie and, to Liv's great despair, nothing in her life had ever been very normal at all.

Chapter 1

Friday, September 9
Jerome, Arizona

"*What on earth possessed you?*" Kiki Condor, Liv's partner and cook, actually yelled at her for one of the few times in their long, long friendship. She grabbed Liv's wrist and pried the remainder of a sourdough roll from her fingers.

Liv let it go reluctantly. Without the distraction of the roll, she knew she was in trouble.

Liv was a master at diverting conversations—six years of running a bed-and-breakfast and having various strangers troop through her home asking personal questions did that to a woman. The exceptions to the rule were Kiki and Hunter Hawk-Cole.

"When you tempt fate," Kiki continued, "you have to be prepared for it to jump up and bite you in the—"

"Hush," Liv warned quickly, automatically, but Vicky was out in the barn. The girl idolized her aunt Kiki, and she was never shy about repeating her words verbatim. Sometimes it was funny. Sometimes it had Liv trooping down to the school for parent-teacher conferences.

Liv tried again to change the subject. "You know, something about that recipe needs work."

"And why are you just telling me now?" Kiki demanded as though she hadn't spoken. "You've been home for five days!"

Because she'd dreaded just this sort of reaction, Liv thought. She licked crumbs from her fingers. "Nothing has happened since we ran into each other. I haven't heard from him."

Dig a hole over there, child, and dump the problem inside. Cover it up and walk away. It's yours no more. More wise words, Liv thought, from her grandmother. She'd dug a hole when she had come home from Delaware, had kicked Hunter in there and had heaped dirt on top of him, and true enough, he'd stayed put.

So far.

Kiki jammed the rest of the roll down the garbage disposal. "I want every specific detail."

Liv gave up. She went to the butcher block table and folded all 5'8" of herself into a chair there. Like their entire inn, the kitchen was done in western tones with an occasional Victorian touch—just as the place had been in its heyday. The floor and one wall were all aged brick. There were pretty rose-colored shutters on the windows instead of curtains. Old copper pots and utensils were strung across the ceiling. But the appliances were modern and state-of-the-art. Kiki had insisted that if she was going to cook for strangers, she was going to do it right. And though it had been Liv's own inheritance that had funded the inn's renovation from 1890's brothel to twentieth-century bed and breakfast, Liv hadn't tried to argue with her.

Liv scraped her long hair off her forehead and held it there. "Well, you already know that it happened at the trade show in Wilmington. Not at it exactly, but while I was there."

"I told you not to take Vicky to that show. Do you remember? Didn't I say I'd baby-sit while you were away?"

"She wanted to go and it seemed like a nice treat for her right before school started again."

Kiki planted her oven-mitted hands on her narrow hips. "You knew there was a NASCAR race in Delaware that weekend and you took her anyway. Are you crazy?"

"The race was in Dover! And the trade show was in Wilmington! These are two separate cities. No, wait, hold on a second." Liv held up a hand when Kiki opened her mouth one more time to berate her lack of judgment. "I got us a room fifty miles away from Dover in Millsboro. Our motel was way down near the southern border of the state. I took precautions. Vicky and I got up extra early every day of that show to drive all the way to Wilmington. What were the odds of Hunter coming to Millsboro the night before the race—for dinner? What were the odds of him suddenly deciding to mingle with his fans?"

"I'd say they were pretty damned good." Kiki shoved another tray of biscuits into the oven, apparently not impressed with Liv's assessment of them, either. "You took your daughter—his daughter—to a state the size of a postage stamp knowing that he would be there on the NASCAR circuit that same weekend. Did you want to run into him?"

"Oh, please." But the pain that flared inside her was every bit as unimaginable as it had been eight and a half years ago when she had sent him away. "It was a calculated risk."

"You always did stink at math."

It was true enough. Kiki handled all of the inn's bookkeeping for just that reason. Liv concentrated on what she was good at— charm, hospitality, service, and an uncanny knowledge of her state's history. Between the two of them, the Copper Rose had prospered.

"I've made it a point to understand this stock car racing," she said. "Hunter shouldn't have been fifty miles south of Dover that night. The drivers keep Winnebagos on the track property from Wednesday through Sunday. They qualify on Fridays. On Saturdays they have two or three practices before the race the next day. They do…I don't know…stuff to their engines. Adjustments. They spend all day Saturday priming those cars. Why would Hunter drive so far south for dinner with all that to do and a driver's meeting two hours before race time on Sunday?"

"Because he's Hunter and he's never played by the rules."

No one who had ever known the man could argue that one, Liv thought helplessly.

But she had never believed that Hunter could buck the rules, either. In a sport dominated by good ol' boys from the south, he had come out of the west—a half-breed Indian raised on a northern Arizona reservation, an intense young man with something of the devil in his eyes and in his soul. When he'd gotten the crazy idea to drive race cars, Liv had never believed that he'd be able to break into the NASCAR network.

She clapped a hand over her mouth as though to hold in the pain of the memories. It had always been something with Hunter, some new idea, some wild hair, taking him off again to a new challenge. She'd thought driving was just more of the same. He'd driven the truck series at first, then the Busch series, finally bursting onto the Winston Cup level four years ago. He was a natural behind the wheel of a car. Now, to Liv's reckoning, he had one Winston Cup somewhere in his possession because he'd topped the point standings last year. He did television commercials for his sponsors and he navigated the talk show circuit. The very thing that should have barred him from a sport filled with Dales and Bobby Joes and Beaus had turned out to be his magic. He was a dark, simmering, laconic American in the most original sense of the word, and he could make a stock car purr like a satisfied animal.

He'd found the one thing he could dedicate himself to…and it hadn't been her. So she had married someone else. Someone who would stay with her. She had never told him about the baby—*his* baby—that she had been carrying at the time.

Liv folded her arms on the kitchen table and slowly lowered her forehead to them. "I just wanted a real home again."

"We all wanted more than hogans and desert, Liv." Kiki banged a cookie sheet into the sink. "That's why we left."

"I never fitted in there, on the reservation. I know it was my birthright—a little bit, anyway—but I was always an outsider there. I spent six years there, craving what I'd lost when my sister and my parents died. I just wanted it back."

"And that is precisely why you shouldn't have gone anywhere near Dover on race weekend. Because Hunter wouldn't give it to you, and you never forgave him for it."

Liv looked up. That dull, hard throbbing came back to her chest, the same feeling that had pressed in on her all week since she had come home from Delaware. After seeing him just once, so briefly, she could taste him, smell him, feel him with every breath she took, all over again.

She *didn't* want him back—that was outrageous. She would never risk Vicky's stability that way. But she dreaded the thought that he would turn up, anyway. And she'd be easy enough to find. She'd never tried to hide.

He'd threatened to find her, after all. He'd promised.

Kiki wiped her hands on a dish towel. "We're going to turn on the cable sports channel right now. We're going to keep an eye on what Hunter Hawk-Cole is up to all weekend, at least as much as they'll tell us."

"The circuit takes him to Michigan this weekend." When Kiki looked at her sharply, Liv flushed then she defended herself. "I checked. I wanted to make sure he wasn't too close by. He can't wander in for a say-hi if he's in the Midwest."

"He could call. The TV will still tell us what he's up to while he's there."

Liv threw up her hands. "Do you think they mentioned on television that the bad boy of racing was going to have dinner in Millsboro last weekend?"

"No. But they might have said that he had a top-notch car and that he was confident. From that you could have deduced that he'd have some free time on his hands, that he wouldn't have his guys poking at that engine all night. If I had been there with you, we would have ordered pizza into the motel room."

Kiki had always been able to think practically in any fix. Liv wondered again, as she often did, why her friend wasn't a doctor or a geneticist. While Liv had been learning the hospitality trade in Flagstaff, Kiki had attended the University of Arizona, majoring in obscure scientific challenges. She'd earned a doctorate. Now she co-owned the inn with Liv, and she was as content at the oven and with their books as she'd ever been over test tubes.

"Okay." Liv flattened her palms on the table and pushed to her feet. "At least we'll know we can't hear from him when he's actually on the race track."

"Not unless he has a cell phone in his car."

"They're moving at better than 180 miles per hour!"

"Do you honestly think that would stop him?"

Liv winced at another onslaught of memories. "No."

"Okay, then." Kiki found the remote control to click on the television that was shelved against one corner of the kitchen ceiling. "But just for the record, I'm tying you to your desk all weekend in case you get any nifty ideas to go have dinner in Michigan."

Liv was in the stock car with him.

Hunter felt her there beside him as he warmed up in Saturday's practice session. There was no passenger seat, just empty space that wouldn't weigh him down, framed by a lot of metal bracing. She sat there, anyway. Sometimes she was a teenager again. At other times she was the woman he had met in Delaware.

"I've thought about it," the teenage Liv said. "I'm not going to chase the wind with you, Hunter. I've found someone who can give me a home, a family, everything I've always needed. You said when that happened, you would go away."

"I'm your family," he told her.

He'd been her family from the first time he'd seen her, Hunter thought now. She'd been living with her grandmother on the Navajo reservation. He'd met her on his first day at the district school there and he'd followed her home after classes to find her tending to Dinny Sandoval and her sheep. He'd been fascinated by her, enthralled by her, so different from all the others with her Irish-Navajo blood and her incredible, exotic face. So he'd kept coming around.

She'd only been twelve then, but the ache in her eyes had been as mature as a full-blown rose—for the life and the parents and the sister she'd lost in a freak accident that had exiled her in an alien land. She'd talked incessantly of babies, a family, and a white house with blue shutters in a city where a symphony played. As soon as she was old enough, she'd told him often, she was going to go and grab that dream.

They'd lain on their backs on the rocky ground and talked about it, the star-strewn desert night etched above them, passing a coveted bottle of ginger ale back and forth. The nearest store had been forty miles away, and neither of them had had access to a car, so they took care not to spill a drop.

Liv Slade didn't belong on that reservation any more than Hunter did—and except for one grandmother, he was pretty much Native American down to his bones. He'd landed in that school because of an ill-fated eagle hunt. It had been one adventure too many. His old man had packed him up and had shipped him off to live with his Navajo mother.

That clan hadn't particularly wanted him, either. He and Liv had both been strangers in a hostile country, and then they had found each other.

After high school, he'd escaped. He disappeared from northern Arizona for weekends at first, then for up to a week. Weeks turned into months sometimes, but he always came back eventually to check on Liv. He'd done passably well with the rodeo, could have been better, but the money wasn't there and it lacked the elusive something he needed. He joined the Army and found the restriction and discipline intolerable. She'd turned fifteen, sixteen, then seventeen while he was away. Her grandmother had died that last year while Hunter was in Louisiana, poling boats through alligator-infested bayous.

Liv had kept up the old woman's sheep on her own after that because if the authorities found out she was a minor living alone, they would come and whisk her off again. The reservation had never been home for her, but Liv was determined that she wasn't going anywhere else until she could do it on her own terms. She kept up the charade for almost a year, and the Anglo authorities never caught on.

That was the way he had left her in January that year, in Dinny's winter hogan alone, the old woman's clansmen close enough for comfort. Then he came back one day in June to find that the girl had gone and a woman had taken her place.

Hunter had driven up in his rattletrap pickup to find her wrestling in the dust with a lamb.

Already the heat had a dry, pressing weight, though it was barely midmorning. The lamb bleated in distress as she chased it, both of them kicking up red-brown dust that hung in the thin air. She had a syringe in one hand, held high as though it were a sword and she was about to plunge it into stone. Hunter stopped the truck and got out to watch her, enjoying the spectacle.

"Hey, you!" he called.

She didn't hear him. She pinned the lamb, straddling it, then she came up on her hands and knees. Her bottom was thrust in his direction, cupped in frayed, hacked-off denim. A horse might have kicked him in the chest for the impact the view had on him.

Sometimes the need to love her actually burned inside him. It was why he never stayed home too long.

He wasn't her dream. He was a man who needed to keep moving. He wasn't what she needed.

But, God, he cherished her.

She hooked her left arm around the animal's neck and raised her right hand again, armed with the needle. Then the lamb wriggled out from beneath her. Liv went after the animal at a fast crawl, her dark hair caught in a ponytail that streamed down her back until it finally splayed over each hip with her movement. Then she got to her feet in one fluid motion that had his twenty-year-old tongue cleaving to the roof of his mouth. She leaped at the little beast, going airborne.

"Jeez, Livie! You're going to kill yourself!"

But she didn't. She came down on top of the lamb, rolling with it, both arms wrapped around it now. She'd lost the syringe, and she swore a blue streak that had his jaw hanging. Still holding the animal, she groped in the rocky dirt for the needle. Just as he moved to get it for her, she found it and finally got it buried in the animal's flank.

When it was done, she let the lamb run off. She flopped over on her back, staring up at a sky that the heat had baked the color out of. She laughed, a woman's throaty chuckle of triumph that almost brought Hunter to his knees.

In all the time he'd known her, he'd never wanted her as much as he did in that moment. It took Hunter a moment to find his voice.

"My money was on you."

Liv sat up slowly enough that he had the sudden, uncanny feeling that she'd known he was there all along. "You didn't

have any money, pal, not the last time I checked.'' Her eyes
were too dark. They were usually a deep, chocolate brown, but
temper could turn them to the charred color of fired wood.
"That's it for the herd. As for you, fish or cut bait.''

He knew what she was talking about, couldn't pretend that he
didn't, even if it made something roar suddenly in his head and
sent his heart galloping.

Liv stood, then she leaned over to brush the dust off her legs.
*"Here's the thing, Hunter. I'm cleaning up my past here. Are
you part of it, or are you my future?''* She straightened and
crossed her arms over her chest. *"Do you want me or don't
you?''*

He thought that if he answered that honestly, he'd probably
be damned to hell for all eternity.

But Liv didn't seem to want words. She walked toward him
with that long, leggy stride of hers, then she yanked her
T-shirt over her head before he could reply and tossed it aside
into the dust. It was the reservation. There wasn't another hogan
for fifteen miles. She wasn't wearing a bra. Her breasts—and
oh, how he had fantasized about them over the years—were as
full and ripe as the rest of her. Her shorts rode low on her hips.
She stopped three strides from him.

*"I love you, Hunter. And I'm tired of waiting for you to grow
up.''*

He almost choked. *"For* me *to grow up?''*

Her voice dipped, losing some of its force. For a moment she
sounded almost as lost as she had been the first time he'd met
her. *"I want to be with you. I want to take at least one good
thing away from this place when I go. I want it to be you.''*

"Babe—''

*"I don't want promises from you, Hunter. I can take care of
the rest of my dreams on my own.''*

She leaped at him suddenly then, her arms around his neck,
her lithe legs wrapping around his waist, her mouth clamping
on his. She gave him no chance for finesse, no time for it. Something inside Hunter broke.

His hands found her bottom, holding her to him. Then they
were both down in the dust while his tongue dove for hers hun-
grily, an agony building inside him too fast. He dragged off her

*shorts, then his own clothes, then he found his way inside her
in one desperate thrust. She cried out, then she made a mewling
sound in her throat and clung to him, riding with him fast,
fiercely, crying out his name. And all Hunter could think was
that this time he'd really come home.*

A voice squawked in his headset, startling Hunter out of his
reverie. It was his spotter, a guy who stood on top of the grand-
stand with radio in hand and an eagle's view of the track. He
warned of pile-ups around the next curve and unseen cars traveling in his blind spots.

This time there was panic in the man's voice, and Hunter's
vision cleared to see the turn-two wall in front of him. He pulled
hard on the wheel, swerving around toward the apron of the
track again.

"What the hell are you doing?" the spotter bellowed. "Man,
you're all over the track!"

"Car feels a little loose." It was the term that described
how—at killer high speeds—the back end of a car could fishtail
and try to catch up with the front. "I'm just playing with it to
figure out how much we need to adjust."

Then he glanced at the nonexistent passenger seat one more
time. The grown-up Liv was there now.

Her perfect face was framed, not by straight, waist-length hair,
but by long layers, brown streaked with russet and tipped by
gold at the ends. She'd wanted him once. She had said she loved
him. Then she'd found someone else in four short weeks, and
she'd sent him away.

Now there was the matter of the child.

His child, Hunter thought. Not Guenther's. What had she
done? Why, Livie, why?

His spotter's voice began crackling in his ear again, so loud
now as to be almost wordless. Hunter focused on the track again.
The turn wall was in front of him one more time. He corrected
too fast, too hard. His reflexes were caught in the past.

The back end of the race car slid around and cracked into the
concrete, crumbling like paper in a giant's fist. Then he was
diving nose first toward the infield, coming down off the em-
bankment. Mikey Nolan, in the 42 car, had been coming up hard

behind him. He tried to avoid Hunter's skid, but he connected with his left-rear quarter panel, rocking Hunter's car around one more time. Hunter slid up the track and straight into the wall with a full-frontal, jarring impact.

When he came to, he smelled gasoline and heard the deadly snap of fire.

Liv screamed.

The sound tore from her throat, raw and unwilling, as she shot up from the sofa in her private sitting room where she'd been watching the practice session. On the television, Hunter's gold car with the number 4 emblazoned down the sides in black flames was smashed against the outside wall of the race track. Its hood was flattened, its rear end was destroyed, and real flames were licking out from behind the left rear wheel.

As she swallowed hard against another reflexive sound, a truck rolled up and suited men jumped out of the bed, armed with fire extinguishers.

Then the net came down from the driver's side window, and she saw Hunter's hand shoot out, giving a thumbs-up sign that he was okay. The TV announcer lamented that he'd qualified for the pole position in tomorrow's race and now his car was more or less demolished. He'd have a back-up available, but changing cars now would put him at the back of the starting line.

"Oh, you stupid, insane fool!" Liv choked. "When is it enough for you? *When?* How damned far do you have to take it?" Her heart was rioting.

A fist thumped against her door. Kiki's voice shouted through the wood. "Are you all right? I heard you scream."

Liv went to open it. Kiki shot into the room, looking around both skeptically and a little wildly. Liv nodded wordlessly at the TV.

Kiki's black eyes took in the scene there as Hunter levered himself out through the driver's window. The stock cars had no doors. The seams and hardware would create drag. "So Michigan doesn't agree with him," Kiki muttered.

Then Vicky hurtled into the room.

Her knees were scraped and reddened as they usually were, and her long, black ponytail was falling loose from some hard play. "What's going on? Somebody said you were all up here." Then she, too, focused on the television screen. "Hey, isn't that the guy we saw in the restaurant last weekend?"

Kiki was closest to her. She caught Vicky's arm and turned her smoothly away from the TV. "What guy?"

"Mom knows who I mean. Some famous guy." Vicky craned her neck around as Kiki steered her toward the door. "It *is* him. He said he drives cars real fast. He's hurt."

Kiki dropped Vicky's elbow to turn back to the TV herself. Liv pushed between them to see. On the screen, Hunter bent over at the waist, in obvious pain. He did it slowly, as though the earth had suddenly produced an exorbitant amount of gravity and was tugging him down even as he fought it tooth and nail.

Liv felt light-headed. The announcers' voices sounded anxious.

"Sit down," Kiki said to her harshly. "You're white as a ghost."

"I'm fine. Vicky, go...do something."

Kiki started angling the girl toward the door again. "Come on. I just made a new recipe for cranberry muffins. I need you to tell me what you think."

"But I want to see what happens to this guy," Vicky argued.

"We can watch on the television downstairs in the kitchen."

Liv knew that Kiki would never allow the TV to go on downstairs until long after this coverage was over. She offered no resistance when the two went out, Kiki closing the door again smartly behind her.

Liv went back to the sofa and sat, fumbling blindly behind her with one hand to make sure the furniture was still there. Then she reached for the remote control and hit up the volume. She'd once seen his car do somersaults down the backstretch, nose to tail, nose to tail, and he'd walked away as steady as a rock. He would be fine.

"They don't seem to be heading for the infield care center," one of the announcers said as an ambulance loaded Hunter and drove off. "Looks like they'll be taking him directly to a hospital."

"What does this do to his chances tomorrow, Hal?"

"I'd say they're minimal at this point, Bud."

He'd driven once with a broken wrist, Liv remembered, taping it for extra support, his jaw set visibly against the pain every time the camera caught him. He'd be in that race tomorrow.

There was another knock on her door. Kiki entered with a tray holding a decanter of brandy and two snifters.

"Where's Vicky?" Liv asked, startled.

"I gave her two of the muffins and sent her out to harass Bourne."

The retired cowboy ran their riding operation. "He'll take the muffins and send her right back again if he's busy."

"Not if he wants to see another of my muffins in this lifetime."

Liv almost smiled.

"Here. You need this." Kiki poured the snifters and handed her one, then she gestured at the television with her own. "So what's the latest? Did he live?"

"They took him to the hospital."

Kiki nodded. "He's too mean to die."

Liv jerked up from her slouch against the cushions. "He's not mean. He's just..." She trailed off at Kiki's expression. "What? Why are you looking at me that way?"

Kiki settled on the sofa beside her. "You've got to get over this. You were fine before you made that trip back east."

Liv took a good swallow of brandy without answering. It burned going down.

"You're the strongest woman I know."

Liv jolted a little. "Me? Get off it."

"I just don't tell you very often because I hate being overshadowed by you."

Liv could only laugh at that, though her voice was hoarse. Kiki was beautiful—tiny, barely five foot tall—with classic Native American looks. She was a dynamo. Liv generally felt pale, clumsy and befuddled beside her. They'd been friends since even before Hunter had entered the picture, from the first moment Liv had set foot on the Navajo reservation.

Kiki got up to move. Like Hunter, she was always moving.

"You made your decision when you cut him loose," she said. "You never looked back—at least not that any of us could tell. You married Johnny and when that didn't work out, we left Flag and came here to Jerome. We established the inn from a ramshackle building that nobody else wanted but that you saw the potential in. You've built a life for your daughter. She's happy, healthy, smart."

"She lives with a bunch of strangers trooping through her home several times a week."

"That's your phobia, not hers. Don't foist it off on her, Liv."

Liv winced.

"You're the one who was always hung up on the traditional nuclear-home thing. You were the one intent on grabbing back everything you lost when your family's car went over that cliff and you were sent to the Res. So what if Vicky has a mother, a doting aunt and a lot of guests from all over the country instead of a mother, a father and a sibling or two? What does it matter if she's thriving?"

Liv found that she couldn't answer.

"My point is, you've got a lot to be proud of. So *be* proud of it. Don't let Hunter Hawk-Cole rock your foundations again just because you made one mistake."

"Which mistake are we speaking of here?" Liv asked dryly.

"Dover."

"Ah, that one. And it was Millsboro."

Kiki waved her hand, telling her what she thought of that particular split hair. "Don't let him drag you down the way you were in those days after he left."

"You just said I never looked back."

"But your eyes didn't see what they were looking at straight ahead, either." Kiki put her snifter back on the tray and picked the tray up. "On that note, I'm going back to the kitchen. If you want to keep wallowing in angst, you're going to have to do it on your own."

Liv nodded absently, her gaze swerving to the television

again. They were showing highlights of Hunter's career on the screen now, while crews cleaned up the track from his crash. Liv watched and tunneled back in time, helplessly and without much resistance.

It was so blasted hot and she had one lamb to go. Without a sheep pen, it was almost impossible to catch the little critter. But her grandmother—the old woman she'd called Ama in the respectful Navajo tradition of "mother"—had stubbornly refused to touch any of the life insurance money her parents had left to make improvements to her land.

Ama had died in her sleep eleven months ago. By hook or by crook, Liv had managed to keep the authorities at the school from finding out. Ama's clanswomen had signed her report cards and they had showed up at mandatory events in Dinny's stead. Liv would graduate in six more days. It was over. Her exile here was done, and there was nothing to leave behind. Even Kiki would be moving to Flagstaff with her to begin college there late in August.

When she turned eighteen next month, she could collect the life insurance money. Everything would be fine.

It scared her spitless.

Why was she suddenly frightened now that the time had come? She'd planned her escape from the first moment her heels had touched down on this arid, forsaken soil. It had taken Social Services and attorneys several days to sort out that she had only one living relative, her mother's mother, an old Navajo woman on a high-country reservation. From the time she'd been delivered into Ama's care, Liv had dreamed of the time when she could go again, back to the city where she belonged.

But she'd been on the reservation for almost six years now, and she worried that she had forgotten how to act in real, conventional society. If she ate in a restaurant, would she even remember which fork to use? She heard Hunter's truck at the same moment the terrifying thought slid through her mind again, taunting her.

He was back. Something in her heart leaped, but she was too stubborn to let it show. *He always left her as casually as though she were one of the lambs she was about to sell off. But that didn't stop her from going giddy with pleasure whenever he returned.*

Liv finally got the animal inoculated and she laughed with relief. The last one. She already had a buyer for the herd, so that was that. She finally sat up to look for Hunter.

"My money was on you," he said, sauntering toward her, wearing that grin.

He was so handsome. Liv drank in the look of him. He still wore his black hair long. He revered his Navajo ancestors, the warriors who had once fearlessly taken on Kit Carson at Canyon de Chelly, though he'd always hated being shoved from his home and onto this reservation against his will. Now his hair shifted against his shoulders, more from his movement than the windless air. His cheekbones were arrogant slashes, and his eyes were an incredible blue.

She never got tired of looking at him, and she never stopped wanting to touch him. Sometimes she squeezed it in, a quick, friendly hug or a touch of her hand to his knee. But he always got so skittish whenever she did that. Kiki said it was because he wanted her, too, but neither of them could quite figure out why he never did anything about it.

She was nearly eighteen now, hardly a child any longer—especially after living on her own this past year since Ama had died.

"You don't have any money," she said, standing to brush the dust off her bare legs. She was going to fix this problem between them, too, before she went to Flagstaff. "Anyway, that's it for the herd. You're next. It's time to fish or cut bait, Hunter. I'm cleaning up my past here."

That fierce heat came to his eyes, the look she loved so much. Liv tingled inside. Now that they might finally be together, she found that she was also a little terrified.

She fought against the fear with bravado and started to move toward him. "I love you. I want to be with you. I want to take something away from this place when I go. And I want it to be you. You're the very best memory of the Res that I have."

She reached for the hem of her T-shirt. She was shaking, wondering if she dared to do it, to just yank it over her head and *bare herself to him to find out what he would do about it. She looked up into those midnight-blue eyes, as sharp as glass now. "Are you going to stop me, Hunter? Don't. I have a good head of steam up here."*

He made a choking sound but said nothing. There was only promise in his eyes.

She tugged the shirt over her head. The hot, arid air licked her skin. Maybe it was that, the kiss of the sun, or maybe it was the fact that she was being so incredibly brazen. Maybe it was everything tied into one, but she felt her nipples tighten, almost hurting. If he turned away from her now, Liv knew she would die.

She held her breath, waiting for an interminable time. Then he brought his hands up almost reverently and closed them over her breasts. She cried out, a sound of relief and release, then she flung herself at him. She jumped and wrapped her legs around his waist and found his mouth with hers.

Finally, finally. It was all she could think. Oh, how she loved him! She'd loved him since she was twelve years old.

They fell together into the dirt, ripping at each other's clothing, and suddenly Liv was no longer shy or frightened at all. She was exhilarated, almost weeping with the joy of it. When he finally found his way inside her, she whimpered his name and rode with him, with every thrust, every glorious beat of his body connecting with hers. Then they lay together in the dust, spent and naked, their hearts rioting.

When she found her air again, Liv just came out and asked him. "How long are you staying this time?"

He hesitated for the barest beat. "I have to be in New Mexico tomorrow."

"Tomorrow? Why?"

"I'm joining the Army."

Her stomach dove. "Write me as soon as you get there. Give me your address so I know where you are. Send it general delivery to Flag. I'll pick it up there."

"I will." *He wrapped his arms a little more tightly around her.* "Livie."

She rubbed her cheek against his chest, sensing what was

coming, trying to savor all the good she could manage before the bad crept in again.

"I love you," he said. "And you're the only person who's ever loved me back."

She wanted to argue that it wasn't true, but she was afraid it was. "We're soul mates," she murmured. It was a game they had played before. "Two of a kind. Peas in a pod."

"I'll always be there for you."

"I might not always need you to be." She couldn't resist the barb. He was leaving again—so soon.

"So when that happens, I'll go and leave you alone."

The possibility hurt too deep for words. Liv hugged him fiercely, suddenly. "Are you sorry we did this?"

"I should be." He kissed her hair. "But no."

"I'm old enough now to make my own choices."

"Well, you sure started out with a bang."

She laughed, her mouth against his skin again. "One more time before you have to go."

"I'm not going until tomorrow."

"Then love me all night."

She rolled on top of him. They didn't make it inside until dark fell over the desert and small, nocturnal animals began rustling through the tufted rabbitbrush. Then they went into the hogan, their arms still wrapped around each other.

When Liv woke the next morning, he was gone again. But he left a note this time, promising that he would find her in Flagstaff the first time he was on leave.

Liv crushed it in her fist and dropped it into her morning fire.

Chapter 2

His doctor was a small man with a nervous Adam's apple. Watching the thing bob up and down was beginning to irritate Hunter in a big way.

"Just say whatever it is you're trying to say," he warned the man. His voice was still vaguely raspy from the effects of yesterday's anesthesia. He was in pain.

"I simply can't clear you to get behind the wheel of a race car in four hours." The doctor stepped back quickly at the change in Hunter's eyes, something that could only be likened to a sudden, solar flare.

"Explain to me why I need your permission."

"I'm your doctor—"

"Do better than that."

"You had surgery for a ruptured spleen twelve hours ago!"

Hunter made a sound of disgust. "I'm driving."

"Actually," said Pritchard Spikes, his longtime friend and team owner, "you're not."

"It's our season! Are you going to throw it away over some stitches?"

"The stitches don't bother me too much." Pritch poured a

cup of water from the jug on the nightstand in Hunter's hospital room. "But throw in the fact that you're now spleenless—and it's going to take even you some time to adjust to that—I'm not going to let you drive my car."

"Don't overlook the seriousness of four broken ribs and a concussion," the doctor warned hastily.

Hunter glared at him again, then back at Pritch. "Ricky Stall is only sixty-two points behind me in the Cup race." There was a calm to his voice now, as though he was confident that he could win this by pointing out the obvious. "If I don't drive today, he'll gain the lead."

"Has anyone told you that you're insane?" Pritch asked. "Stall might well take home the Winston Cup this year. You're not getting in a car again for at least another month."

The idea was so absurd that Hunter didn't even hear it. "I'll hang back in the pack today. I don't have to win. Anywhere from fifteenth to twentieth place will do me. I just have to finish so I can keep the points close going into next week."

"I talked to Alan Carver this morning about running your car. Damn it, Hawk, you're going to need four weeks to recover from all this—six before your body could tolerate another crash."

"I heal fast."

Exasperated, Pritch put down his paper cup. "People won't forget you if you come in second for the Cup. Is that what you're afraid of?"

It wasn't fear, Hunter told himself. It was loathing. Free time was the antithesis of everything he was made of. He hated being still.

Especially now.

Free time meant not losing himself in the pressures of the race as he had done for more than a week now. Free time meant that there would be nothing to quench the fire of fury that burned in his gut whenever he thought about Liv and that little girl.

People wouldn't forget him because of a few weeks off—and if they did, he could remind them again in a hurry. But he was afraid of what he would find when—if—he had time on his hands to corner Liv Slade for a few answers.

Damn you, Livie, what did you do?

"Find Chillie for me," he said to Pritch, his throat more raw than ever.

"Your business manager? Why?"

"If I've got to take a month off—"

"Six weeks would be my recommendation," the doctor interjected.

"Stay out of this," Hunter growled. Then he turned back to Pritch. "I need Chillie to find me a place to stay in Arizona for a little while."

He'd checked into it once, years ago. She was still living there. She'd left Flag and had opened up a bed-and-breakfast in Jerome with a partner.

It was time to pay Livie a visit.

Liv let her mare choose her own footing down the trail off Cleopatra Hill. Daisy was a champion climber, and all she needed from her rider was to leave her alone and let her do her thing. Liv gave her her head and kept her own attention on the sixteen people riding single file in front of her.

Six of them were guests of the inn. The others were tourists visiting town for the day or staying at one of the more modern hotels. The tours were a side business she'd begun two years ago after being peppered by questions about the area at the tea they served each afternoon at the Copper Rose. Liv knew a lot about Jerome, about Arizona in general. Her knowledge came free with a stay at the inn, but then she started wondering, why not charge the other tourists? Why not combine local lore with a little Western riding?

Riding had never been her strong suit, but she was better at it than most, thanks to Hunter's relentless tutoring. Her horseback tours of the area had become a thriving success.

Don't think about him, she warned herself. But her mind had worried over him ever since he had disappeared from the Michigan hospital two days ago. News reports said he was "recovering" at an undisclosed location.

Hunter wasn't the type to lie about and heal. Liv had the nagging, unsettling feeling that he was up to something.

The walkie-talkie at her waist suddenly crackled and spat noise. Bourne was riding at the head of the pack and his voice came through. He thought that an overweight woman wearing a voluminous pink blouse was starting to seem short of breath. Her poor horse was doing all the work, Liv thought, but she also suspected that the woman's nerves were screwed up just about as tightly as they could go. She decided it was time for a scenic break.

She told Bourne to stop the group at the next clearing. A few minutes later the riders gathered in a rocky enclave with a spectacular view of the Verde Valley beneath them. In the opposite direction, the homes and buildings of Jerome climbed up the hill like diligent ants.

Liv dismounted. "A hundred and twenty-five years ago, this area was nothing more than a settlement of tents," she began conversationally. She'd learned never to sound as though she was lecturing. "Our Native Americans were the first miners on these hills, then the Spanish came along, looking for gold but finding copper instead. Along about 1876, Anglos staked the first legitimate claims and Jerome sprang to life. It called itself the wickedest town in the West."

"Why?" someone asked as Bourne began handing out juice packs.

"The men who came here were—for the most part—young and single and rowdy. They were drawn from all over the world—Mexico and Croatia, Ireland and Italy and China—by the prospect of finding their fortunes here. Jerome became the darling of investors, and there was always some corporation willing to buy these guys out. Then, of course, the men needed something to spend their money on, so more people moved in to provide that. At one point Jerome boasted twenty-one bars and eight houses of...well, ill repute." She grinned. "And where there are liquor and loose women and men of different cultures, there are bound to be a few fights and a handful of murders."

"Especially if one of those women played her man like a fiddle."

The voice was smoky, an idle notch above dangerous. Recognition jolted through Liv. She turned quickly.

Hunter.

Liv had the bizarre thought that at least she knew where he was now. He sat on a black horse just at the mouth of the path. Already his hair seemed vaguely longer than it had on television a week ago. But everything else about him was treacherously familiar.

How many times had he ridden up to her hogan looking just like this? With that careless, masculine slouch on a gelding with no saddle…his movements making his hair shift and catch the light. But this time he didn't grin at her. She had the half-hearted hope that he was in pain—it hadn't been that many weeks since his accident—and maybe that glare didn't mean that he had every intention of destroying her for what she had done.

Liv flipped her own hair behind her shoulder. "If she got what she wanted, then I'd say she was a wise woman."

"Or the man was a fool. I'm no fool, Livie."

"Don't call me that." No one but Hunter had ever called her that.

"Folks are ready to move on here, Liv," said Bourne.

Liv glanced at him helplessly. It occurred to her that he had no idea who Hunter was. She planned to keep it that way. "Start out again without me."

"Not sure that's a good idea. The insurance—"

"Do it." Liv swallowed carefully and softened her tone deliberately. "Please."

"You're the boss."

She looked back at Hunter. She heard Bourne's saddle creak as he mounted again behind her, then the plodding sound as seventeen sets of hooves hit the rocky soil, moving out.

Something strange was beginning to happen in the area of her chest, something airy and light that almost felt like relief. They'd settle this now. Liv discovered that she was ready for combat. It was better than living in dread. She couldn't go on leaping out of her skin every time the phone rang.

"Boss," Hunter repeated so softly his voice might have been a caress, but there was nothing warm about it.

"You knew that or you couldn't have found me. Someone had to have told you I was leading this ride."

"The desk clerk at the Connor suggested where I might find you. You have a few of his paying customers astride."

"Yes." It seemed safest to keep things simple until she could gauge his intent.

"I'm staying there."

She forced herself to nod. "How nice."

"I thought the Copper Rose might be a little…too close for comfort."

"Well, don't let me keep you."

He made no move to go. She hadn't expected him to. "Where's Johnny Guenther? Back at the inn cleaning the toilets?"

"Don't you *dare* disparage him!" Outrage hit her with enough force to take her breath away. "He did more for me than you ever did!"

It was cruel, and his eyes showed it. "I thought he might be the type who would jump to do your bidding. That's what you wanted, right, Livie?"

She clamped her jaw hard, refusing to rise to the bait. "Right."

"So where is he now?"

She was all out of lies. And there was no sense in them anymore, anyway. She'd devised them all to keep him away. "Flagstaff, I would imagine. We're not together anymore. You knew that, too. From Delaware."

He nodded. "Get up on your mare, Livie. Let's ride a bit. We need to talk."

"I have to catch up with my group."

"Do it later."

She brought her chin up. "No. You need to go."

He was off his horse in a flash. She'd forgotten how he could move like that, as though he were part of the wind. Liv backpedaled quickly enough that she almost stumbled. When he reached out to catch her, she jumped again. "Don't touch me!"

"Scared you might still like it?"

Yes. "I got over you the day I knew you weren't coming back."

"Why would I bother? You were the only thing in Arizona worth seeing, and you closed the door."

It cracked something inside her and she made a sound she despised, something low and throaty and pained. Liv turned away from him. "I'm leaving."

"Fine. Then I'll see you at the Copper Rose tonight."

It stopped her in her tracks. "Don't come there!"

"Why? Do you think I'll figure out that that little girl is mine?"

Liv felt her knees fold. Hearing him say it aloud had her reaching quickly for the saddle horn to regain her balance. Her mare sensed her tension and skittered cautiously out of reach. Liv fisted her hands and turned back to Hunter.

She was many things, but she had never been a coward. "I'm afraid that *she'll* figure out she is."

It stopped him like stone just as he began to approach her again. Liv wanted to see his eyes, had to know what she'd find there. But when he reached up and pulled off his ultradark sunglasses, all she saw in that dark, dangerous blue was betrayal.

"I could kill you for this." He nearly snarled the words.

Things inside her went cold. It happened gradually, starting in her heart, then spreading out through her limbs. If he had loved her once—and that was a big *if*—then he clearly hated her now.

Liv told herself she didn't care. Not anymore. "Cut me a break, Hunter. You're the last man in the world likely to spend time shaking a rattle over a bassinet."

"I never knew I had a bassinet worth rattling over." He moved in her direction again.

Liv rounded to the other side of her horse. Fast. "Don't you dare take another step toward me."

"I want to choke you."

There was enough of a vibration in his tone to tell her that he meant it. "Which is precisely why I want you to stay right over there."

"I'm not leaving, Olivia. Not until we settle this."

"You already left. Eight and a half years ago."

"That was your choice. This time around, I'll decide."

It snatched the air right from her lungs. Liv looked into the dark-blue midnight of his eyes. Midnight was when all the most dangerous animals came out in the desert, she thought, the ones that could kill. "If you drag Vicky into this just to tell the world you had a part in it, I will hunt you down and destroy you."

"Spoken like a mama protecting her cub."

"I am."

His grin was slow and cruel. "Damn, Livie, could it be that you're capable of loving someone after all?"

Then he closed the distance between them. The mare skittered away, spooked. He brought his hand up to close it around Liv's throat.

His palm was calloused as it had always been, the splay of his fingers broad, and that was the same, too. The thumb stroking under her right ear made something inside her convulse.

"I'm not Johnny Guenther, babe. I don't know what you did to him or where he went, but I won't let you snap your fingers and tell me where to go."

"I've got a few good suggestions." She couldn't breathe.

"It's too hot where you're thinking. And even the devil won't have me there."

"He might be afraid of the competition."

"With good cause."

Liv slapped his hand away. "I'm not nineteen anymore. You don't impress me, and you can't touch me and make me crumble and forget everything I need."

"We'll see."

She spun away from him to find her horse. This time she managed to get hold of her saddle horn. Liv swung into the saddle.

"Eight o'clock," he said. "Tonight. We'll finish this then. Meet me in the Spirit Room at the Connor Hotel. I'll buy you a drink...for old time's sake."

Her gaze whipped to his face. "There really wasn't anything worth commemorating, Hunter."

"If you're not there by eight-thirty, I'll come looking for you."

Liv didn't acknowledge the threat with an answer. She put

her heels to her mare and trotted past him, then she let the horse break into a canter when they reached the trail. But no matter how fast they moved, she couldn't get past the fact that he looked much better in person than he ever had on TV—and so much more volatile.

God help me, she thought. I'm in trouble.

Hunter watched her go. That long dark hair of hers, all woven with gold, bounced against her back with the horse's jog, just the way it had all those years ago. She wore a tight red tank top that told him she hadn't put on a pound in eight years, except maybe in the right places. Her legs were still trim and lean and long, clasped in denim as her thighs gripped her mount.

What a shame that she could still make his mouth water, Hunter thought, because he had every intention of unraveling her lie, thread by thread, piece by piece, even if it hurt her.

"You're sitting on that pony like you've got one of Dinny's broom handles down the back of your shirt!" he shouted at her as she rode the horse in circles around him. "Loosen up!"

"I'm loose!" But then the horse broke into a faster gait and she squealed and grabbed the saddle horn.

She'd been afraid of horses from the first moment he'd met her, Hunter thought. Her father had been a college professor, her mother an artist. Though she'd been born and raised in Phoenix, Livie had never set foot near a horse until she landed on the Res.

He'd done his best to ease her out of her fear, if only for the sake of her survival. It had been a long distance from point to point back there in Navajo land. But Liv had always preferred to walk or stick her thumb out whenever she needed to go somewhere.

Now her new job demanded that she know how to manage a horse. She'd been hired by one of the major Flagstaff resorts to work in their stables and guide their group rides. She'd let her past speak for itself, implying that a girl from the high-country could gallop with the best of them. She needed the job, so she hadn't bothered to mention that she preferred her heels planted solidly on the ground. She'd written him a frantic letter for help instead.

So Hunter had come back from New Mexico. He'd picked her up at dawn at her apartment and they'd slipped out to this isolated ranch north of the city. The owner was the father of a guy he'd crossed paths with in the Army.

Hunter was suddenly struck by inspiration as he continued to watch her critically. "You know what you're doing wrong?"

"Besides sitting on top of a thousand pounds of unpredictable animal?" But her fingers loosened on the saddle horn.

Hunter grinned. She was the only person he'd ever known who could make him do that—grin himself right out of frustration. "It's in your hips, Liv."

She wiggled her brows at him. "You like my hips."

"Not on a horse, I don't."

She sighed and reined the animal in. "Okay. Tell me what's wrong with them. I'm all ears."

"You don't move them right. You're all rigid. Move them like you do when I'm inside you."

Her reaction delighted him. Her breath caught and her eyes went wide, then she looked around quickly to see if anyone was close enough to overhear them. They were alone.

She grinned wickedly. "Um, I forget exactly. Better remind me."

He hadn't been angling for such an invitation…and for the life of him he couldn't walk away from it. Hunter started toward her horse with slow, deliberate strides. She made a move as though to dismount. Then something—maybe the snap of a twig as his heel came down on it, or the sudden tension that he could only imagine was zinging through her body—made the horse spook. It reared, and Liv went head over heels off the back of the saddle.

Hunter shouted and closed the rest of the distance at a run. When he reached her, she had a wild look in her eyes and she was breathing hard, but he knew in an instant that she was unhurt. She was spitting mad.

"That nasty beast tossed me!"

"Did it hurt?" He helped her sit up, brushed her off.

"Of course it did! It jarred the breath right out of me!"

"Will you live?"

She narrowed her eyes at him. "You'll never touch me again if you don't show a little sympathy here."

"Sorry. But think about it. The worst happened. You got thrown. If you're going to ride, it had to happen eventually. But how bad was it? Something to be so terrified of that you can't do this job they're offering you?"

He could tell by the way she refused to let herself smile that he'd made his point. "I hate you."

"You love me."

"Some days less than others. You did that on purpose, didn't you? You spooked my horse to make a point."

"Nope. It was an accident."

She finally let herself grin. "I'm still not exactly sure how to move my hips."

He had her flat on her back before she could breathe again. "Ah, Livie." There was no one like her, no other woman who could make him crave and ache and smile during long nights alone in the barracks.

As they began fumbling with each other's clothes, Hunter maneuvered her to her feet. "Not here." They weren't on the Res anymore.

"The barn," she gasped against his mouth.

They headed that way, trying to walk decorously, but her mind was on other things and she stumbled once. Liv giggled. He caught her elbow and propelled her inside, into a stall. And they laughed and touched and feasted and it ended too soon because he had to leave again, but for that one high noon, everything was the way it had been before. He slid inside her as they rolled on bales of hay, and he whispered the truth in her ear, that she was all he ever needed.

There was never any doubt that she would go to the Spirit Room.

Liv prowled her sitting room at 7:30, her hands scraping restlessly through her hair then fussing with the belt of her robe. Her stomach was alternately a knot, then something squishy and weightless. She tried a glass of wine to calm her nerves, but it only made her nauseous.

"Okay," she whispered aloud to walls that undoubtedly knew many more secrets than her own. "I'm fine."

All that mattered was Vicky, Liv reminded herself. She would die to protect her, would keep any of this from affecting her, and that was that. Liv paused in her pacing to swig more wine, then her throat closed and she found it hard to swallow.

She had lied to Hunter all those years ago for one reason— to make him go before he realized she was pregnant. She'd known by then that he wasn't ever going to stay with her, and she would not subject their child to a fly-by-night father slipping in and out of their lives. He would do the same thing now— fade in and out, a tantalizing wish—if she let him. So somehow she had to make him go away again, once and for all.

Kiki was right. She'd given Vicky a reasonably stable life. Maybe it wasn't everything she'd ever dreamed of for her child, because in the end, she hadn't had it in her to stay with Johnny. But it was enough. She would not let Hunter change that.

Liv moaned aloud, her stomach heaving. She had never been able to make Hunter do anything he hadn't wanted to do. That was how she'd known that he'd never really been in love with her. Because when she'd told him to leave, he'd gone.

Liv was so grateful to be out of the stables, she almost didn't mind the hokey uniform they'd given her for her promotion to barmaid. She ducked into the rest room to check her appearance before her shift started, reminding herself that this was actually a step up.

She'd lasted with the riding operation for five months until it had closed for the season right before Christmas. Hunter had come back three more times to hammer the tricks of the trade into her. She'd done well because she'd made it a point to do well. She'd hadn't been thrown again. But she wasn't about to spend the remainder of her life on horseback and mucking out stalls.

In January the resort had transferred her to their child care facility. The tips from road-weary parents anxious for some time to themselves had been great. The children, for the most part, had been impossible. Still, Liv had stuck it out for ten months until this opening had come up in the bar.

She intended to learn the hospitality business from the ground up, from the stables to the food and beverage facilities to the head office. Tonight she would entertain a few drunks and begin to learn the workings of the back of the bar. Unfortunately, she was going to have to do it looking like a cross between a beauty pageant queen and Annie Oakley.

The cowboy boots weren't bad, she decided, except they were red. Her legs were good enough to tolerate the very short skirt. Personally, she thought the boots would look better with shorts, but it wasn't her call to make. If she ever had her own place, she thought, the barmaids would wear boots with shorts. And the boots wouldn't be red.

At the moment, however, she was stuck with petticoats—bustling white petticoats, layers of the damned things—under the full short denim. Liv turned this way and that in front of the mirror, but the contraption really didn't afford her a good side. It was topped by a tiny denim vest that was laced up the front with red ribbon. In all her years on the reservation, she'd never once seen fit to put on a cowboy hat, but she wore one now.

Liv stuck her tongue out at her mirrored image to show what she thought of the whole getup.

"Yeah, but it presents some interesting possibilities for getting you out of it again."

Liv squealed and spun away from the mirror. "Hunter!" He stood in the rest room door. "Where did you come from? You didn't say you were coming back! You can't be in here!"

"Nobody stopped me."

"You can't go through your whole life just…just doing things because no one locked the door on you!"

His face changed. For a crazy moment while it felt like the bathroom tilted on its axis, he actually looked confused, Liv thought. She realized that she had never commented on his life before, on the way he flew higher and danced faster and did everything better simply because it was there to be done.

But she had never needed so desperately for him to calm down and stay put before, either.

She wasn't ready for him, Liv thought, her heart jumping oddly—and that was new, too. She'd always been just purely elated to see him again, but this time nerves scurried in her stomach. She'd been planning to buy a pregnancy test kit this weekend, to be sure. Then she'd thought she would write him, either asking him to come back so they could talk, or putting it right down in her letter.

Hunter, I'm pregnant.

She hadn't anticipated that he would just show up like this out of the blue.

The rest room tilted back again and Liv felt light-headed. She closed the distance between them unsteadily, framed his face with her hands and kissed him soundly. "Sorry. You just surprised me."

He wrapped his arms around her, the moment forgotten. "I had some time off so I came back. The guy out at the bar said you were in here. He said it was okay for me to come after you because they hadn't opened yet."

Liv lifted her left arm behind his shoulder to see her watch. "I've got five more minutes before they throw the doors open. Come back to the kitchen with me. My locker is there. I'll get you the key to my apartment. You can wait for me at home."

"What time do you get off?"

He was nibbling on her mouth, making it hard for her to think. "Um, midnight. But it will be one o'clock before I clean up my station here and get there."

His lips claimed hers fully. "I can't wait that long."

"Then maybe you should stop going away."

She hadn't meant to say that, either. Maybe it was just hormones making her shaky. Or maybe it was just that night after lonely night, she watched her friends with their men, aching inside for her own as Hunter chased wild dreams a continent away. He'd spent the past month in New England on a fishing boat. And she'd slept by herself, and sometimes she'd cried with frustration. Why couldn't she just have a normal relationship? Why couldn't he love her enough?

Unconsciously she put a hand to her tummy, wondering if a baby would make the difference. She pulled out of his arms.

"Let's go. I can't be late starting my first night."

"Liv, are you all right?"

"I'm fine. I just wish I wasn't working tonight, now." She managed to grin for him. "Why didn't you write that you were coming back?"

"Because I didn't know until two days ago, and then I just hit the road. I figured I'd get here before the mail could."

"There's always the telephone." She scowled at him. "Did you get fired?"

"Actually, I quit."

"You didn't like fishing?"

"I found something I might like more."

Her heart lurched. *Please, please, please let it be me.*

"It's a long story," he continued. "I'll tell you when you get home tonight. You're going to be late, babe. Better get moving."

Liv had no choice but to agree. Her shift had started one minute ago.

They went to the kitchen and she gave him her key. She kissed him goodbye at the back door and somehow she got through the night. She didn't learn much about the bar business, but then, she hadn't expected to under the circumstances. Everything inside her tugged her toward the door, toward home and Hunter and whatever it was he had finally found. Only a tiny corner of her mind was on the patrons, the bar, the tips she shoved relentlessly and absently into the pocket of her gruesome petticoated skirt.

At 12:45, she fairly burst out the bar door. She jogged to her car and drove home faster than she should have. *Hunter, Hunter, Hunter,* her mind chanted. He would tell her he was going to stay this time—he had come home unexpectedly, after all, and in the rest room he had hinted that he'd finally figured out what he wanted to do with his life. He would stay, and she would tell him about the baby. Her period was a month late. The test was only a formality, after all.

When she parked her car outside her apartment building, her palms were slick with perspiration and her heart felt as though a riot of microscopic beings was going on in there. She pressed her hand to her tummy again as she raced up the stairs to her *second-floor unit. He was asleep on the sofa when she let herself inside.*

For a moment Liv just stood, watching him. How could a man be so beautiful? He made something ache inside her. Most of it was loving him, but part of it was pure appreciation. Even in repose, one arm tossed back over his head, the other dangling over the edge of the sofa, he looked as arrogant and magnificent as the hawk his mother's family was named for. Liv went to kneel on the floor beside him. She kissed his mouth to wake him.

"You look just like those ancestors you used to talk about all the time when we were kids," she murmured. "You look like a warrior."

"Maybe a dead warrior." He sat up. "I was out cold, wasn't I?"

Liv chuckled. "Well, that's one way to pass the time until you could see me again."

His eyes narrowed on her as she stood. "That is the ugliest outfit I've ever seen."

She cocked a hip. "Then get me out of it."

Her gasp turned to laughter when he leaped off the sofa, caught her about the waist and tossed her over his shoulder. A moment later they were in the bedroom, and the pieces of her uniform were strewn all over the floor. And finally, as her hands flew over his skin and she arched up to press herself against him, her nerves were gone and the only thing that ached for him was her body.

When they were spent and wrapped around each other, Liv decided to tell him about the baby now, right now, while her heart was still thudding from their lovemaking. They were so close, skin to skin, heart to heart. It was perfect.

"Hunter."

"Hmmm." His fingers played absently with her hair. "Hey, you cut it."

She frowned, impatient. "I do that every fall. Listen to me. There's something—"

"I know," he interrupted. "The thing I started to tell you about at the bar. You sidetracked me with all that white frou-frou there under your skirt."

Liv set her teeth. "They're petticoats."

"They're still ugly."

"Well, I'm not wearing them now, so—"

"Come here." She'd started to sit up, but he pulled her close again. "There really is something important I need to tell you."

Okay, Liv thought. He could go first. "Spill." She laid her cheek against his chest.

"I'm heading for California tomorrow."

For a moment she lay perfectly still. She wasn't sure she could move. "What's so different about that? Louisiana, New Mexico, Maine…now California. You're always heading somewhere."

"I have a chance there, Livie, a great chance. I met some guy in Bangor. He's got a garage in Anaheim."

"A garage?"

"Stock cars."

"What's a stock car?"

"Pared-down, fast-as-lightning, zoom around the race track."

"Zoom," Liv repeated.

"Livie, I was talking to him. He thinks I have the right stuff. This could be the one thing I've always wanted to do."

"Chasing alligators was the one thing you always wanted to do."

"This is different. I can't explain it."

"Try."

He was quiet for a very long time. "From the time I could walk, people were always putting me somewhere. My parents couldn't stay together. I lived with relative after relative while they tried to sort out their own mess, until I acted up enough and the auntie or uncle of the week would call them home. You know that."

She nodded against his body, back in his arms again, waiting, praying…for something, some word that would make all this right.

"My father always said I was trying to kill myself."

She knew that, too.

"When they finally broke up for good, when Mom stayed on the Navajo res and Dad went back to Tuba City, she sent me

*with him because I was too much of a handful. Then he sent me
right back for the same reason.''*

"Hunter," she said, exasperated. *"You went eagle-hunting,
fell down a cliff, lay there with a broken leg for three days while
the whole town frantically combed the mesas looking for you.
Then you practically crawled home on your hands and knees
and the Feds arrested you for poaching. You* were *a handful.''*

*"I was just looking for…I don't know, something that made
me feel right.''*

Tell me it's me.

"I sort of feel that way when I'm driving. Complete.''

*Her heart couldn't have fallen to her feet any quicker if she
had been standing.* "This guy let you drive a race car in Bangor?"

"No, no. I gave him a ride home from a bar. But there was
nearly an accident and I avoided it and he liked what he saw."

Liv was quiet for a long time. "You're not coming home,
then."

*"Livie, you're my home. Wherever you are. That's all I
need.''*

But I need more. *She punched his shoulder as she sat up.*
"Home *is a place you go to each night to lay your head on
your pillow!''*

"I lay my head on dreams of you."

"That's not enough!"

"I want you to come with me this time. Can you?"

Her heart staggered. "Where?"

*"I just told you. To California. You can find a resort to work
at there.''* He sat up slowly, watching her, looking both sad and
confused again, maybe even a little angry. *"Babe, you're really
off the wall tonight.''*

He didn't understand.

*It hit her then, in all its enormity. She was probably pregnant.
And he was going to run off to California tomorrow to try his
hand at racing cars. When that failed, it would be something
else. God help her, it would always be something else.*

She wasn't—had never been—enough to hold him in one

place. Whatever it was that he was looking for to make him feel complete...it wasn't in her arms.

She drove her hands into her hair. She slid out of bed, shaking. "I can't do this."

"Do what?"

Raise a child like this, while you chase the wind.

This time she didn't say it aloud. She snatched her bathrobe off the hook on the back of her bedroom door. When was it going to stop? Never, Livie, never, and you always knew that. The voice in her head mocked her and scoured the life right out of her soul.

She'd accepted him on his terms, and their crazy life together, apart more than they were in each other's arms. She loved him with all of her heart. But how—oh, God, how?—was she supposed to explain his whereabouts to a child when he was gone for months, here for a day? How could they go with him? How could she tell this child, "No, baby, this isn't home, but maybe the next stop will be?"

How could she pawn off on this little one the same kind of upheaval her parents had destroyed her with when they had died?

"I'll have to learn the business from the ground up," Hunter said from the bed, "and a lot of drivers have a head start on me. They cut their teeth in their daddy's garages. And, granted, they're all pretty much a bunch of Southerners, so I'll break the mold. But this guy—his name is Pritchard Spikes—he says he'll let me test drive at his track in Anaheim and he'll see what I can do. If I really have the right stuff, he'll give me a chance."

"What?" Liv turned to him vacantly, belting her robe. "What are you talking about?"

"The stock car circuit. This chance. This is it, Livie, I feel it in my bones."

She stared at him. She couldn't think of a single thing to say. Liv went to the bathroom to throw up.

Liv found herself leaning against the bathroom sink now, fighting nausea again. Only this time she wasn't pregnant. She hadn't been with a man since...that night.

She'd done the test kit that weekend after Hunter had gone again. It had turned up positive. That had been in October.

He'd written, once, to tell her that Pritchard Spikes had indeed liked the way he handled his cars. He was going to give him a shot in his NASCAR garage in Winston-Salem, North Carolina. Not driving, not yet, but in the background, learning. Hunter told her that starting in February, he'd spend the next ten months in a different part of the country every weekend, on the race circuit.

He'd said he would stop in Flag on his way to the East Coast. She'd told him not to bother. It was over for them.

She had a child to raise. So she had married Johnny Guenther. He'd given her security, a home, everything she'd always needed. She had given him...nothing.

What she had done to Johnny out of sheer desperation had been cruel and despicable. She'd never been able to be a wife to him. She'd ended up alone after all. But she'd raised her daughter in one place, in one home, if not conventionally.

Shuddering, Liv went back to her bedroom and slipped out of her robe. She pulled on a pair of khaki slacks and a sleek, black top. Shoved her feet into black sandals.

She was ready for the Spirit Room now. Hunter had made his choice. She had made hers. There was nothing left now but to say goodbye—for good this time.

Chapter 3

Hunter wished he didn't remember the look Liv wore when she entered the bar, but he had seen it before.

Elegant, he thought. She'd always been able to look elegant, even in cutoffs and work boots, with dust coating her skin. It had been in the way she moved, in the dip of her shoulder when she would glance back with a cunning grin, in the way she tunneled her fingers through her hair, pulling it straight back from her forehead, then letting it fall. Everything about her said that she'd been born for a better life than the Res.

Sometimes, in their last years together, he'd marveled that a half-breed troublemaker like himself could find her in his arms, skin to skin, that she was his. It had all been a mirage, but it had overwhelmed him while it had lasted.

As Liv paused to look for him in the Spirit Room, she reminded him of an unbroken filly trapped in a corral for her first saddling. He knew that when she stepped closer, he'd see a certain wildness at the edges of her eyes. She'd tremble so imperceptibly that it would be little more than a hum in the air around her. Livie had known fear, but like a proud and wild horse, she would never let it show.

He *had* trapped her tonight, Hunter thought, as surely as he had ever herded a mustang into a pen. He'd given her the choice of meeting him here or playing this out in front of her daughter. *His* daughter.

She was right to be afraid.

The mirrors behind the bar were smokey and bronzed. The whole room was brown and gold and dimly lit. Watching her reflection as she spotted him and approached, Hunter thought it looked a little like a tintype. He rolled his stool around to face her as she stepped up beside him and dropped one hip onto the neighboring stool.

"Punctual, Livie. As always."

She'd already told him not to call her that. She wouldn't give Hunter the satisfaction of protesting again. She scraped her hair back as the bartender approached and stared at the bar in front of Hunter. It was bare burnished walnut. She wondered how long he had been waiting. "Who's paying for this little shindig?" she asked.

"I am." Hunter glanced at the bartender. "Remy. Straight."

"No more Boone's? You've come up in the world."

"I've always burned it as fast as I earned it. Now there's just more to burn."

"In that case, make it two." She thought Hunter almost smiled, but his mouth was too hard to allow it.

Liv felt dazed. She couldn't believe she was here with him like this. In a bar. Again.

She'd known he'd come to Flag even though she'd told him not to. Liv willed herself, schooled herself, to be cold when she saw him walk in the door. She could show nothing. Hunter was like a wild cat when it came to scenting doubt, fear, pain. And he'd always known what she was feeling.

He couldn't know it this time. Her baby's future depended on it.

She was still angry at him, so angry that it hurt with a physical pain. Maybe that was all he would sense.

It had been a month since he'd left her bed for California, and Liv had already worked her way up from cocktail waitress to tending bar. No more frou-frou for her. She'd graduated to black trousers and a silk vest that nipped her waist and plunged down to her cleavage. She leaned forward when Hunter sat at the bar, giving him a good view of what he would be missing.

If he let her go.

"I told you not to come," she said, her tone flat. Then her heart sank. He was watching her eyes. Trying to read them.

"Yeah, well, I couldn't figure out why so I stopped to see for myself."

"North Carolina is a long way away from Arizona, pal. Better hit the road."

"After you tell me what's wrong."

You won't stay put. You won't just stay put and love me! Liv *straightened from the bar as someone gestured for another beer. She went to draw the draft.*

He was still waiting for her when she came back.

All she could do was take a deep breath and plunge in. A lot had happened since he had left.

"I'm getting married, Hunter. I've found someone who can give me a home, a family, everything I've always needed. You said when that happened, you would go away. So go."

Oh, dear God, the pain on his face. It snatched at her air. She couldn't bear to see it, so she went to wash glasses instead. But his voice followed her.

"Not you, Livie. You were the only one who ever knew when I was gone."

She looked up from the sink and steeled herself. "Are you still here?"

"Talk to me."

"I just did."

"Why?"

"I've thought about it. I'm not going to chase the wind with you, Hunter." *Fight for me. Oh, please, God, let him fight to keep me.*

His face went to stone. Any emotion there was just suddenly gone, as quickly as he blinked. He stood from the bar stool. Things screamed inside her.

"I really wanted you to come with me this time," he said.

"I never had your wings. I just plummet to the ground again when I try to fly. It's where I belong."

He'd gone. He'd moved on to North Carolina and a spot on one of Pritchard Spikes's pit crews, and she hadn't laid eyes on him again until the weekend in Delaware. Now he was back and he looked…dangerous.

She'd never feared him before, she realized wildly, but she did now. Even that first day when he'd turned up on a piebald gelding in Ama's grazing yard, his dark-blue eyes narrowed to slits against the sun, his long black hair tickling itself in the wind, looking as heathen as her worst nightmares. Even then, she hadn't been afraid. He'd asked her if she wanted some help. She'd said sure. She had loved him. Instantly, childishly, with a wild excitement and an obscure yearning for things she didn't yet understand.

Now the golden light in the bar turned his dusky skin to amber. His hair was swept back off his forehead, but it was long enough in the back to nudge his collar. His cheekbones were still slashes, and his eyes were still narrowed against something, but this time it wasn't the light. It was her.

"What do you want from me?" she asked bluntly.

His mouth didn't exactly soften, but he grinned like a shark. "Once you wouldn't have had to ask me that."

Heat slid through her. Liv gulped Remy and coughed a little. "That was then. I don't know you anymore. Now you're some kind of national sports icon, used to getting his own way."

"I've always gotten my own way." Except once. But Hunter couldn't let himself think about how she had sent him away. Not now. It would buckle something inside him. And this was war.

"This brings us back to my original question," Liv said. "What is it you're after with this little surprise visit?"

"You weren't surprised." He'd thought about it a lot since their meeting that morning. She'd been jarred, yes. But surprised? No. She'd known he'd come.

He watched her open her mouth as though to deny it, then she did that thing with her shoulder. A hitch, then a dip. On any other woman, it would have been called a shrug. With Liv, it meant, I'm not giving you an inch unless you earn it.

So he started back at the beginning. "Tell me about Johnny. The guy who *didn't* father your daughter. Tell me why you never mentioned a baby that last night I passed through Flagstaff. Damn it, Livie, you never said anything about being pregnant at all!"

He knew because he remembered every word.

"I never had your wings," she said. "I just plummet to the ground again when I try to fly."

No. She belonged in the sky with the sun, Hunter thought, burning bright while he flew. Why couldn't she see that? "Who?" he rasped. "Who is he? Who had you?" His fists hurt, cramped tight, ready to kill.

"No one." She brought her chin up to challenge him. "Yet."

"You're going to marry someone you've never even been with?"

"Sex isn't everything."

He laughed, and the reflex was flame-hot sand in his throat.

"I need a picket fence, Hunter. Will you give it to me? Stay here? Get a job?"

"I've had jobs, Livie! I've always had a job. Is that what this is about? What do you think I've been eating with and buying gas with to drive back here all the time?"

Her eyes said it was the wrong answer. They went to charred black. "Go to hell, Hunter Hawk-Cole."

He was reasonably sure he was already there.

"I called Flagstaff City Hall for your marriage license," he said now, watching her expression. "About a year later."

Liv felt bony, white knuckles grab her heart and squeeze. "Apparently, you never bothered checking for the divorce decree, too."

"I figured you had enough grit to make it last. But I was wrong about a lot, wasn't I, Livie? Did he know the baby wasn't his?"

Johnny had known. It was why he had married her. Johnny had been her knight in shining armor. He'd loved her and was decent enough to try to give her what she'd needed most—a father for her child. "That," she said hoarsely, "has no bearing whatsoever on this conversation."

She saw him clench his jaw. "I really have a keen interest in finding out whether or not you passed my daughter off as someone else's."

She'd never done that. "You have a really rock-bottom view of my integrity, don't you?"

"Why should my opinion be higher?" He saw her flinch and was glad. But Hunter had always loved the way she could recover.

"He knew." Her chin came up. Her eyes narrowed haughtily. "Does *she?*"

"*She* has a name."

"Victoria Rose. I looked that up, too." He hadn't wanted to admit it, but the words were out before he could stop them.

"When?"

"Two weeks ago. Just to check. She was born eight months and twenty-nine days after the last time you and I were together."

"Bingo."

"You've still got that attitude, don't you? The world can kiss your butt and you'll give them directions to find it. Why that name?"

He wanted to know everything, he realized, and that surprised him. He had never wanted a child. He knew what adults could do to a kid. His Anglo relatives had dragged him to their churches when he was little. He'd been caught between three cultures—Christian, Hopi and Navajo. But all three of them had one theme in common. *The sins of the father...*

He had never intended to visit his own shortcomings upon progeny. He was damaged, baggage-laden, and he had always craved anything that would make him forget that for a while. Speed. Alligators. Spitting in death's face. But whether he'd looked for her or not, Victoria Rose was here.

And he wanted to know about her. Every detail.

"The name," he said again when Liv didn't answer. "It's not in your family, it's not in mine. Was it his? Guenther's?"

Liv hesitated, then she got that glint in her eyes. "Desert Rose was a little avant-garde for the life I envisioned for her."

"So it was supposed to be Desert Rose."

Again she hesitated. "Yes. But Victoria was more traditional."

"Was she ever one of those kids who hated her name?"

He watched her expression spasm. "You don't need to know this."

"I do."

"Damn you, Hunter, just go away again!"

He could do that, he thought. Maybe. Maybe. Because letting himself love the daughter meant being near the mother. But he needed to put more pieces together. *"Tell me, damn it."*

He watched her gasp for breath, then the words tumbled out. "She always liked the Hawk bit better than Slade. She never took Johnny's name."

Hunter sat back suddenly, though there was no part of the stool to support the reflex. Something punched him, something unseen. "Then she does know."

"She hasn't watched racing. She makes no connection to you."

"She will."

"Over my dead body." Liv felt things riot inside her. "Leave her alone. What do you have to gain by any of this?"

"I need to see her."

"Why, Hunter, *why?*" Liv played her last ace card. "Is what you think you want more important than what she needs?"

"Yes. Because I'm the adult here. Her father. And I have a right to decide what's best for her."

"You've been gone her entire life!"

"Not my choice."

There was that, Liv thought. Oh, bless her, he'd never let go of that. "Please. Trust me."

"Never again."

It killed something in her soul. "Not as a lover. As a mother."

"I don't know what kind of mother you are."

She felt heat stain her cheeks. "A good one."

"Prove it. Give us both time to come to terms with this."

"You and me?"

"The hell with you, Livie. You don't matter anymore. Me and Victoria Rose."

He said it tonelessly. Something hot and wet hurt her eyes. She refused to cry.

"If she knows Guenther wasn't her real father," he said, "what does it hurt to introduce me into her life?"

You'll go again. He was still the same man who hadn't wanted her enough all those years ago to just stay put and make a life with the two of them.

She'd given him the option. He could have grabbed her back from marrying Johnny. He hadn't done it. The wind he'd chased had been more important to him than catching her as she fell to earth.

"What are you afraid of, Livie?" His voice was suddenly silken with challenge. "That your little girl will tell you that you made the wrong choice in men?"

Her heels found the pine floor. Liv felt a little jarred, surprised by the impact when she slid off the stool with such force. She was even more surprised to find her snifter in her hand. There was little more than a mouthful of Remy left. She tossed it at him.

He came off his stool like lightning. It was one small thing she'd managed to forget about him, how fast he could move when he was angry. Not angry, she thought, feeling something shrink inside her. Furious. This time when his hand caught her chin, his touch hurt. His fingers did not clench. His grip did not tighten. But there was something there that threatened her, a certain heat that terrified her.

Liv wrenched away.

"There's an easy way to do this," he said, "and a hard way. It's your choice, Livie."

"Go to hell."

She took a step away from the bar, then turned toward him, her whole body flowing into the movement. From her expression, he knew that if she had access to another drink, he'd be wearing that, too. When she finally turned away again, Hunter decided to let her go.

And simmer on it some.

That hadn't solved anything.

Liv's hands were like claws on the steering wheel as she rocketed her little BMW back up Main Street toward the inn at the edge of town. Even her heart was shaking. *He wasn't going to go.*

She knew him far too well to delude herself into wishful thinking. He just wasn't going to leave their lives again, at least not without kicking up a good bit of dust first.

Meeting with him had been an utter waste of time. All it had done was stoke more old memories. It had rekindled all the old pain. "Damn him, damn him, damn him!" She banged the heel of her hand against the steering wheel, jumping when the horn sounded. She almost swerved off the road.

She couldn't drive right now, not like this.

Liv pulled over. She let the fury blaze through her, so immense, so alive it literally made red dots dance in front of her vision. How *dare* he?

She'd given him every opportunity eight and a half years ago to love her enough to stay put. *To fight for her.* To give her the simple sweetness of knowing that he'd do whatever it took to keep her from marrying another man. Instead, he'd walked out. Out of that bar and the Flagstaff resort, out of her life. He'd gone.

Now he dared to act as if he had some sort of rights in this situation. As a *father.* He dared to threaten her. To imply that *she* had done something wrong.

He wanted a fight? He'd have one, Liv decided.

It took Hunter five full minutes to remember that Liv Slade had never been able to drive worth a damn.

He went upstairs to his room and washed the Remy from his face. He shoved his damp shirt into the bag for the laundry. His blood was pumping.

Over the years he had learned to curb his temper. Bumper-to-bumper, quarter-panel-to-quarter-panel traffic at 180 MPH was no time to give vent to anger over some infraction committed by another driver. A retaliatory tap of metal against metal at that speed could send another man to his death. He'd learned to contain anger, to control it, to wait to finish things off after the race if need be. By then his fury had usually waned.

But now it was liquid fire in his blood, scouring the inside of his veins with something painful and blistering, and it showed no signs of abating. He couldn't get rid of it.

She'd dumped him eight and a half years ago like a minor inconvenience. She'd gone chasing after her picket fences with *his* child. He'd taught her to laugh, to love, to ride, to drive—

To drive.

She'd once plowed his pickup right into the side of a barn. And she hadn't been angry at the time. She'd actually been concentrating.

Hunter rubbed the back of his neck at the remembered whiplash pain and went to the phone on the nightstand. He picked it up, held it for a long moment, then he slammed it down again. Who the hell was he supposed to call to let them know there was probably a maniac on the road? He didn't quite hate her enough to bring the cops down on her head.

Well, he did, but that would be a particularly low blow. Not his style.

Damn her. She hadn't needed him eight and a half years ago, and she hadn't needed him once in all the time that had passed since then. If she was angry now and erratic, that was her problem.

Except she was somebody's mother. His kid's mother.

Hunter swore and grabbed a T-shirt out of one of the drawers. He snatched the keys to his rented SUV off the top of the room's television. He jogged down the stairs and outside.

As he peeled out of the parking lot, he double-shifted for more immediate speed. The engine of the SUV gave a squeal of pure shock at what was being asked of it. Hunter didn't know what he was looking for as he sped down Main Street. He didn't know what kind of car she was driving these days. His eyes scanned the roadsides for a heap of smoldering metal. Mountainsides were harder than barn walls.

Then he spotted the BMW pulled to the side up ahead, just idling there. She was fine. She'd had the sense to pull over.

He stopped behind her. His headlights threw the interior of her car into a glare brighter than full noon on the high desert. He saw her fumbling with her armrest as he jumped down out of the SUV, probably trying to find the lock button. He ran to drag the door open before she could manage it.

She screamed.

"It's me." Hunter caught her elbow and dragged her bodily out of the little car. She fought him like a madwoman. Maybe his words hadn't penetrated. Then again, maybe they had, and she really hated him this much.

He caught her wrists as she pummeled his chest with them. "Stop it!" He shouted this time. *"Stop it!"*

"I hate you!" she screamed.

Right on the second try, he thought. She'd known it was him. "No problem. You're real low on my list of favorite people, as well."

She reared back. "What are you doing here?"

Losing my mind. "You can't drive when you're upset. Hell, you can't drive on a good day." He sounded like an idiot, even to himself.

"This from Mr. Anaheim," she spat.

He scowled at her. "Mr. Who?"

"Anaheim! That's where you went when you left me!"

It took him a moment, but he made sense of it. Pritch's trial track.

"Let me go." She tugged against his grip.

"Calm down first. And *you* left me."

"The hell I did! But I will now if you'll get your hands off me!"

Hunter let her hands go but grabbed her shoulders. He wanted to shake her. *"You were pregnant when you told me to leave that bar!"*

"And you left!" she shouted back.

Then she started shaking.

He felt it under his fingertips, tremors that grew and shuddered. Hunter pulled his hands back fast. For more than eight long, cold years, he'd imagined ways to punish her for leaving him as if he was yesterday's garbage. Now he couldn't let her emotion rock him.

"I'm going to be a part of that little girl's life," he said more quietly.

For more than eight desperate, aching years, she'd imagined ways to make him hurt as badly as he'd hurt her, Liv thought. Her breath chugged a little, then she finally got her voice back. "No. You're not. Because I won't allow it."

He leaned closer, pinning her back against her car. He stopped only when his face was inches from hers. "You have no options here, Livie. I'm bigger than you are. You can't stop me if I decide I'm headed somewhere."

"Try me." Liv's fist found his gut. She was rewarded by a grunt of breath.

She started to twist away, but then something in his eyes stopped her. His gaze turned heated and speculative at the same time she realized what she had just said. "I didn't mean—"

"Why, Livie. Was that an invitation?" He pulled her back and his mouth found hers.

She managed, just managed, to work her hands up between them and get them against his chest. *Oh, no. Don't let me remember this part!* It was too cruel, much more than she could stand. But one of his hands found her shoulder and he eased her back against the car again. And his mouth pummeled hers.

Why was he doing this? Had he lost his mind? No, she thought desperately. He'd always been capable of doing anything at any given moment.

And she'd always melted into his kiss as though nothing else in the world had mattered. She'd always been so at home tangling her tongue with his. It all came back to her, flooding, hot, debilitating. The way she used to tease him, pulling back to nip his lower lip. She did it again. The way she'd once loved to stroke her fingers through his hair. Her hands moved up, up, searching to tangle in it.

The way he could swallow her breath.

The way she needed him.

The way he made her whole.

The scent of Liv was different, he realized. The impact of that rolled through him. She smelled spicier, sharper than before. More woman than girl. But the taste of her was the same, dark and sweet and tantalizing. The flick of her tongue was the same, part challenge and part desperation. The heat had only grown, and it damn near drove him to his knees.

Liv felt things coming undone inside her. Unraveling, spinning faster and faster, parts of her hurling off into space with each hot, wet slide of his lips. And she knew she was never going to get those pieces back this time if she didn't stop this *right now.*

She brought her knee up.

He felt it, sensed it, just in time, and turned half away from her, breaking the kiss, avoiding the blow. He scrubbed a hand over his mouth. "Damn you, Livie. You never used to play dirty."

"*Don't call me that!* And don't you ever, ever, *ever* do that to me again!"

He wasn't sure why he had. To make her remember what they had once shared? The memories had been gnawing at him all night.

"Scares you, doesn't it, that we still strike sparks?" It had taken her three full minutes to think of hurting him, he realized. Something moved in his gut, a triumph of sorts, then it died.

She turned back to her car and slid into the seat, behind the wheel again.

"So where does this leave us?" he wondered aloud.

Liv pulled the door shut hard, almost taking off parts of his anatomy that shouldn't have been awake in the first place. Hunter stepped back fast. Then she lowered her window.

"It leaves *you* in whatever city you were planning to call home next weekend," she spat.

"Guess we'll be running into each other again then."

"Hunter, *no!* This is insane."

"It's overdue. We would have gone through this a long time ago if I'd only known the truth then. So let's just set things to rights this time and be done with it."

"You should have just asked me to marry you in the first place!"

"How could I? I didn't know about her!" That, he thought, seemed to be something she refused to get through her head.

Then he watched her expression cave. He saw the tears gather in her eyes, shining and wet.

"Exactly," she said, clipping off the syllables.

She put the car in gear. He moved around in front of it to stop her from driving off. She wouldn't actually run over him. At least, he didn't think so.

He was willing to risk it.

"Exactly?" he demanded. "What does that mean?"

Liv stuck her head out the window as she took her foot off the brake. The car coasted forward. Hunter jumped back. And jumped back. Again. She kept coming.

"Damn it, Livie!"

"Why did you need to know about the baby, Hunter, to want to stay with me?"

She gunned the engine. He leaped aside just in time to avoid being flattened. She'd turned out to be not an altogether bad driver after all. He watched her car smoke up the road and silently wished for a cop to nail her spiteful backside right to a speeding ticket. Hunter realized his hands were fisted.

He forced himself to relax them, then he scrubbed a palm over his mouth, still tasting her. Still wanting her.

He realized he could hate her for that alone.

Everything about him kept filling her head all the way home.

Liv veered into the garage at the back of the inn's property and hit the brakes hard. But she didn't do it soon enough. Her tires skidded. She drove the nose of her precious little BMW squarely into the far brick wall. She heard the metal squeal in pain.

A keening sound of frustration and helpless anger filled her throat. She turned the car off and jumped out, kicking a tire. "This is your fault, Hunter, damn it! I haven't had an accident in almost ten years!" She slammed the door. "Do you know what it costs to fix one of these bumpers?"

"No," Kiki's voice said flatly. "What?"

Liv whipped around. "What are you doing here?"

Kiki folded her arms over her breasts where she stood in the open garage door. "You asked me to spend the night so someone would be with Vicky."

Liv gritted her teeth. "Don't you think I remember that?"

"I don't know. Do you?" Kiki threw her hands up in a question. "Or are you just insane and beside yourself with…what? Temper? Lust? Regret?"

"None of the above." Liv stalked toward the door and reached up to grab the panel to pull it down. "You want to move," she warned. "I almost just ran him over, so I probably can't be trusted with this garage door, either."

"You need me. You won't hurt me." But Kiki stepped back. "What happened?"

"Were you waiting up for me?" Liv challenged without answering. She headed for the back door of the inn.

"I was sound asleep when I heard tires burning rubber in the driveway."

"Liar. You're a night owl."

"Okay, I was making brownies—an extra treat for tea tomorrow." Kiki pulled open the kitchen door and they went inside together. "I'll get the brandy."

Liv stopped just over the threshold of the kitchen and paused to sniff deeply. *This* was her life. Kiki's cooking, aromatic in the air. Her home, her livelihood, a restored brothel, an aging whore restored to youth and civility by a virgin's pretty clothes. *This,* she thought fiercely, was hers. It was what she had done, what she had made, when he'd left her.

She would not let him shatter it—her—all over again.

Liv sank down in one of the kitchen chairs, dropping her forehead to the wood of the table. She stayed that way until she heard the crack of the brandy bottle hitting the butcher block.

"Sit up and stop wallowing," Kiki said. "If it went that badly, then we need a plan."

Liv's spine snapped straight again. "I'm not—"

"Wallowing? Of course, you are. You've been crying," Kiki observed. She poured and pushed a snifter in her direction.

"You know, when you went to Delaware, you should have simultaneously bought stock in the nearest distillery. Something tells me we're going to be buying a lot of this before you straighten out the mess you've made."

Liv felt everything inside her stiffen and she hurt with the betrayal. "You think all of this is my fault?"

"In a nutshell? Yes." Kiki tossed back a shot and gave a delicate shiver. "Remember on the Res, when this was illegal?"

"I don't want to remember anything about the Res." She was still stinging from her friend's last comment.

"You and me and Hunter would drive clear to Winslow and back that last winter there, just for a bottle of Boone's," Kiki reminisced. "That truck he had was *horrible*."

"Yeah, well, it died when I drove it into his aunt's barn," Liv muttered. "And he doesn't drink Boone's anymore."

Kiki sat back and sipped her next shot. "Tell me all about it."

Liv felt the shaking start inside her again. "He wants to see her. He wants to see Vicky."

"You couldn't have expected anything else."

"Why not? He left once. I was hoping to make him do it again. Tonight."

"You're simplifying."

"Who's side are you on, anyway?" Liv demanded, grabbing her own snifter.

"That's easy. Vicky's." Kiki wiggled her brows to soften the impact of her words. "Hey, I'm her godmother."

"You're Navajo, and I had to drag you kicking and screaming into the church for her christening."

"But God didn't kick me out again, so it stuck."

Damn it, she was *not* going to smile. "What do I do now?" she asked, her voice hollow.

Kiki thought about it. "What are the odds that he could meet her once, then just take off again?"

"I can't let that happen." Liv's bones went to cement at the mere thought. Cold and heavy.

"Why not?"

"Do you know how much that would rock her world?"

"Maybe not as much as it would rock yours." Kiki held a hand up when Liv would have protested. "Look, I'm not the enemy here. If I had had my way, you never would have gone to Delaware in the first place. But I couldn't stop you. You've heard that expression about beds and lying in them?"

Liv put her head down again. It hurt, throbbed, in deep recesses. "Damn it."

"Give him what he wants, Liv. Get it over with and stop fighting him. Any day now, he'll catch scent of the wind again and he'll go. He always has."

Liv tilted her head to peek up at her friend. "And how do you think Vicky would feel about that if she knew he was going?"

For the first time, Kiki had no answer. She hesitated, then she shook her head. "That was my best advice."

"It stunk."

"In retrospect…yes."

They were quiet for a long time before Kiki cleared her throat again. "Does he look the same as he does on TV these days? Kind of fierce? Drop-dead gorgeous?"

Liv sat up and let out her breath. "More or less."

"Wow. He grew up nice, then."

Liv's eyes narrowed. "Why didn't you ever go after him?"

"Because he loved you."

A tremor went through Liv. He hadn't. Not enough. "I meant before I got to the Res. You had to have known him then, before I was part of the equation. You two were in school together."

But Kiki shook her head. "He was definitely a loner before he met you."

Why did that hurt so much? Liv took more brandy, swallowing deeper this time. Then she spit out the words. "He kissed me."

"I know."

Her eyes bugged. "What are you, psychic?"

"Just very wise. You two sizzled off each other back then. I couldn't see it changing, especially with all the anger between you right now. Anger is hot. Also, your lipstick is all over your face."

Liv scrubbed her hand over her mouth just as the oven timer buzzed.

"That's my cue." Kiki got to her feet again.

"You're not going to drive back to your apartment tonight, are you?" Kiki was a loner, too, a woman with a silent, still soul deep inside. She liked her solitude, which was why she didn't live at the inn, though Liv did keep a room for Kiki there. They'd revamped the attic for her.

"And come back here at five-thirty to get ready for breakfast?" Kiki asked. "Not worth the gas or the effort." She pulled the brownies out and dropped them into a warming tray to cool them down gently. She said it made a difference, kept them from hardening up. Something about their microscopic particles, Liv thought. Which was why Kiki's brownies were better than anyone else's.

So she was staying, Liv thought. That was good. Because she didn't want to be alone. "Let's have another, then." She reached for the bottle.

Kiki sighed. "Okay. Twist my arm. At least it's not Boone's. Remember when you used to do that to me?"

Liv cracked up. "What were we? All of eighteen?"

"*I* was eighteen. You were seventeen, and wondering why Hunter would never touch you. It was right after your grandmother died and I used to sleep over to help you ease into all that new silence. You'd keep me up all night talking about him."

Liv nodded. There was nothing so quiet as being alone in the desert without even the sound of another human being's breath. "I remember."

"You stayed awake and bleated about Hunter all night."

"I didn't *bleat.*"

Kiki shrugged. "Maybe that was the lambs." She came back to the table and sat again. "I guess Hunter has no similar qualms about touching you this time around."

Liv felt his mouth on hers all over again. She refused to shiver visibly. "Why would he do such a crazy thing?"

"Power play? I don't know. Anyway, it's not going to help this situation."

"It's not going to have the chance to affect it one way or the other. I'm not going to see him again."

"Sure you are. He'll be on our doorstep in the morning."

Liv's whole body spasmed. "I know."

"Well, we agree on something, then." Kiki held her glass up in a toast. "Now all we have to do is figure out what do to about it."

They clicked their crystal together. Neither one of them noticed the door to the center hall ease quietly shut again. Neither of them heard the soft patter of bare, little-girl feet moving back up the stairs.

Chapter 4

Hunter wasn't waiting on their doorstep in the morning. That scared Liv just a little bit more than if he had actually turned up. A silent Hunter was always more dangerous than one who was grabbing her and kissing her.

With the memory, Liv's fingers fumbled as she wove Vicky's hair into a braid. "Ouch!" Vicky squealed.

"Sorry, baby."

Liv finished up, trying to pay attention, half waiting, braced, for Kiki to sound the alarm from downstairs that Hunter had shown up. But there was only the distant rustle of the guests moving about, gathering for breakfast.

Then the intercom they'd installed between the kitchen and the private rooms finally crackled with gentle static. Liv stiffened.

"The buffet table is laden with sausage, eggs, fruit, potatoes, and Hangtown fry," Kiki said. "Come and get it."

"Uh…we'll be right there." Liv got her breath back with the reprieve.

"Mom, I look like a show pony," Vicky complained.

Liv scowled at her daughter's reflection in the vanity mirror.

Okay, so the ribbons she'd woven in to her braid stuck out a little here and there. But the end effect was charming. "You look fine."

"I'm not leaving this room like this."

"Live with it. Please?" When had Vicky turned eighteen? Liv was frantic, rattling in her skin. She had to get Vicky out of here in case Hunter showed up.

Vicky started to reach up to undo Liv's whole last ten-minute toil.

"Didn't you hear Aunt Kiki?" Liv asked quickly. "She made Hangtown fry!"

Vicky hesitated. "Oysters."

"Oysters," Liv said solemnly.

"For breakfast."

Most kids lived for pizza. Hers critiqued five-star restaurants. "You'll miss them if the guests have enough time to dig through it all before we get there."

Vicky sighed. "Oysters...or I don't look like a geek. Oysters...or I don't look like a geek." She flipped her hand back and forth with each phrase. "Tough choice."

"Go with the oysters," Liv advised.

Vicky finally turned away from the mirror to hunt up her book bag.

"Guitar," Liv reminded her. "Music lessons today third period. And don't forget your riding stuff for after school." Vicky had lessons every Tuesday and Friday.

The little girl went to the corner of her room to grab her guitar case and a small duffel bag. Liv watched her prance to the door, laden with everything she would need for her day. *I've done well.* Maybe Vicky wasn't normal in the conventional sense of the word, but she didn't shoplift at five-and-dimes, either.

"I've done okay by her," Liv muttered under her breath. "I did the right thing. Damn it, Hunter, leave us alone."

"What?" Vicky asked.

Liv jolted. "Nothing. Let's go. Swallow a few oysters, then we'll head down the hill for the bus."

"It's only 7:30!"

"We'll be early for it, then. We'll wait in the car and share some quality time."

"Mom, you're acting weird."

Liv didn't answer that. She went out and shut the bedroom door behind them.

Only a desperate man would pair oysters with eggs, Hunter thought, putting the menu down in a restaurant he'd found on Main Street. He'd be hard-pressed to decide which was slimier.

"Two eggs over hard, pancakes and bacon," he told the waitress.

"All on one plate?"

"Pancakes separate to allow for the syrup goo."

She grinned. She was young, maybe all of nineteen, and she reminded him so painfully of Liv at that age, Hunter felt something inside him literally cramp. Her hair was blond, her eyes were blue. It didn't matter. She had that same love-me-and-tip-me ferocity about her, something that said there was a lot going on behind that cheeky grin.

She picked up his menu and took off. Hunter reached for his coffee mug and drank deeply.

He really hadn't needed to go back to the bar last night after he'd left Liv. Somewhere en route to the Connor he'd determined that another shot of cognac would take the taste of her off his tongue. It hadn't worked, so he'd tried a few. Even that hadn't allowed him to sleep. Now, muddleheaded, he had to decide a plan of attack for today.

He'd wanted to be in her driveway when she took the child to school. Liv would have to drive her there, he figured. The inn was way out on the edge of town. What were the odds that a school bus would go that far? But he suspected that his eyes were just bleary and bloodshot enough to scare the bejesus out of the little girl. So he decided to jolt himself with caffeine first. And he'd use the time to plan a little.

Damn you, Livie. Damn you. I had a right to know. He couldn't get past that. He had to figure out what to do about it now that he *did* know.

His breakfast came, and Hunter polished it off, feeling better for it. He paid the tab and went out to his SUV. Sorry excuse for a vehicle, he thought. He needed to *drive*. He needed to get some of this tension out of his system. He was still ticked off at Pritch, but now, at least, he had other things to occupy his mind.

It was already 8:45 so he headed straight for the school. He parked half a block away from the entrance and watched a lot of buses roll up, but there was no sign of Liv's BMW. Maybe she'd cracked it up last night after all. The thought offered him both a rush of satisfaction and a spasm of panic. He got out of the vehicle and stepped up to the schoolyard fence.

A pretty redheaded woman stood there, her fingers hooked into the metal mesh. She pulled one hand back to wave to one of the kids.

"Boy or girl?" Hunter asked conversationally.

She looked at him, startled.

"The one you're waving to," he clarified.

"Oh." She flushed, smiled. "Girl. Dandi Jane. She's right over there. She's eight."

Right on target, Hunter thought, then he lied because there were things he needed to know. "My daughter is only six. I guess I have a lot to look forward to."

The woman laughed. "That you do. Six was easy. Just wait until you get into piano and gymnastics."

"Hmm."

"Oh, and ponies. As soon as she turns seven, you'll probably have to buy her a pony."

He gave a mock shudder. "They're expensive."

"Right. By the way, I'm Adele Trawley." She held out her hand.

"Joe Smith." Hunter lied again at the last minute and almost stumbled over the name, but he shook her hand.

"Something tells me you're not a custodial dad," Adele said.

"A what?"

"You're divorced and you don't have custody, right?"

"Uh, no. I don't."

"Not even joint?"

"Joint?" Hunter echoed.

"I was divorced six months ago, so I'm up on the lingo," she explained, grinning again. "That's all the style right now."

"Joint custody," he repeated, to be sure.

"Four nights a week with me, three with her dad. Equal opportunity parenting. Family court judges are big on it these days, except with infants. Infants really need their moms full-time."

"That makes sense." His mind was buzzing. Victoria Rose wasn't an infant.

"If you don't have joint custody, you should find another lawyer," Adele advised. "Go back to court."

He would definitely think about it, Hunter decided.

"Do I know you from somewhere?" she asked suddenly. "You look familiar."

Gig's up, Hunter thought. NASCAR was getting entirely too popular for his comfort these days. "I think I look a lot like that stock car driver. People tell me that all the time."

She studied his face and a light dawned in her eyes. "Sure. Hunter Hawk-Cole. Wow. You're a dead ringer."

"Maybe I should pretend and start handing out autographs."

"Or pit passes."

A race fan, he thought. Just his luck. How long would it take her to remember that the Hawk was temporarily off the circuit? "Hey, if you'll excuse me, I've got to run."

"Sure. Maybe I'll see you here again some morning."

Maybe, he thought. Joint custody.

Now that he had a few choices regarding what little girls did with their extracurricular time, his next order of business was to find out what Victoria Rose's preferences were. He turned away from Adele and in a split-second time frame that froze him, he saw his daughter get off one of the buses.

Her black hair was all done up in a braid with red calico ribbons tied through it. She wore jeans, red sneakers and a red denim jacket. She lugged some sort of duffel bag that had the words MUSTANG RIDGE RIDING ACADEMY printed on it in peeling white letters—the satchel obviously got a lot of use. She also carried a guitar case.

A guitar and horses. Not so far removed from pianos and ponies at all. Adele Trawley was a genius.

Hunter turned back to her. "Can I ask you one more question?"

She smoothed her hair in an entirely female gesture. "Sure."

"Do the kids get music lessons in school?"

She nodded. "It's part of the curriculum. Boy, you are new at this."

"Yeah," Hunter said. "I am."

He left her again and went back to the SUV. So the guitar was for school hours and the riding stuff was probably for after, he decided. He got behind the wheel just as the little girl with the red ribbon in her hair headed up the steps into the school.

He stared at her. She had Liv's stride. A little arrogant, but there was that hint there that said maybe she was forcing it. Maybe there was a bit of marshmallow inside that she didn't want anyone to find.

Then someone must have said something behind her because the little girl turned around suddenly just as she reached the doors. She flashed a grin and Hunter saw...himself.

"Ah. Ah, God."

In an instant he could no longer breathe. His heart stretched, yawned, pulled to new capacity, and it hurt. She had his black hair, he thought. His blue eyes. All of that he could bear. But in that second, with that grin, he'd seen something else in her eyes, something he recognized intimately and it undid him. *Come on, dare me. See if I'll do it.*

In an instant Victoria Rose dropped the guitar case and the bag. She leaped for one of the stone pillars holding up the porte-cochere entrance of the school. She wrapped herself around it like a monkey and shimmied up, then—one hand groping and grasping—she pressed her palm to the roof. She was laughing when a teacher came to scold her and pull her down again. She tucked her head, pretending to be abashed, but before she did, Hunter saw the devil's own grin in her eyes.

She was his. His blood. His flesh. That beautiful little daredevil was *his child.*

Hunter sat there long after she had finally gone inside, his hands gripping the steering wheel. His eyes hurt. A lot. He finally loosened a hand to rub one of them. And he realized that he was crying.

Liv was late getting to Mustang Ridge.

Over the years it had become a point of pride for her that she never missed an afternoon tea at the inn. She hadn't done it after a nasty fall out of the barn loft when they'd been renovating out there, or through a relatively minor bout with pneumonia. Kiki was the accounting brain and the scrumptious food behind their operation. Liv had vowed from the beginning that her contribution would be more than just the money needed to get the place off the ground—and it was.

She was a hostess, and she was a good one. She'd learned the art first on horseback then in the bar, and finally in hotel operations in Flagstaff. Her gift was her charm...even when it hurt.

She was not going to let a little thing like Hunter Hawk-Cole's arrival in Jerome knock her off her stride.

She'd just keep things short and sweet with the guests, she decided. She didn't want to leave Vicky alone at her riding lesson while he was in town. Liv glanced at her watch. It was five minutes before three. She leaned closer to her vanity mirror to slash lipstick over her mouth and fluff the long layers of her hair. Then she stepped back to inspect herself. Her blue chambray shirt had been pressed to within a wrinkle of its life. She rolled the sleeves up a little. She wore jeans and a braided belt and boots, and tiny, dangling copper roses in her ears. She dressed for tea...but she didn't. She was, after all, just welcoming guests into her home.

Liv left her rooms and trotted downstairs.

The week's group was an eclectic bunch. She joined them in the parlor that she and Kiki had had gutted and enlarged to accommodate a sideboard and two separate seating areas. The nuns from St. Joe's in Brooklyn—two of them—were holding court on the navy-blue divan with two teenagers from Myanopie, Louisiana. The girls had been a temperamental handful since their arrival late yesterday. Jade was sixteen, Ruby was seventeen, and they clearly did not consider a family vacation to be their lifelong dream. But now Ruby's cheeks were flushed and her eyes sparked. She was in a heated debate with Sister Ann over the value of confession.

The girls' parents enjoyed the brocade sofa on the opposite side of the room with a widowed writer from Oregon and a pair of newlyweds from Kansas. Liv joined that group. She never argued politics or religion.

"These brownies," Mrs. Endelmen, mother of the teenagers, gushed. "There must be some secret to keeping them so moist. You'll share it with me before I go."

"No, I won't." Liv grinned, helped herself to one and poured the tea. "I really don't know it. At least not entirely."

"You don't do the cooking?" asked the writer.

Liv flailed mentally for his name. She didn't usually forget, but it had been an extraordinary few days. Ed something-or-other, she thought. Ah… "No, Mr. Stern. That would be my partner. She actually has her doctorate in science. She earned it while she was working here."

"She must be a bright woman. And she cooks for a living?" asked Mr. Endelmen, clearly startled.

"She says her success is based on the molecular breakdown of each ingredient and the ghosts of campfires past."

"Ghosts?" Jade piped up. She left the divan to join their conversation. "You have ghosts here?"

"Sure. Jerome is a bona fide ghost town." And Liv was off and running.

She told them about the jail that had relocated itself by sliding downhill in a mudslide and the clanging chains that could still be heard there at night. About the woman in red who could be seen higher up on the cliff face under just the right conditions— a full moon in warm weather. And about the young girl of ill repute who had once lived in the inn when it was still a brothel, who occasionally made her presence known in the attic where she had reportedly died at the hands of a jealous lover who hadn't a clue what she did for a living until he found her there with another man.

"Can I see it?" Jade asked avidly. "The attic room?"

Liv shook her head. "Sorry. No can do. That's my partner's quarters."

"Doesn't she mind sharing it with a ghost?"

"Kiki doesn't spend the night here often. But she's a force to be reckoned with. When she's in residence, Sweet Sarah tends to mind her manners. It's only when the room is empty that we can hear her crying. The sound echoes down the stairs."

Ruby came to join the conversation. The nuns looked a little disapproving of the subject, Liv thought. She glanced at her watch—3:15. She needed to get out of here and head down the hill to the riding academy. The bus would land Vicky there at 3:30.

"You mean the stairs there off the third-floor hall?" Ruby asked.

"Right. The door at the very end goes to the attic," Liv said. "You can sit there and listen for a while tonight if you like."

"Your partner won't be here?"

"Probably not."

"What do we do if we hear her?" Jade asked.

"Run like hell," Ruby advised.

Ed Stern cracked up. Mrs. Endelmen looked resigned. The newlyweds seemed relieved that they did not have a room on the third floor. Liv polished off her tea and hitched her position in the general direction of the door.

"I do a horseback tour of the area every morning, if any of you are interested. We can check out the sliding jail, and I can show you where the lady in red turns up on a good night. There are lots of other interesting things, too."

"Like that stock-car-driving hunk?" Ruby asked. "Talk about sweet. I heard he's vacationing here."

Liv's heart vaulted for a beat, then it froze. Now Hunter was invading her home—her livelihood, her sanctuary—if only by topic of conversation. But before she could react—or school herself not to—the girl's mother spoke up.

"That's not him," she said.

"How do you know?" Ruby demanded.

"I-it's not?" Liv asked.

"I heard a couple of women talking about him in the drugstore when I stopped in this morning to pick up some things,'' Mrs. Endelmen said. "One of them actually met him. She says he only looks like the Hawk, but it's not really him. He said so himself.''

What the hell game was he playing? Liv felt her heart begin moving again with an ache that was both old and new. Then it bounced with something like panic.

He was up to something.

Liv glanced at her watch. She had to go. It was nearly 3:30.

She took another step toward the door. "Enjoy yourselves, everyone. I'll see you at breakfast tomorrow. If any of you would like to join the tour ride, you can let me know then. I think we still have three or four mounts available.''

"Sidesaddle?'' asked one of the nuns.

Liv looked at her quickly. "Um, I don't think we have one of those.''

The nun looked down at her habit and sighed. "I'd like to try it, but it would be difficult with this skirt.''

Liv understood. "Let me see what I can do.''

It was going to cost her another few minutes, but she jogged to the barn to talk to Bourne before she left. He was wrapping the bowed tendon of a filly that had been really promising. She might still do for children under Bourne's healing ministrations. "Where can we lay our hands on a couple of sidesaddles?'' she asked him.

He answered without looking up from the stretch-wrap he was applying. "How 'bout the place you're heading out to right now?''

He was still annoyed with her for bucking the insurance guidelines and sending him on alone with the tour group yesterday. Liv closed her eyes briefly as a feeling like helplessness rolled over her. What else could Hunter possibly interfere with? Now he had her help ticked off at her, too!

"Mustang Ridge,'' she said, her voice sounding a little strident, even to herself. "I should ask at Mustang Ridge. That makes sense.''

"'Bout the only place I can think of might have one or two,'' he said.

Liv turned away and headed to the garage. Nuns sidesaddle on a trail ride. What next?

She was halfway down the cliff road that zigged and zagged back and forth on its way down the slope when she came to the overturned semi. Trucks weren't even supposed to be on this road, but once or twice a year one of them thought they could get away with it and gave it a try. The result was usually predictable.

"Damn it." Liv put her car in park and took her foot off the brake. Her nerves were coiled.

She thought of turning around, of going back up the slope and heading down the other road at the opposite end of town. It would take her forty minutes to get to Mustang Ridge that way. She glanced at her watch again. Now it was a quarter to four. If they cleared this mess within forty minutes, it would still be faster for her to just stay put and wait it out.

A police cruiser came whining down from town. She inched the BMW closer to the shoulder to allow it to pass.

It was 4:15 when traffic started moving again. She'd get there just as Vicky's lesson was over, Liv figured, grinding her teeth. She cursed the semi driver, then felt instantly contrite because this one might well have been really hurt. Her foot punched the accelerator.

Vicky was dismounting in the ring when Liv pulled up in the parking lot. Liv scanned the area and saw nothing amiss. No Hunter. Her heart settled down for the first time in an hour. Her panic had been ridiculous. He couldn't possibly know that Vicky took riding lessons or when.

She let herself into the arena and crossed to Vicky. "Sorry I'm late. How did it go today?"

"I got tossed."

Memory rained through Liv, of Hunter and a barn in Flag and what they had done there after he'd scraped her up off the ground. *She had to stop remembering.* She snatched herself back from the brink. "Are you hurt?"

"Nah. Landed on my butt."

"It's been a long time between falls," said Lila Severn, the instructor, stepping over to join them. "She was due." She tugged affectionately on Vicky's braid.

"Lila," Liv said. "I need to talk to you about something."

"Likewise. Vicky, you know the routine. Cool that pretty lady down." She motioned at the horse.

Liv frowned as she watched Vicky lead the mare off. She looked back at Lila. "You need to talk to me? Is there a problem?"

"I'm not sure. You tell me." She inclined her head to the left.

Liv looked that way. And saw Hunter.

He was standing with one shoulder against the far side of the barn, his arms crossed over his chest. The open barn door had blocked her view of him when she'd pulled up. The earth suddenly vanished from beneath her feet and her energy, her bones, her very *being* spiraled down into the vortex that was left. Liv opened her mouth to respond, but no words would come.

"Do you know him?" Lila asked.

"Yes." Liv finally hissed the word.

"Well, he's been here for most of the hour, watching your daughter."

"Did he approach her?"

"No."

Liv crossed to the edge of the ring without another word. She climbed the fence and landed hard on the other side, then strode toward him. By the time she reached him, her blood was humming. She shoved him hard in the chest. "You're way out of line."

His expression had been dispassionate as he watched her approach. Now something happened to his eyes. Temper leaped there then got cold. "Calm down. I didn't say a word to her."

"I don't care!" Liv realized she was shouting.

"So what you're saying is that you would prefer it if I didn't even observe her?"

"I would prefer it if one of your escapades would wipe you off the face of this earth!"

"Won't happen, Livie. I have the devil's own luck and, anyway, I would only come back to haunt you."

She found her fist wrapped in his shirt front at just the same time she heard Vicky call out from inside the barn. "Mom?"

"One word," Liv spat at him. "One single *word* to her and I'll kill you myself."

"You did that a long time ago, Liv."

Her heart clenched. Damn him for making her feel regret! "This isn't about you. Or about us."

"Isn't it?"

She dropped her hand and stepped back quickly. "No. You were never big on insight."

"I could always see straight through you. Except that last time. I still can't understand why you did what you did."

She was shaking. Damn it, he was making her shake again. *"Mom!"*

Vicky's voice went through her, sharp and demanding. "I've got to go see what she wants," Liv said.

"I'll wait."

"You need to *leave.*"

"Not when the show's just getting interesting. Go on, Livie. Let me see what kind of a mom you really are."

Vicky catapulted out of the barn and found them. She caught Liv's hand and tugged. "Mom, I put the horse on the hot-walker to cool down. Lila said that was okay. I can go now." Then she grinned up at Hunter. "Hi, Mr. Car-Driver. What are *you* doing here?"

"It's not the same guy," Liv said quickly. Her heart was pistoning. "He just looks like the man we met in Delaware. He told someone so today."

Vicky frowned. "Really?"

Liv begged him with her eyes. For one of the few times in her life, she begged. Once had been with the social worker after her family had died, a woman intent on sending her to some alien land, an Indian reservation. Once she had done it with her God and all her grandmother's deities that this man would fight for her, would not walk away when she was carrying his child.

None of that had worked at all.

"Please." She mouthed the words at him silently. "Don't."

He ignored her and looked at Vicky. "I'm the same guy. I

just told some people today that I wasn't because I didn't want them to recognize me.''

"Damn you," Liv spat. *"Damn you."*

"How come you don't want to be recognized?" Vicky asked.

"Sometimes life is easier when I'm not."

"We're going," Liv said. She pulled on Vicky's hand hard enough that the girl almost stumbled. An apology would have jumped to her lips, but she was too busy swallowing back helpless tears.

Vicky let Liv lead her away but she looked back over her shoulder. "Catch you later, Mr. Car-Driver. What's your real name, anyway?"

Daddy. Liv's heart stopped, waiting for him to say that, too.

"Hunter," he said. "Keep my secret for me, okay?"

Vicky giggled and pressed the fingers of her free hand to her lips. "Sure. Hush-hush-hush."

"There's a girl."

Liv looked back at him, and her eyes shot daggers. Then she hurried off, dragging Vicky with her.

Dear God, he could have just grabbed her and taken off with her. She'd been an hour late, Liv thought. He could have taken Vicky, could have kidnapped her. He could have—

"Stop it!" she grated aloud at her own spiraling and desperate thoughts.

"What?" Vicky asked. "I didn't do anything."

"Get in the car."

"I'm getting." She dove into the back seat. "You don't like that guy, do you?" she asked when Liv was behind the wheel.

"Not even a little bit." She'd loved him so much. Her hands fumbled with the keys. Liv started the engine.

"Why not?" Vicky asked.

She had to skate the edge of honesty here, Liv realized. Delicately. Carefully. "I knew him a long time ago, and he hurt my feelings."

"Is that all?"

"That's a lot." Liv drove hard out of the riding academy lot, her tires kicking up dust.

"Mandy Singapore hurt my feelings, but I only hated her for one day."

"Because you have a heart of gold, baby," Liv said. But her tone was a snap, belying her words.

"Well, you should try it."

Liv didn't answer. She just kept driving. There was no reasoning with a teenaged eight-year-old.

Hunter watched the BMW spume out dust from its rear tires and head for the highway. His eyes narrowed. If Liv had still been nearby, she would have recognized the look. Bulls reacted pretty much the same way when confronted with a red flag.

She wasn't going to let him anywhere near the child, Hunter realized. Victoria Rose. His Victoria Rose.

He'd given Livie his last, best chance. And she'd betrayed him. One more time. She hadn't let him speak more than a few words with his little girl. But if he was getting his facts right, he didn't need her approval to have a part in his daughter's life.

Hunter stepped away from the barn just as the riding instructor headed his way. He'd had enough confrontation for one day. Now it was time to start lining up allies.

Chapter 5

Three days passed without another skirmish or sign of Hunter. By Friday Liv was almost able to convince herself that he'd given up and left town.

Almost.

She thought about it as she sat at the computer in their little office beside the kitchen, checking the e-mail on their Web site and confirming reservations. Then she rested her chin in her hand and stared out the window at the barn and the garage until her frown started to hurt her forehead.

She groaned and rubbed the ache there. It was possible, she supposed. The wind *could* have called to him again. But that would be predictable, and the only predictable thing he'd done since she'd met him in Delaware was turn up in Jerome in the first place.

She'd thought he'd come pounding at the door here to see Vicky, but he'd gone to Mustang Ridge instead. She'd thought he'd harass her hourly, but now it seemed that he was lying low.

Why?

Impulsively Liv reached for the telephone. When she got the

desk at the Connor Hotel, she asked if Hunter Hawk-Cole was registered.

"No, ma'am."

No? Liv thanked the man and hung up again. That told her nothing, she realized. Hunter wasn't admitting to being who he was—except to Vicky—so his room could very well be in another name.

Liv gave up trying to concentrate. She signed off on the computer and pushed back from the desk to go upstairs and change. Tea today would probably be a quiet affair. The Endelmans had gone, and the nuns had taken avidly to riding with their sidesaddles. They'd barely come in from the trails for two days running now.

She arrived in the parlor to find only the writer and the newlyweds. More guests were expected that afternoon, but they hadn't arrived yet. Liv shared what she knew of the old Phelps Dodge Mine with Ed Stern and wondered idly what he was writing about, then she slipped out in time to get to Mustang Ridge by 3:30.

She never made the same mistake twice.

Vicky was just getting off the bus when she arrived. She flung herself at Liv for a quick hug, then she raced off to the barn to change her clothes and saddle her mare. Liv looked around for Lila and found her in the feed room.

"Hi," she said, sticking her head into the room. "I'll have those saddles back to you by Sunday. The nuns are checking out tomorrow."

Lila looked up from the grain bin and laughed. "That must be some sight. Wish I could have seen it."

Liv found a smile. She cleared her throat. "Um…by the way, has that guy been back? The one who was hanging around here on Tuesday?"

Lila shook her head. "I haven't seen him. I would have called you if I had." Her eyes said she wanted to ask what was going on.

Liv stepped back out of the door quickly. "I'll go see how Vicky is coming along."

She found her backing the mare into cross ties for saddling.

"Hey, baby, I meant to ask you. Have you seen that guy who was here the other day? The one we met in Delaware?"

Vicky didn't even look at her. She was concentrating on hefting the saddle onto the mare's back. "Hunter?"

"Right. Him."

"Nope."

Liv almost breathed. "Not at school or...or...I don't know. Anywhere?"

Vicky rolled her eyes. "Mom, I just told you."

"Okay, okay."

"You know, you're paying good money for this lesson. You shouldn't distract me while I'm getting ready."

Liv wondered if there had ever been a time when Vicky had actually been a kid. "I'm leaving now," she said, chastened.

She went to lean against the railing of the arena and pretended to spend the next hour watching the lesson. Her gaze hitched restlessly. To the barn. To the parking lot.

He didn't show up.

There was a strange, settling feeling to her heart by the time Vicky was finished. Relief, she told herself. Pure relief. She wouldn't have to tangle with him today.

He'd always lit up her life like no one else had ever been able to do—with anger, with passion, with joy. But she didn't want that. Not anymore. She wanted peace. She'd moved mountains to achieve it. It was hers now and maybe...just maybe, he really had gone.

She stopped at the mailbox on the street when they got home and left the car to grab the day's mail. When she turned around, her gaze fell on the BMW's wrinkled bumper again. She *had* to get the car fixed, she decided. The sooner she got that bumper ironed out, the sooner she'd be able to live without reminders of him again.

Except when you look at your daughter, a little voice whispered in her head.

How long had it taken her to get over that the first time around? she wondered, rubbing her forehead as she got back in the car. She tried to remember as she headed up the drive to the inn. She'd spent months praying that Vicky's blue eyes would eventually go dark like her own. The baby had been as bald as a cue ball for six of those months, then her hair had come in jet black. To the best of her recollections, Liv hadn't been able to stop seeing Hunter in her daughter until sometime between the chicken pox and that shocker of a ballet recital when Vicky had suddenly determined in midact that her solo needed a handstand and a cartwheel for a grand finale.

That, Liv thought, sliding the car into the garage—yes, *that* was when Hunter's memory had finally receded a little, just enough that she had begun to feel like Vicky was *her* baby, *her* girl, something she had maybe done by immaculate conception. Because Hunter hadn't been there to bring down the pox fever and he hadn't been there to face the horrified ballet teacher who had, in spite of Liv's pleas, never given Vicky a solo again. Hunter hadn't been there to go to the school when Vicky had suddenly piped up with one of Kiki's pet phrases, and he hadn't been there when Liv would have given her eyeteeth for a break during those first colicky months.

Now he wanted to come back into their lives. He wanted to be a happy-good-times parent, here today, gone tomorrow. Resentment bubbled up in Liv again, hot and acidic.

She followed Vicky back toward the inn, flipping through the mail, not watching where she was going. She came across the certified-mail envelope at the same time she tripped on her own feet. The envelope was from a lawyer. She felt her blood drain.

"That was graceful," Kiki said dryly.

Liv looked up sharply to see her partner standing on the back porch. "What?"

"The half gainer you almost just did on the asphalt. Anyway, tea's cleaned up and I'm taking off. I'll see you in the morn—" Then Kiki broke off. "What's wrong?"

"He got a lawyer." Liv's voice was a croak.

"What? How do you know?"

Liv held up the envelope.

Kiki bounced down the steps to snatch it from her hand. "Don't rush to conclusions. Maybe we gave someone food poisoning and they're suing us. Hey, come on," she said sharply when Liv swayed a little. She caught her elbow and shoved her forward again, not gently.

"Where's Vicky?" Liv asked.

"She headed straight upstairs to her room. We'll open the envelope. We'll see what we're dealing with." Kiki got her inside and planted her at the table. "Where's the brandy?"

"We can't keep drinking brandy every time Hunter acts up," Liv said feebly. "This is getting ridiculous."

"We'll stop as soon as he's gone and people quit suing us. As it is, I'll pour." Kiki began opening and closing cupboards.

It wasn't like her not to remember where she'd put something. She was rattled, Liv realized. She tore open the large legal-size envelope. Then her gaze flew over the caption, and her gut seized. The papers fell from her hands to the kitchen floor just as Kiki found the brandy and turned back to the table.

"Not food poisoning?" she asked, her voice uncharacteristically soft.

"He wants custody of Vicky."

Kiki took a deep breath and nodded. She put the bottle back. "Then we don't need this. We need a lawyer."

It took them several hours on the phone to find a good one. Adele Trawley—the mother of one of Vicky's classmates—swore by her attorney. They actually got more recommendations for a man in Sedona, but his name already appeared on the top of Hunter's Petition for Custody.

Liv found herself in the lawyer's office at 11:30 the next morning. She felt dazed, half wondering how she had gotten there, barely remembering the drive. It was a small place, little more than a storefront, with a secretarial area off to one side of a tiny, two-chair lounge. The art on the walls was cliché and the secretary was pretty, harried and abrupt. Liv told herself that that was a good thing. The attorney obviously had a thriving practice if she brought in a secretary on Saturdays—and that woman could barely take a moment to look up from her keyboard.

Ingrid Small swept into the waiting area five minutes later. She was short, pleasantly plump, with a dark-brown pageboy she had tucked behind her ears. She wore blue slacks beneath a man's oversize shirt. She didn't *look* like a high-powered attorney, Liv thought, but then again, Ingrid was seeing her today on an emergency basis.

Liv came to her feet.

"Hi," the woman said, holding out a hand. "Come on into my office and let's see what you've got there."

Liv wasn't sure if she should shake Ingrid's hand or put Hunter's envelope into it. She was *so* out of her element. Hunter had destroyed something inside her when he'd walked out all those years ago. Now he was trying to snatch away all she had left. Liv started to shake.

Ingrid solved the problem for her. She took both the envelope and Liv's hand, as well. "Coffee?" she asked, leading the way back to her office.

"Maybe arsenic," Liv whispered.

The woman heard her. "For you or for him?" she asked, sitting behind her desk. "I've specialized in family law for ten years now, so I always keep some on supply." She grinned— and in that moment Liv decided she liked her.

"You weren't my first choice," Liv admitted, sitting as well.

"No, that would have been Max Montague down in Sedona."

Liv felt her mouth pull into its own smile. "That's the guy."

"Well, I'm better than he is. He just charges more. Gives people the impression he's worth all that money."

"Exactly how much *is* this going to cost me?"

"I don't know yet," she said honestly. "Let me see what you've got first." Ingrid upended the envelope and poured the papers out onto her desk. She motioned at the coffeepot in one corner of the office. "Help yourself while I read."

Ten minutes later, when Liv's foam cup was drained, Ingrid looked up. "There's not a judge in this country who's going to give this man full custody."

The rush of relief that swept through her was so sweet, so intense, Liv almost felt light-headed. "Amen."

Ingrid began ticking points off on her fingers. "A—he's had absolutely no relationship with the child since her birth. No judge is going to yank her out of her home and drop her into one with a stranger. B—she's a little girl and she needs at least some quality time with the same-sex parent who's all she's ever known. And C—Max is going for full custody because he knows he'll never get it. He's shooting for the sky and hoping for joint, figuring the judge might give him half of what he asks for.''

''Joint?''

''Custody. Some time with you and some time with…'' She glanced down at the papers again. ''Hunter Hawk-Cole? No way. The race car driver?'' She blinked, obviously picking up on the name for the first time. Except on the petition's caption, he was referred to as Plaintiff.

Liv's elation vanished. She sank a little lower into her seat. ''Right.''

Ingrid put the papers aside. ''Okay, big whoopies. Now tell me *your* side of the story.''

Liv did. She tried desperately to keep it cut-and-dried, but her heart bled through into her words, rang in her voice. Ingrid listened; she nodded sympathetically; she shrugged. She got up to pour them both more coffee. She didn't interrupt. Liv talked for nearly an hour.

''Your weak spot is that you never told him,'' Ingrid said finally, sitting again and leaning back to twine her fingers behind her head. ''Normally, I'd angle to get this before a female judge who would be more inclined to understand that decision. Unfortunately, we only have one of those in Verde County. Samantha C. Woodingham. She has a reputation for somewhat outlandish verdicts. I'd like to stay away from her if at all possible.''

Liv sat forward worriedly. ''*Is* it possible?''

''Maybe. Mr. Hawk-Cole's petition is being heard under what's called an Order to Show Cause. That means he's in a hurry to get it in front of a judge because he has limited time.''

''I can't imagine that he'd want to take too many weeks away from the NASCAR circuit.'' The simple truth tweaked Liv's temper all over again. ''He was hurt a few weeks ago, which is probably the only reason he's in Jerome now. He probably *can't* drive for the time being—at least not safely.''

''I saw that race.'' Ingrid nodded. ''Of course, Max Montague is implying that the child is going to suffer irreparable harm if this isn't heard by a judge right away. He's not uttering a peep about his client's famous schedule.''

"'Irreparable harm'?" Liv was staggered. She hadn't read that part. She hadn't read all of the petition. She'd tried, but it had sickened her. "How?"

"He says that your Victoria Rose shouldn't go a day longer without knowing her real father, not while she's tucked into her formative years as she is. Ya-da, ya-da, ya-da."

Liv felt her blood boil. "He wants to be a father but he doesn't want to interrupt his season for it any longer than his health demands?"

"That would be my take on it. If Max didn't submit this as an Order to Show Cause, a normal petition wouldn't come up on the docket for at least a month. As it is, it's set to be heard in a week—this Friday. In front of Judge Woodingham."

Everything was pounding inside her, Liv realized. Her pulse, her brain. "That's the judge we don't want."

"Right." Ingrid nodded. "But here's what we can do. I don't want you to officially retain me until Monday. That is, no money can change hands until then. Got it?"

"What good will that do?"

"If you've only just hired me, I can conceivably plead that I need more than a couple of days to prepare. As it is now, our answering petition would be due on the judge's desk no later than Wednesday. If you don't hire me right away, I can call the court on Tuesday and beg a few days' extension. If I can get this bumped off Friday's docket, chances are we might end up with a different judge."

"That's sneaky," Liv said, rubbing her temples.

"That's law." Ingrid brought her hands to the desk again. "So, what do you think?"

"I think you're hired."

"Okay, then. Bring me a check for twenty-five hundred dollars on Monday. If we can settle this in one hearing, that's all it'll cost you. If it somehow mushrooms on us, it'll be more."

Liv blinked at her. "For that kind of money, you ought to have more than a storefront."

The woman looked startled, then she laughed. "Max Montague charges six thousand up front and he drives a Porsche. I, on the other hand, give generously to the women's shelter. Does that help?''

Liv rubbed the ache in her head again. She stood. She wasn't sure if she felt like dancing or crying—she had someone on her side. ''I think so.''

Ingrid stood as well. ''There's no way in hell that man is going to walk out of that court with custody of your daughter. I'd bank my reputation on it.''

Liv nodded woodenly. Fear still clawed inside her. ''I'll see you on Monday.''

When Liv pulled up to the garage, Vicky was inside, sitting Indian-style on the concrete like a skinny Buddha. Liv lowered her window and leaned out. ''What does this mean?''

''I want to go to Mandy Singapore's house. She called and asked if I could come over.''

Liv hesitated. Her head was still pounding and she didn't want to drive back into town any more than she wanted, well, to meet Hunter in court. But the inn was so far out on the edge of Jerome that she tried not to complain about scooting Vicky hither and yon to see her friends. There was no one to play with nearby unless one of the guest parties included children, which wasn't the case at the moment.

''I thought you hated Mandy Singapore,'' Liv said, hoping for a miracle.

Vicky rolled her eyes. ''Mom, you weren't listening. I said I only hated her for one day.''

Liv sighed. Then she had an insidious thought—if Hunter had his way, maybe she'd never have another chance to drive Vicky around again.

''Hop in,'' she said, her voice going a little thin.

Vicky scrambled to her feet and ran for the car. Liv backed out of the driveway again.

''Where did you go?'' Vicky asked.

Liv scowled into the rearview mirror. Her thoughts were snarled and distant with visions of courtrooms. ''What do you mean? When?''

"Just now. Aunt Kiki said you had to go into town."

Liv's stomach somersaulted. She felt her heart race off in a way that couldn't be healthy. In that moment she felt the full enormity of what Hunter was doing.

For nearly twenty-four hours now, all she'd considered was what he was doing to *her*. Trying to strip her of the one thing he had left her with all those years ago: a child who had become her reason for living. She knew he was punishing her for not telling him the truth all those years ago. He was tearing her soul right out of her. But now, finally, she realized that he would be punishing her little girl, as well.

He would uproot Vicky's life. He would dismantle her world. He would change it, rock it, take everything that was good and sweet and trusting in her and turn it into something unsure and unsteady. Just like what had once happened to Liv.

So she lied to her daughter for the first time in her life. To buy time. Because maybe, *maybe*, if she won this, Vicky would never have to know how close she'd come to disaster.

"Business," she said shortly. "Inn stuff."

Liv was as glad to see Mandy Singapore's driveway as she had ever been to see anything. She watched Vicky scamper out of the car and thought briefly of tracking Hunter down now— right now. She wanted to find him, to hurt him, to scream and cry at the man who had once healed her own heart only to visit the same nightmare upon their child now.

She didn't trust herself to do it, Liv realized. Because she knew, in that moment, that she might well be capable of killing him.

Sunday passed without a word from him. On Monday morning Liv ran into town and took a check to Ingrid Small's office. The woman was in court. Her secretary took Liv's money and promised that Ingrid would call her.

Ingrid did, the next day. Liv was chatting with the week's new guests at tea when Kiki appeared in the parlor door. "Excuse me," she said, smiling around at everyone in a brittle, too-bright way. Kiki wasn't a people person.

Liv rose from the settee and went to join her in the door. "What is it?"

"Phone."

Liv's legs turned to water. She could only think of three people Kiki might interrupt tea for, and one of them, Vicky, was getting on a school bus and heading for Mustang Ridge right about now. That left Hunter or Ingrid.

Liv hurried from the room without even asking which it was. She jogged through the kitchen and grabbed the phone in the office. "Hello!"

Ingrid's voice came back to her. "I've got an update."

Liv sat quickly in the desk chair. "Good or bad?"

"A little of both. Which would you like first?"

"The bad." When she'd been little, she'd always eaten her vegetables first, too, loathing every bite, so she could finish off each meal with something she loved.

"Woodingham is our judge," Ingrid said.

Liv had gripped the edge of the desk, but now she relaxed her fingers. She'd expected much worse. Maybe Judge Woodingham was a little unorthodox, but that was better than having someone unilaterally decide to snatch her child away from her without even the mercy of a court hearing. "What's the good part?" she asked finally.

"We got the postponement. Woodingham has backed it up to the following Friday. She didn't much buy Montague's bid for expediency. Unfortunately, in the process of making that decision, she read his petition and the case intrigued her. She wants to keep it for herself. Seeing as how she's presiding judge of the family court, it's her call to make."

Liv breathed again. "I can live with all that."

"You haven't heard the other bad part yet."

"There's *more?*"

"She wants to see all parties in her chambers tomorrow morning at 8:30 sharp."

All parties? Liv felt her blood drain. "Vicky," she whispered.

"No, no, not the child," Ingrid said hastily. "Woodingham doesn't like to put the little ones through the court scene unless it's absolutely necessary. Just me, you, Montague and your ex."

"He never married me," Liv said helplessly, inanely. "Why? Why would a judge do something like this?"

"Truthfully, I have no idea. I warned you. I just can't read this woman." Ingrid paused. "I'm sorry, Olivia. I really would have preferred to avoid Woodingham, but it was the luck of the draw."

Liv nodded as though Ingrid could see her. She tried to think through the clamor inside her head. "Exactly how did she get this reputation for being eccentric?"

"She tends to go to the wall for the kids, to preserve the rights and the hearts of the children caught up in custody battles and divorces. She doesn't much care for adults. She's come up with some outlandish decisions."

"I see." That was a *good* thing, Liv decided. She *wanted* someone to protect Vicky.

"Olivia, what I'm trying to tell you is that I doubt she'll be sympathetic with your reasons for not telling Hunter Hawk-Cole he was a father eight years ago. She won't give a damn about your broken heart. The only thing that will concern her is that your little girl doesn't have a father."

"She *does!* She sees Johnny Guenther occasionally!" Oh, God, Liv thought, would Woodingham take Vicky away from her just to prove a point about the merits of a nuclear family? "If she sends Vicky to Hunter, she won't have a *mother!*" she cried.

"There's that," Ingrid allowed. "But you're missing the gray area I mentioned the other day. There's always joint custody."

Liv's heart stalled. "Tomorrow? She'd order this tomorrow?"

"No, no, she won't render a decision until the hearing. I'm not sure what tomorrow's all about. And I'm hoping Mr. Hawk-Cole's unstable lifestyle might sway her even from that. It's how I'll argue when the time comes."

"I guess it's the best we can do," Liv muttered.

"There's the spirit. I'll meet you in the coffee shop in the courthouse at 8:15 tomorrow," Ingrid said. "It's on the second floor."

Liv hung up the phone.

Kiki poked her head into the office. "Well?"

"I need to get to Mustang Ridge," she said absently, glancing at her watch. It was 3:30.

"The *lawyer!* What did the lawyer say?" Kiki demanded.

Liv pushed to her feet and paused for a moment to make sure her legs would hold her. "The judge wants to see us all in the morning. Can you finish tea for me? Make my apologies? I've got to run."

Kiki pasted on her too-perfect smile again. "Sure."

"Just don't talk about microbes this time." Kiki had done that once, much to the bemusement of the guests.

"It was *photons*. I was explaining why ghosts can scientifically exist."

Liv headed for the back door. She didn't want to hear it. If Kiki's theory was right, then Hunter would probably haunt her for all time.

What did one wear to impress a judge who hated grown-ups?

Liv stood in front of her closet the next morning feeling physically ill. Her Vicky, her baby. She had to do everything right. Dear God, she couldn't lose her. Her stomach heaved.

She worried about the effect that a skirt or a dress would have on the judge. Would it look as though she was *trying* to impress her? That might tick her off. Or worse, it could look as though Liv was such a savvy and enterprising businesswoman that she had limited time for her child.

Liv groaned aloud and gripped her head in her hands. She wondered if she was getting the flu. It was early in the season for it, but she felt achy and groggy and feverish. Then again, she hadn't slept. That could account for the first two symptoms. The third could be pure unmitigated fury at what Hunter was doing.

She finally went for what she thought of as her "mom" look—nothing too fancy, the sort of thing that normally took her from tea to soccer to riding lessons without missing a beat. She chose turquoise jeans, a white turtleneck, and a teal-turquoise-and-white cardigan sweater. Flats or boots? Boots. She brushed her hair, kept her makeup to a minimum and rushed downstairs at 7:30.

"Can you give Vicky a ride to the school bus?" she asked Kiki, hitting the kitchen.

Her partner was at the sink, and she turned away to dry her hands. "What do I tell her if she wants to know why *you're* not doing it?"

"Inn business."

"That's going to get old in a hurry."

"Maybe not." She would *not* drag Vicky into this until a gun was held to her head. But Hunter was busy gathering up the ammunition, she thought. "I've got to go."

Thirty seconds later Liv peeled out of the garage. She arrived in the coffee shop before Ingrid and she ordered tea. Maybe it would settle her stomach, she thought, pressing a hand to it. She sat and took her first sip just as Hunter walked in. It nearly came back up through her nose.

He took several strides into the room before he noticed her, then his face went to stone. Her heart began thudding. There were no other tables available.

He crossed to hers and scraped back the other chair, lowering his frame into it. He looked arrogant and sure of himself, she thought helplessly. He hadn't gone for the "dad" look. He wore a suit. Was that good or bad?

She had never seen him in a suit before in her life.

It was navy blue and it made his shoulders look like slabs of mountain. He'd gotten his hair cut, too, though it still swept back from his forehead and tickled his collar. But there was something in his eyes that looked dangerous and primal no matter how civilized he tried to appear. The polished clothes couldn't conceal the hunger in his gaze or the restlessness that seemed to move right beneath his skin like something palpable.

Liv found her voice. "That seat's taken."

"Stop making everything so difficult." He settled back, getting comfortable.

The pressure inside her head made her eyes hurt. "*I* didn't file this suit!"

"Got your attention, though, didn't it?"

"Hunter. Don't do this." Oh, God, she was pleading with

him again. She would, she thought. For Vicky, she would—again and again and again until her voice went hoarse.

Something flared in his eyes. "I just want to see my daughter, Liv."

"You saw her last Tuesday."

He leaned forward so suddenly she jerked back. "You snapped her out of that riding academy before I could say two words to her."

"Because I didn't trust what you might say! Obviously, you're capable of anything!" She realized she was shouting. Other patrons were looking their way. "Please," she said more quietly. "Don't put her through this."

"Knowing me won't hurt her, Livie. It only threatens *you.*"

His voice dropped a notch, too. It reminded her of what it had once felt like when his breath had touched her skin, whispering things both sweet and provocative. A fist grabbed Liv's throat, and yearning rocked through her. It was too fresh, too real, now that he had touched her again the other night.

She couldn't allow that—all those treacherous old feelings—to complicate this.

Before she could recover enough to answer, Ingrid stepped up beside their table. "Mr. Hawk-Cole," she said in greeting, then she looked at Liv. "I didn't expect to find you two so cozy. Have we resolved this without the need of court intervention?"

Liv pushed to her feet. "No," she breathed. She kept her eyes on Hunter. "I'll fight you to the death."

"Those are dangerous words, Livie. They sound like a challenge, and you know how I react to challenges."

"I don't remember. You were a long time ago, Hunter, and not that memorable in the first place."

Liv fled from the table, from the coffee shop, stopping only when she reached the second floor lounge area because she had no idea where to go.

Ingrid caught her elbow. "Calm down," she cautioned.

Liv felt tears stinging her eyes and she blinked furiously. Ingrid switched her briefcase to her opposite hand and pointed down the corridor. Liv fell into step beside her.

A law clerk showed them into the judge's chambers and told

them to have a seat, though Woodingham wasn't yet present. The moment the man left and shut the door again Ingrid seemed to transform. She placed her briefcase on the floor beside one of the chairs and crossed her arms over her breasts almost militantly. She'd gone from slacks and a man's shirt—on the one other occasion when Liv had personally met with her—to a charcoal-gray pantsuit that did nice things for her robust figure. She looked taller, more imposing, colder.

"Woodingham won't turn up until Montague and your ex get here," she explained. "She doesn't want either side to think the other had any time alone with her."

"He's not my ex," Liv said again halfheartedly.

She went to sit on a sofa against the rear wall. Then she sprang to her feet again when it occurred to her that Hunter could well arrive to sit right beside her. There was only one other chair. She started to move that way, then the door opened again. She swiveled.

Hunter and Max Montague entered the room.

The appearance of the other lawyer shocked Liv. She'd expected someone sleek and sharklike. But he was short, round, with a balding, freckled pate and wire-rimmed glasses. His suit looked slept in and she was reasonably sure that a bit of food was stuck in his bristly mustache. But she'd heard too many tales of his courtroom prowess to be misled by any of it. Liv felt sicker by the moment.

Hunter and his lawyer sat next to each other on the sofa. Liv could feel Hunter's gaze pulling at her. She refused to meet his eyes.

The door opened again and the judge arrived. *She* looked like a shark, Liv thought—a pretty, intimidating shark with the unique kind of grace only a tall woman could really muster. Her hair was strawberry-blond and thick, sweeping just past her shoulders. She rounded her desk and sat seamlessly, crossing long legs under her robe.

"Good morning, ladies and gentlemen."

"Same to you, Judge," Montague said shortly, almost rudely. Liv was surprised by his manner.

"Good morning, Your Honor." Ingrid took a place beside the

chair in the room, pushing down on Liv's shoulder until she sat hard there, like a bullet shot to earth.

Judge Woodingham smiled and showed teeth. "Get up, Max. Let the other lady have that seat."

He did, grumbling. "You ought to be prepared for more than three people in your chambers at any given time."

"I detest crowds," Woodingham said mildly, then she sat forward and linked her hands together on her desk. "I particularly loathe being forced into these prehearing conferences."

What did that mean? Liv thought desperately. *She* had called this conference! Liv looked questioningly at Ingrid who had gone to sit on the sofa. The lawyer seemed to shrug.

"I'll get right to the point, as I have a docket piling up, waiting for me in Courtroom A," Woodingham continued. "Did any one of you frustrated, angry people even bother to determine if we genuinely have a case here?"

Ingrid's jaw dropped a little. Montague's face went florid. Hunter showed no expression at all.

Liv had no idea what the judge was talking about, but she felt her pulse shift, going sluggish with dread.

"*Is* this little girl the biological product of Mr. Hawk-Cole?" Woodingham continued. "It strikes me that we ought to ascertain that right off the bat. Obviously, the plaintiff and the defendant had an affair several years ago. Clearly, a child exists now. But I'll be damned if I'm going to drag that child through the legal mire until I know for sure that she's the result of that liaison."

"You want a paternity test," Montague said flatly.

"Yes, before I waste any more of the court's time."

"No!" Liv cried.

She felt the eyes of the others come around to her. Wings of panic beat in her chest. Needles, she thought. Doctors. Blood. And Vicky would have to know why it was happening to her.

She shot to her feet again.

"You're declining to produce the child for such a test?" Woodingham asked.

"I—"

"Excuse me," Ingrid interrupted, coming to her feet as well. "I'd like a private word with my client."

"Make it quick," Woodingham warned her.

Liv found herself guided forcefully out of chambers by her elbow. "Not cool," Ingrid said when they were outside in the hallway. "You need to let me do the talking. Olivia, you never denied to me that Hunter Hawk-Cole was your daughter's father."

Liv swallowed. "Because he is."

"Then what the hell was that all about?"

"I don't want to put Vicky through a paternity test. I...I..." Liv trailed off and dragged air into her lungs. "She has no idea any of this is going on. I haven't told her yet."

"Oh." Ingrid pursed her lips together. "You know, this test could be to our advantage."

"How so?" Liv pleaded.

"If we walk back in there and admit paternity, Woodingham would probably accept that and forgo the test for the child's benefit. But then we'll be in court next Friday. Whereas if we *don't* admit paternity and we force the blood test, that's going to take some time. It'll be a week before we can arrange the test and another two before we get conclusive results. We could successfully drag this out for another month and that's precisely what Montague *doesn't* want. He knows—as you've implied yourself—that Mr. Hawk-Cole won't stay in town that long." Ingrid paused. "Think about it, Olivia. But think fast. I'm not sure how long Woodingham's patience is going to hold with our little private conference out here."

Think about it. Liv jerked away from the lawyer. There was nothing to consider.

She had a sudden, mental flash of a day long ago in her own life, of lawyers in their suits—one had smelled relentlessly of mothballs—and of a dour-faced judge who'd looked like he'd had a few years on Methuselah. She remembered a social worker with icy hands holding one of hers. *"Your Honor, we've determined that the minor has only one remaining relative."*

"Does this relative admit kinship?"

"Yes, Your Honor, she's the child's maternal grandmother. She's willing to take custody."

Liv flinched visibly as that long-ago gavel cracked again in her memory. She'd been in a car with the social worker, heading north for the Res that very afternoon. No one had stuck her with needles, but that courtroom had changed her life.

She would *not* let this one affect Vicky. She'd fight it until the last possible moment.

"Hunter has never backed down from a fight in his life," she said hoarsely.

"You're saying that, even if we delay the proceedings with this test, he'll hang around?"

"If he doesn't, he'll just come back for the hearing at the appointed time."

"You want to place the admittance on the record, then."

Liv took a shuddering breath. "I have to." She was the only one willing to give her heart and soul to protect her daughter.

Chapter 6

The judge spared Vicky the test.

She seemed to approve of Liv's decision. Liv found herself wondering if that was a good omen as she left chambers. Hunter went off with his own lawyer, and she refused to meet his eyes, though she felt his gaze probing at her.

What had she just done? It was entirely possible that she had given herself less than one more precious week with her daughter. She felt sick. She watched Ingrid sail off down the hall to another hearing and forced herself to keep walking, as well, before her legs had the chance to give out from beneath her completely.

She stepped outside into the sunshine and blinked in the brightness. The day should be cold and damp and dreary, she thought. It should be raining. The angels should be crying.

"You surprise me, Livie."

She gasped at Hunter's voice and jerked around. He was leaning against one of the white stone pillars. *Lying in wait for her.* She should have known that he wouldn't go away easily, that he wouldn't leave her alone in her misery.

He pushed off the pillar and came toward her. "Montague

says you could have dragged this out for another month if you had gone for that test.''

"At whose expense?" Liv hissed, feeling adrenaline shoot back into her blood. "You would have let her be stuck with needles, a strange doctor poking at her—"

"It's a simple procedure, Liv," he interrupted. "Painless."

"Tell that to an eight-year-old who hates needles!"

She had the satisfaction of seeing him flinch.

"I didn't know," he said finally. "And I blame *you* for that."

Liv clapped her hands to her ears. She couldn't stand any more accusations. Her muscles hurt with the strain of tension. There was a constriction in her throat and she couldn't swallow around it. She turned her back to him.

Then words scraped out of her, anyway. "I always knew you'd be furious if you found out the truth. But I never thought you'd try to destroy her, us."

"You were the one who said this wasn't about you and me."

His voice was so close behind her, she would have felt his breath on her nape if her hair hadn't been in the way. Liv cupped her elbows in her hands and realized she was shaking. Flu, she thought again. She couldn't stand knowing that his nearness still affected her. "You changed that. You're doing this to punish me, and you're using Vicky for a pawn."

"Turn around, Liv. Let me see your eyes when you say that."

"No."

"Damn it, turn around!"

She jumped a little, but she didn't move. He didn't want to touch her again. He didn't want to put his palm on her shoulder and make her do it. He still hadn't gotten past the insanity of that moment when he'd kissed her. Sometimes, in his sleep, he was sure he could still smell the spicy hint of her perfume. Waking at dawn, he could still feel her breath mingling with his own.

But she wasn't going to budge, so he stepped around her again, holding on to her elbow to keep her from running. He felt the heat of her through her clothing. "Just once, before we leave this courthouse," he grated, "we're going to be honest with each other."

Her chin lifted, even though her skin was waxen. "What for?"

"I want to end this. All you have to do to stop it is let me have some time with her."

"No," she whispered wretchedly.

"That's it? You're not going to give an inch? Ah, Livie. Who's punishing who, here?"

She felt as though he had slapped her. Her face stung as blood flew into her cheeks again, because her skin had been cold as death just a moment before. "I'm trying to protect her!"

"From me? When did you get it in your head that I was such an ogre?"

"You bastard. Don't twist this around on me! You *know* why I don't want her to learn to love you! Look what it did to *me!* You'll *leave* her!"

He touched her again. This time it was reflex, desperation, a helpless feeling that he hadn't once felt since he'd walked out of that Flagstaff resort. She'd been everything he'd ever needed, and now she was trying to rob him of things he hadn't known he wanted.

And he knew—he knew—that she was doing it for no other reason than to watch him bleed for some age-old slight that had been at her own instigation.

How the hell had they ever come to this?

His hands found her shoulders, and he shook her a little. "Of course I will—temporarily! I have a life on the circuit! I'll be back!"

"That's not enough! I want her to have a normal life!"

"By whose standards?"

His words lashed at her. She couldn't breathe. "Mine." Yes, she thought helplessly, yes, hers. She'd given everything to ensure Vicky had a normal life. She'd turned her back on the only man she'd ever loved. And she was damned if she was going to let him undo that now.

"You're willing to risk losing her entirely rather than give her something different?" His voice was too quiet. "You're free now, Liv. Free of the Res. Let your own horrors go."

She pulled away from his hands and whipped around again,

then her feet stalled. She turned back. "What are you going to do if you win this, Hunter? Are you going to drag Vicky from city to city with you every weekend while you race?"

His jaw hardened. "She'll travel with me."

"What about her schooling?"

"Tutors."

Her laugh was giddy. "Those are *your* standards?"

"If that's the only way she can know her father, yes."

She'd meant to be the one who walked away first. But he stepped past her and trotted down the steps. Arrogant, she thought again. Sure.

He would have made a hell of a gambler, she thought. To her knowledge, it was the one thing he had never tried.

Liv barely let Vicky out of her sight for the rest of the week. She wasn't protecting her from Hunter's sudden appearance any longer. She knew him too well to believe that he would do anything other than wait now, like a wildcat watching its prey, knowing his moment would come. She did it because she was spending every last minute with Vicky that God would give her.

"You're overdramatizing," Kiki said Thursday night, making them a pot of tea. The weather had turned suddenly into winter, as it could do in Arizona's higher elevations. It had been sixty degrees that morning. Now the dark sky outside the windows was gathering moodily into heavy clouds.

Liv took her cup. "Thanks for staying over again."

"Think nothing of it. It's not like I'm a single woman in a town full of sexy-hunk tourists or anything."

Liv shot her a look, then sat at the table. She curled her legs beneath her. She sipped, wondering if the warmth would melt some of the ice in her chest. "Let's talk about the weather. I don't want to think about tomorrow."

"That's because you're leaping to panicked, farfetched conclusions that have very little basis in reality."

Liv sighed. "Kiki, this situation isn't a scientific equation. There are variables. Personalities."

"Equations can have variables."

"Excuse me. I didn't go to college. I learned this business by the seat of my pants."

"Thank our stars for that. Someone's got to shmooze with the guests. In the meantime, use that people-instinct you've got going for you to throw a sensible light on this situation. What judge in her right mind would yank a little girl out of school and a consistent home life to send her out on the NASCAR circuit with a tutor? Ten bucks says the lady judge will just order you to let him see her whenever he's in town."

Liv's heart skittered. "Thank you for the vote of confidence." She stood suddenly. "I'm going to go hug her good-night."

"You did that already. She's been asleep for an hour now."

"Sometimes she reads with the flashlight under the covers."

"Stop it. You're making yourself crazy." Kiki surged to her feet, and Liv suddenly found herself in her arms for a hard, quick hug.

Kiki was not a physical person. She was glib, strong, fiercely independent. She was the most solid friend Liv had ever known. But she didn't hug, which only told Liv that Kiki thought she really needed it right now…and that she was afraid, too.

Liv felt tears sting at her eyes. "You're hurting me."

Kiki stepped back. "I'm half your size."

"You're hurting my heart."

Ten bucks says the lady judge will just order you to let him see her whenever he's in town.

Not you, Livie. You're the only one who ever knew when I was gone.

The voices, the words, tangled in Liv's head as she arrived in the courthouse coffee shop the next morning for the custody hearing. Kiki would be coming, too, as soon as she finished up with breakfast at the inn. Liv wished desperately that her friend was here now. Instead Ingrid was waiting for her.

Hunter and Montague were nowhere to be found. Liv's gaze cruised for them, then she let out a bated breath.

"Montague and your ex are in the courtroom," Ingrid said, standing from her table. She gathered up her briefcase and tossed her coffee cup in a trash can. Liv followed her down the corridor.

It was something she couldn't quite wrap her mind around, she thought. In all the days that had passed since that meeting in chambers, she kept trying to imagine life without her daughter. Every time she bumped up against the concept, everything inside her recoiled from it in pain.

She knew that what Kiki had said last night made absolute sense. And she did not believe that Woodingham was insane. But she felt the life she had built for herself and for Vicky spilling through her fingers like sand, and panic built inside her.

They stepped into the courtroom. Hunter and Montague were seated. Liv fumbled with the chair beside Ingrid's at the defense table and sat, as well, just as Judge Woodingham swept into the courtroom, her robe flowing.

There was the usual legalese. Liv waited through it, her pulse hitching erratically. Finally Woodingham rapped her gavel.

"Hearing postponed," she said mildly.

Montague and Ingrid were on their feet as though someone had lit fires under their respective chairs. "What?" Montague demanded.

Woodingham waved a hand as though she found him tedious. "Sit down, Counselor, and hear me out." She glanced at Ingrid. "If you want equal time to give me an outburst of your own, please do so now so we can move on."

Ingrid shook her head. "Not at this time, Your Honor."

Liv thought wildly that she thought she saw the judge smile.

Woodingham looked at Montague again. "I've read the defendant's responding papers to your petition, Mr. Montague. Ms. Small has a point. Your client is in no way prepared to raise a child on his own, given his choice of career. He has not married and has no spouse to assist in this endeavor. My feeling is that he really hasn't thought this through, that he filed the petition under emotional impetus. I don't blame him for that, but you should have known better. In any case, I won't remand custody of this child to a housekeeper or a baby-sitter, or send her on a lickety-split, round-the-country excursion while she should be in school."

Liv hadn't believed her heart could beat any faster. But it did, and she felt even more light-headed. *This was good!*

"However," Woodingham continued, "I do want to give this little girl every opportunity to know her father. I can't choose sides in this matter when the plaintiff has had absolutely no contact with the child to date. So how about if we give him some? Say, the next ninety days. If Mr. Hawk-Cole still wants to pursue this matter then, I'll rule at the end of that time."

Liv's heart stopped racing. It seized on midbeat. *She was going to take Vicky away from her for three months!*

Montague looked elated. Ingrid's complexion was livid. Judge Woodingham held up a hand to forestall more argument. "Here's how we're going to do this. You—" she lifted her gavel and twirled it in Hunter's general direction "—are going to reside in Ms. Slade's home for the next ninety days, with the child, so Victoria Rose can get to know you on her own turf, without her life being uprooted in any way. And both of you—" this time she included Liv in the gavel motion "—are going to make very sure, during that time, of your motives in this war before I alter the child's life. This matter is hereby postponed." She clunked the gavel again.

Montague couldn't hold his tongue any longer. "Your Honor! That's not acceptable! My client has a very demanding career, and he needs to get back to it within the next couple of weeks! Literally hundreds of thousands of dollars of income rest on that!"

"Point denied," Woodingham said. "Ask your client which is more important—his career or the child he purports to want a relationship with."

"Judge!" Ingrid shouted. "You can't order two unmarried people to cohabit!"

"Of course I can. I'm presiding judge. And let's keep in mind that they got rather intimate without a marriage license eight and half years ago. Your point is denied, as well, Counselor, especially in light of the fact that Ms. Slade cohabits with strangers on a regular basis. I believe you own a bed-and-breakfast, Ms. Slade?"

"I—" Liv began, but the judge cut her off. It was just as well. She was going to throw up, anyway.

"I fail to see the difference between Mr. Hawk-Cole taking a room and a tourist from Topeka."

"Ms. Slade's rooms are reserved months in advance, Your Honor," Ingrid argued. "She's booked through the winter. It would be detrimental to her business to ask her to cancel reservations to accommodate Mr. Hawk-Cole."

"She'll have to. And his income will be taking something of a hit here, as well," Judge Woodingham replied. "So let's keep things even. Yes, I like that idea."

"Why is it necessary for him to *live* there?" Ingrid was almost begging now.

"Because he wants to be a father." Woodingham rose from the bench. "This arrangement will begin within seventy-two hours, no later than Monday. Mr. Montague, you brought this petition before me so you can see my clerk for a return date. I'll render a decision in ninety days."

The judge left the room. Liv looked up dazedly at Ingrid. "This is insane."

"Well," the lawyer said, "I did warn you about her. And you didn't lose custody."

"Not yet." Liv swallowed. Her throat felt like sandpaper. "You're fired."

Hunter was thunderstruck. He was also angrier than he had been since...well, since Liv had walked out of the Spirit Room at the Connor Hotel after refusing to work with him on this and tossing a drink in his face. Then he had handled it by going after her and kissing her—but he was damned if he was going to pucker up for Montague's pudgy little mouth.

"Hold it right there!" he warned as the man headed down the courthouse steps ahead of him. "Think twice if you're planning to just walk away after that debacle!"

Montague paused, glanced at his watch, and looked back at him. "I have an appointment in fifteen minutes."

Hunter trotted down the steps to catch up with him, feeling like a jerky marionette as rage yanked at his muscles. He fisted his hands so he wouldn't grab the man by the shirtfront. "You told me there was no way in hell that judge was going to disallow me time with my daughter!"

Montague blinked at him owlishly. "Well, she didn't."

"She put me on some kind of *probation!*"

"She's giving you a chance to live with Victoria Rose."

"I'd have to live with her mother, too!" The mere thought made panic cavort in his chest. It raced around in circles in there, and it had claws.

"I warned you when you asked me to file this suit that if we pulled this judge in the rotation, anything was likely to happen," Montague said.

"You said we'd win!"

"We did."

"Like hell! Can I get out of this?"

"Certainly. You can walk away from the whole affair. No one can make you move into that inn."

They couldn't, Hunter thought. They damned well couldn't.

"Or we can appeal Woodingham's decision," Montague continued.

Hunter liked that idea even better. For the first time in ten minutes, he actually felt his lungs expel breath. "How long will that take?"

"The Appellate Court limps along. Depending on their docket, three to five months. And I've got to tell you, they'd likely uphold. This was a fair decision."

"Fair for who?" Hunter roared.

"For the child, of course. I've heard of the Copper Rose. It's got five guest rooms and a handful of private suites. The judge has a point. It would hardly be like sharing an apartment with the woman."

Hunter's air left him again, riffling out of him this time. He raked his hands through his hair. "I can't do this."

Montague looked at his watch again impatiently. "I've got to go. Think it over and give me a call on Monday if you're not already in residence at the Copper Rose."

He walked away again. This time Hunter let him leave.

He followed more slowly, heading for his SUV in the parking

lot across the street, feeling dazed. Pritch had been willing to let him back in a car next weekend. He'd driven down to see a doctor in Phoenix yesterday and had gotten a clean bill of health. It was already October first; he would have five weeks, five races, to scramble back into points contention. It was a long shot but it wouldn't quite take a miracle. He could still do it.

If he tucked into one of Liv's guest rooms for three months, his season was over.

He wanted to punch something.

"My money is on you flying off again," said a familiar voice from behind him.

Hunter cued the remote to unlock his SUV and turned. Kiki Condor. How long had it been?

"Where's your sidekick?" he asked shortly.

"What happened to 'Hello, old friend, how have you been?'" She came up beside him and leaned her shoulder against his vehicle, crossing her arms over her chest. She hadn't changed, Hunter thought. She had that ageless quality that so many Native American women shared when their lives weren't riddled by poverty. Her black hair was still long and lustrous, her eyes were still deep and clear. She was still a knockout, Hunter thought.

In the beginning they had circled each other suspiciously and antagonistically. Kiki had been absolutely sure that Hunter would hurt Liv, and Hunter had been convinced beyond doubt that Kiki would do her best to turn Liv against him. Neither of those things had happened, and the three of them had ended up being the best of pals.

"Liv made a side trip to the rest room. I believe she's going to be sick."

"Good." It gave him a sharp edge of satisfaction to know that Liv was as upset about this as he was.

"So what are you going to do?" Kiki asked again.

"I'll win this eventually." As Montague had said, no judge was going to prohibit him from contact with his child—assuming he wasn't an ax murderer.

Hunter felt a tightening across his forehead—slick, hot tension. It would be best to head out to Charlotte tomorrow, he thought. Have Montague file the appeal. The Appellate Court could chew on it all off-season.

And they would probably come back with a decision sometime in mid-February, he realized, just when the new season was kicking off in Daytona.

"So Liv was right." Kiki pushed off the vehicle in disgust. "You'll fly away and come back when it suits you."

"Wait a second," Hunter said harshly, stung. "How did this get to be your business?"

"Vicky is my goddaughter."

That stalled him. He realized he was glad. Then the heat across his forehead gripped tighter as images of the child danced in his mind's eye.

"I'll let Livie know what I decide," he said gruffly. He reached for the door handle and got into the SUV, driving off hard, just as Liv came through the courthouse doors.

Liv was calmer when she caught up with Kiki—which was to say that her pulse hiccuped instead of rioted, and there was only a dull ache at her temples instead of a pounding. She narrowed her eyes on the SUV as it sped off. "Were you just talking to him?" she demanded.

"Yeah." They fell into step together, heading toward Liv's car.

"Some moral support you turned out to be."

"You wanted me to stand up in court and beat my chest in angst over the decision?"

"You were just caught red-handed consorting with the enemy!"

"I was trying to figure out if I should clean out my room for him. We can't cancel reservations."

"No." Liv's footsteps stalled. "What did he say? Did he say he was going to do this?" Her voice rose.

"He evaded the issue."

They stopped beside the battered BMW. Liv stared at the bumper. "Damn it. I really need to get this fixed." It seemed safest to concentrate on the car. That didn't make her heart flip over and spin.

Kiki wouldn't be sidetracked. "I'd wait until he leaves town," she advised. "Otherwise you'll probably just end up having to do it twice."

"He's not going to miss the rest of the NASCAR season." Liv had almost convinced herself of that in the time it took her to apologize and rehire her attorney and to catch up with her friend. "Hunter Hawk-Cole has never stayed in one place for ninety days in his whole sorry life."

Kiki went on to her own car. "We'll see."

Hunter stopped at a liquor store on his way back to town and picked up a bottle of Remy. He'd thought of visiting the Spirit Room, but he knew he wasn't fit for human company at the moment.

He knocked back a shot in his room and glared at the telephone as though it were somehow responsible for this nightmare. He could call Pritch and tell him that he would be staying in Jerome. Or he could go back to driving and let Liv win this.

He jerked out of his suit jacket, throwing it on the bed. Somehow he'd convinced himself that when he hit Charlotte at the beginning of the week, he'd have Victoria Rose in tow. The judge had been right about one thing—he hadn't thought beyond that. He figured he'd have to bring her back to Livie eventually...but this would have been *his* time. A drop in the bucket after the eight long years when Liv had had the child to herself.

His turn.

He'd show her the cars, Hunter thought, give her a spin in one until she shrieked and giggled. But she wouldn't be afraid. Not his kid, not his little girl with the devil in her eyes. They'd go from Martinsville to Talledega, and from Alabama they would swing through Phoenix then head back east to Atlanta. They'd live his life together for a while.

Hunter swore at the thought and sat down on the edge of the bed. Hard.

He would have established a link with his daughter, he realized, would have had a blast with her through the short remainder of the season, then he would have let her come back to her mother. And he would have visited whenever he could after that. He would have paid Liv back for all this, then he would have gotten on with his life. Because the NASCAR season was a long one—ten months, thirty-six races—and he had to be with his crew, working to strike that delicate balance between mechanics and serendipity. He'd go back to that because it was where he'd finally found peace after Livie had pushed him out of her life.

Words rolled through his head, things that had been said in court just hours ago.

Why is it necessary for him to live there?

Because he wants to be a father.

Suddenly he understood the way the judge had grinned to herself when she'd left the courtroom. And he understood why his skull had been tightening steadily ever since Kiki had faced him down. If his only motive was to pay Liv back, he wouldn't be willing to live at her inn, he realized. The judge was going to find out just how much Victoria Rose mattered to him before she ruled and rocked the child's life. She was going to find out how far he was willing to go to be a father.

"Ah, damn it." Hunter rubbed his temples and shot to his feet again.

He'd taken several snapshots of Vicky that day at the riding academy, before Liv had arrived. He'd stopped off and bought one of those disposable cameras on his way to Mustang Ridge. Now he grabbed the packet of photos from his dresser drawer.

His favorite was her narrow-eyed look of pure betrayal when the mare had dumped her. No, he thought, flipping through them, his favorite was when she had gone nose-to-nose with the horse right afterward, her little jaw jutting as she faced the beast down. Then there was the one of Liv dragging her away, when she glanced back over her shoulder at him, grinning conspiratorially.

His heart shifted painfully. This really was his turn with her. It just wasn't under the circumstances he'd asked for.

Hunter picked up the phone to call Pritch and kiss off the rest of his season.

Kiki made duckling l'orange for dinner. It was her idea of comfort food. Though she usually left the inn after tea, they occasionally shared dinner at the big butcher-block table in the kitchen.

When Liv felt reasonably steady again after some solitude in her room, she followed her nose downstairs to find Vicky. She knew her daughter would be helping Kiki.

"Ah," she murmured, pushing through the door into the kitchen, sniffing deeply.

Vicky was crowding Kiki at the oven door. "You forgot the garnish," she said accusingly.

"Move over, Chef Boyardee." Kiki gave her an elbow. "If I put the oranges on while it was still roasting, they'd wilt."

"That's true." Vicky nodded sagely and skittered out of the way. Then she saw her mother. "Kiki's cooking for us!" Her joy told Liv what she thought of her own efforts—usually frozen entrees, take-out and sandwiches.

"Get the brandy," Kiki said, lifting the duckling out of the oven.

"What for? Hunter's not—" Liv broke off quickly, feeling the avid weight of her daughter's watchful gaze.

"What's the race guy got to do with dinner?" Vicky asked.

"Nothing to do with dinner and everything to do with brandy," Kiki muttered under her breath. "Besides, we don't have any wine. I didn't have time to buy any, what with chasing all over the county today."

Liv's pulse started again gradually. She could protect Vicky from this until she heard from Hunter, she thought, until she got word that he was actually going to do this, to move in. Aside from a slip of the tongue, she was damned well determined to do just that.

She moved to the cupboard without answering.

"Take this while I serve up the rice and the salad," Kiki said to Vicky, handing her the duckling platter. "Careful. Use the potholders. I kept the platter warm."

"Duh. I've been helping you since I was *born*." Vicky grabbed oven mitts and pulled them on at the same time a distant knocking sounded at the front of the inn.

"Got to be that writer," Kiki complained. "How long has he been with us now?"

"Four weeks." Ed Stern kept extending his stay and it had played hell with reservations. He was definitely working on something that had to do with Jerome, Liv thought again. And he was absentminded. He generally went out for a while right after tea and forgot his guest key on a regular basis.

"I'll get it," Vicky said, sliding the duckling platter gently onto the table. "I like him. He tells great stories." She raced off, the oven mitts still on her hands.

"What kind of stories do you suppose he tells her?" Liv asked worriedly, watching her go.

Kiki shrugged and put the salad and the pilaf on the table. "All I can tell you is that Vicky hasn't asked me what a brothel is yet so he must be minding his tongue."

Liv brought the brandy to the table at the same time Vicky's voice rolled excitedly down the hallway. "*Mom!* It's Mr. Race Car Driver!"

The bottle slipped from Liv's hand. Brandy spilled and spewed. Into the rice. Over the duckling. It pooled in the salad. She didn't even bother to grab it up again as it chugged out its contents. She stood frozen.

Kiki recovered first to snatch the bottle before it emptied completely. "Uh-oh. Sounds like we're going to need this."

Liv grabbed her friend's arm. Her fingers dug in like claws. "What's he doing here?"

"I'd say he's either moving in or he's throwing in the towel."

"*Mom! Come here!*" Vicky's voice came again, more urgent this time. "*He's got a suitcase!*"

Liv's legs folded and she sat at the table. "The judge gave us seventy-two hours!"

Even Kiki looked a little pale. "Well, the sooner he moves in, the sooner it'll all be over with, right?"

"I don't want him to move in!"

"Neither do I, particularly, but I'm not sure there's anything we can do about it short of blowing the place up."

"*Mom!*" Vicky called again.

"I've got to take care of this." Liv pushed to her feet and felt unsteady.

"I'll get another plate," Kiki said.

"No!"

Kiki paused in midmotion and lifted a brow at her.

"Woodingham said I had to let him sleep here," Liv grated. "She didn't say I had to *eat* with him. As far as I'm concerned, he's just a...a nonpaying guest."

"Tell that to your daughter."

Liv held the table for support. She was going to have to tell Vicky *something* now. The room spun.

She finally pushed off the table and headed for the hall. Vicky was nearly jumping up and down with excitement at the front door. Liv's heart seized as she wondered what they had been talking about. She picked up her pace and put a hand on Vicky's head when she reached her.

"Aunt Kiki needs you."

"But—"

"The race car driver isn't going anywhere. Yet. Go help Aunt Kiki."

"Mom, everything was already on the table! What does she need help with?"

"There was a little spill."

"I'll just bet," Hunter drawled.

"Shut up," Liv said in a deceptively pleasant tone as Vicky left. When her daughter was gone, Liv took his arm and yanked him into the parlor. "Damn you! Have you never heard of a telephone?"

He crossed his arms over his chest and looked around without answering. "Nice place."

"Don't make yourself at home."

He quirked a brow at her. "Ah, Livie, you're going to make this a long three months."

"Count on it. What did you say to Vicky just now?"

He brought his gaze back from all the brocade and the brass and the raw, dark wood. One wouldn't have thought it would go together, he thought, but that was Liv. The bland, the blasé and the trite didn't stand a with against her.

She'd even made that frou-frou skirt look good all those years ago.

But he didn't want to remember that, and when his eyes fell

on her face, everything else washed from his mind, anyway. She was white as a sheet.

"I didn't tell her who I am," he said finally. Then he left her to wander around the room.

Things stiffened inside Liv with every silver demitasse cup and candle snuffer he picked up to inspect. "Stop that."

"Sorry. Guests can't touch?"

"You're not a guest," she snapped.

"Probably more like your worst nightmare."

"Finally. We agree on something." Liv wondered if she was shaking with fury or fear. "Why are you doing this, Hunter?" She had never really believed he'd do it.

"Because if I don't, someday you'll tell Victoria Rose how I walked away rather than give this a chance."

She heard the honesty ring in his tone. Liv deliberately softened her own. "I won't tell her. I swear. Just go."

"Livie, with all due respect, I gave up on believing you a long time ago." He turned back to her. "I won't hurt her that way."

What was he saying? "You're trying to make me believe that you're doing this for her?"

He picked up a copper lion sitting on an end table, turned it over in his hands, put it back. "Maybe I'm doing it for me. I can't stomach walking away from her. Don't say it," he said sharply, glancing back at her when she opened her mouth. "I didn't walk away the first time. Let's put that behind us right now. I didn't know, and you told me to go."

"Would it work if I did it again now?"

A corner of his mouth almost lifted into a grin. "No."

Liv lowered herself gently onto the divan. She hugged herself. "You wouldn't have done it then, either, if you had known the truth."

"That's why you didn't tell me."

She refused to respond. She supposed he could read the answer in her silence.

"Someday she's going to be eighteen," he said, starting to prowl again in that way he had. "She won't stay small and complacent forever with whatever you've told her about me. As the years go by, she'll ask you more and more and you'll end up telling her that I had this chance and I walked away from it.'' He turned back to her. ''I'm not going to be that man.''

Liv covered her face with her hands.

So many years, she thought desperately. So many careful words. Making everything just so for Vicky. Arranging it neatly. And now he was going to blow everything wide open. She dropped her hands and stood again. ''If she sheds one tear over you, I'll kill you.''

''Duly noted. What's for dinner?''

''Whatever you can scare up at a restaurant in town. You won't be joining us. But I'll make sure there's a room available for you by nine o'clock.''

Liv left the parlor, her spine so straight and brittle she thought it crackled with her every move.

Chapter 7

The duckling was delicious. Liv couldn't swallow.

"He says he heard our place was better than the Connor," Vicky chattered at the table. "That's good, right? Word of mouth?"

"Word of mouth is good," Liv agreed, forcing the words through her tight throat.

"Their kitchen is *definitely* inferior to ours," Vicky decided, shoveling in rice pilaf.

"That's because their chef doesn't know an ion from his own—" Kiki broke off at Liv's warning look. "Patootie," she finished.

"Patootie!" Vicky put her fork down and laughed hard. "It sounds like something to eat! Patootie, potato-ie."

"Just keep it to yourself that I said so," Kiki warned. Her expression said that they already had one too many lawsuits going on in this household.

Liv moved her food around on her plate one more time, then she pushed her chair back abruptly and stood. She had to know if Hunter was still out there.

She left Kiki and Vicky frowning after her and went to the

swinging door that led into the hall. She pushed it open a crack and peered toward the front door. There was no sign of him. That didn't mean anything. He could well be sitting in her parlor, smoking one of those skinny cigars he'd gone crazy over for a short spell during his stint in Louisiana.

She'd lied in the courthouse coffee shop last week. She remembered everything about him.

Liv left the kitchen and moved quietly up the hall. She realized that she was holding her breath. She peered into the parlor. His suitcase was still there, but he was gone.

Liv glanced at the staircase. Even Hunter wouldn't knock on doors, disturbing her paying guests, until he found an empty room. Would he? She decided she would have heard a complaint by now. Still, she headed for the stairs just to make sure.

By the time she got back to the kitchen, Vicky was helping Kiki stack plates in the dishwasher. "Didn't you promise Bourne you'd check Nutmeg's tendon before bed?" Liv asked her. The injured filly was one of Vicky's favorites.

"I will. Bed's a long way off, Mom. It's not even eight o'clock yet."

"By the time you check the filly and take a bath, it will be nine."

"I'm speedy!" Vicky protested.

"You haven't sped since Bourne took after you with that riding crop for spilling a whole fifty-pound-bag of sweet feed," Kiki reminded her.

"Ouch," Vicky said. "That was an accident. I was trying to help."

"He might forgive you someday if you take good care of his filly," Liv said.

"Right." Vicky grabbed her jacket off a peg in the mudroom and hit the back door.

Liv breathed again and started loading pots and pans into the other dishwasher, the high-powered restaurant model. "He's gone," she said.

"Of course he's gone," Kiki agreed. "If he hadn't left, he'd have been sitting at the table with us. Give the man points for delicacy."

Liv choked. "He barged in here three days early!"

"Well, he always did prefer the upper hand."

Liv leaned back weakly against the counter. "I guess you're going to have to clear out your room after all. I don't know where else we can possibly put him."

Kiki turned the knob and started the dishwasher. "It won't take me half an hour to get my stuff together. And to have a word with Sweet Sarah."

"You're going to tell our resident ghost to mind her manners?"

"I'm going to tell her not to."

For a brief, priceless moment, they grinned at each other. Then Liv's smile wobbled. "I hate him."

"There's a very, very thin line between love and hate." Kiki grabbed a dish towel and dried her hands. "That's because it's difficult to work up such an intense feeling as hatred without an equally strong emotional foundation."

"I haven't loved him in a long time."

Kiki studied her face. "I'm not sure if you're lying to me or yourself."

Liv felt the room spin a little. "I can't."

"Lie or love him?"

She shook her head back and forth, helplessly. Something like desperation was beginning to chug through her veins. "I don't know if I can do this, Kiki. I don't know if I can live with him here. I don't think I can survive it. *Ninety* days!"

"You can do it because you love your daughter. And because you owe it to yourself."

Liv narrowed her eyes. "Stop talking like a philosopher. The love-hate thing was skirting the line as it was."

Kiki combed fingers through her long hair and knotted it at her nape to keep it out of the way. Then she pushed her sleeves up for the job of loading her personal possessions from the attic room. "You never had closure on this, Liv."

"Of course, I did! He walked out. That was a pretty loud door banging shut!"

"He left on a lie of your own implication."

Liv felt her skin going cold. She didn't answer.

"And that's why you went to Delaware. I've thought about that a lot lately."

"Stop this," Liv hissed. "Stop this right now."

"No. Because I can't sleep over and share brandy with you for the next three months, so I'm going to say what I've got to say right now."

"You can sleep on the sofa in my sitting room. You can't leave me here alone with him!"

"Thanks, no. I prefer a bed."

"Traitor."

Kiki tapped her forehead. "I'm the proud possessor of a 160 IQ. There's a difference."

"I did *not* go to Delaware because I needed closure!"

Kiki headed for the door, but she stopped and looked back. "You two were so young before. You were just kids playing at being in love."

"He was twenty-two."

"And you were nineteen. With all the worldly wisdom of a teenager, you thought you knew what you wanted. What your baby needed."

"I'm not liking this, Kiki," she warned. Please, she added silently, stop now before you hurt me. She had enough on her plate at the moment.

But Kiki didn't relent. "Now you're going to be forced to interact as adults with one precious little girl at the center. Do you see the irony? This court-ordered arrangement is unwelcome territory, just like the Res was for both of you all those years ago. You've been forced into this the way you were forced back then. And like before, you're either going to have to link hands and get through it together, or you'll kill each other."

"My money's on the latter."

"I'm going to go clean out my room." Kiki started to push through the door, then she turned back once more. "You know, this time if you part ways, it will be forever."

Liv opened her mouth to argue. There was no *if* involved. Then Vicky careened through the back door again.

"The race car driver is back! He wants to know where he should put his truck."

"In the Styx," Liv grated.

"Where's that?" Vicky frowned.

"Never mind. I'll take care of it. Go upstairs and hit the bathtub."

"Mo-o-o-m."

"Now."

She rarely used that tone of voice with her. Vicky took a quick step backward, maybe in hurt, maybe in surprise. "Sorry. I'm going."

"Thanks, muffin." Liv deliberately toned her voice down.

"I'm not edible," Vicky complained, but she headed for the hall door.

Liv clenched her hands and unclenched them. She breathed in. Breathed out. She pushed her shoulders straight and headed for the back door.

He was standing in front of the garage next to the shiny, red SUV that had pulled up behind her on the main road the night she'd met him at the Connor. The way the moonlight slanted across his face made him look dangerous. Or maybe that was just her perception. Maybe she felt threatened because so very many of her memories with him had taken place beneath the glittering stars just like these. Liv crossed to him. "Guests park on the asphalt apron to the side of the inn. Over there." She pointed.

"How many of them stay for three months?" he countered.

"You'll never make it that long."

"Want to bet?"

Her pulse skipped. "Just move that thing." She thrust a thumb at the truck.

"You're not using your head."

"You have no idea what's going on inside my head!"

"Sure I do. You're conniving ways to make this as miserable for me as possible."

The thought of Sweet Sarah popped into her head again. Oh, Liv thought, what she wouldn't give to have the ghost act up this very night and send Hunter Hawk-Cole hightailing it out into the night and out of her life again!

"Look," he said with enough patience to scare her a little.

"This is a rental vehicle. I'm going to turn it back in to the company on Monday since I'm going to be here for an extended period of time. Chillie is going to have my Monte Carlo brought up from home over the weekend, and it's customized. I don't want it sitting out in the rain."

"I guess you should have thought of that before you asked him to send it. Where's home?" Oh, God, had she asked that? Liv hugged herself against a chill.

"Pacific Palisades. California."

She snorted. "I guess you fit right in there. The half-breed bad boy and the rich folks."

He didn't react. "I'm rarely home. And I haven't stolen anyone's hubcaps yet."

She squeezed her eyes shut. "Sorry."

"No, you're not."

Her eyes flew open again. "No. I'm *not!* Because you wouldn't settle down for me, and now you're holed up in some kind of millionaire paradise!"

"I don't live on the beach. Does that help?"

She clapped a hand to her mouth before she could laugh giddily. "Who's Chillie?"

"My business manager."

Something else she could sink her teeth into, Liv thought. "You'd have one of those. Can't get too tied down with details, can we? That would clip your wings."

"I'm not good at details. I never was. I need someone to handle the endorsements and channel the money so I don't botch it up."

Liv dropped her hand. "Why won't you fight with me?"

His face changed. For a moment he just looked broken again, the way he had when she'd sent him from the Flagstaff bar. She turned half away from him so she wouldn't have to see it.

"Don't worry, Livie. We'll get around to it sooner or later."

She took a steadying breath. "We need to work out some details. Set some ground rules."

"Beginning with where my car goes."

"As I said, the guests—"

"The last time I warned you there was an easy way and a

hard way to do things you wouldn't listen. Don't make the same mistake twice.''

She jerked back to him. "Don't you dare threaten me!"

"Then act civil."

It stung. And she hated him for that, for getting one in on her. Then Liv opened her mouth and honesty tumbled out. "If I start giving an inch now, you'll walk all over me by the time this is finished. I *know* you."

He looked genuinely startled. "I never walked all over you."

"You *owned* me! Every breath I took was yours, even when you were away!" And that had been most of the time, she reminded herself.

He scrubbed a hand over his jaw and looked up at the moon. "We're not going to be able to separate our past from this, are we?"

Liv made a choking sound. "Our past brought us to this." And, she thought miserably, there was no way to untangle it.

"I want it to be just about our daughter."

Our daughter. She wanted to shout at him again that he hadn't been here, not through the pox or the disastrous dance recital, not through any of it. But she knew how he would answer. She knew he would only remind her that he'd never had a choice.

He was right about one thing. It was time to let that part go.

Liv gathered her dignity. She pulled her spine straight again. "There are four stalls in the garage, and Kiki and I only use two. You can have the third. But leave the last one for Vicky's mechanical bull."

"Her *what?*"

"She went through a stage of wanting to be a rodeo queen. I wouldn't let her practice on a real bronc so I picked it up at a bar down in Sedona that was going out of business."

"A mechanical bull," he repeated.

"She hasn't touched it in six months, so I suspect I'll be able to move it out soon. In the meantime, don't crowd that space. I don't want her using it again, flying off the damned thing and going noggin-first into a Monte Carlo."

Hunter's eyes narrowed. "I'd die before I hurt her, Liv."

"Good. Here's your chance to prove it."

Their eyes met. This time there were no memories there, just challenge.

He looked away first and peered into the open garage stall. "Do you have mats down in there for her? Around this bull?"

"Of course I do. I picked them up used from a gym in Winslow."

"A mechanical bull." He shook his head again.

"She's like you in leaving no possibility unexplored."

As soon as the words left her mouth, Liv would have given her life to pull them back. Because what she saw in his eyes almost undid her. A softness. A yearning. She *couldn't* let him touch her heart again. And loving Vicky was the quickest way to her heart.

"More ground rules," she said, quickly, hoarsely.

"Hit me with them." It took a moment, but his face cleared.

"The Copper Rose is a large establishment and we should be able to successfully avoid each other without too much trouble, but we'll need to set some kind of meal schedule. We're not going to sit down all cozy together, like one big happy family."

"God forbid."

"The inn serves breakfast and an afternoon tea to guests. You can have your morning meal with everyone else in the dining room, and I'll just eat in the kitchen."

"What about…Vicky?" He'd caught her use of the diminutive form of the child's name, but he liked Victoria Rose better. Though she was no hothouse flower. He wanted to grin again at that thought. Hunter scrubbed a hand over his mouth instead.

"She can eat with whichever one of us she wants to. I won't interfere with the court order."

He thought about it. "Playing your cards, Liv? Strategy? You won't take the chance of flying in the face of the judge's intentions with this arrangement." But he'd never expected anything less from her, not from the girl he'd known.

"Exactly." Liv brought her chin up.

He shrugged his acceptance of the rule. "Okay. That's all fine with me."

Her eyes narrowed. "When did you start getting gallant?"

"Somewhere between the Busch and the Winston Cup series

when they started pushing me onto television and into the company of starlets.''

It hurt. How could it hurt after all this time? ''You probably broke hearts all over Hollywood.''

''Monique Shaughnessy's comes to mind.''

''You dated Monique Shaughnessy?'' She was flabbergasted enough to forget all her ground rules for the moment.

''She's actually pretty vapid,'' he offered. ''I ended it before she was ready to.''

She didn't want to hear this.

''She's also self-absorbed,'' he said.

''Ha. You two should have been like peas in a pod, then.'' Her voice went thin.

''Now, now, Livie, we were just getting along.''

''No, we weren't. We were setting ground rules.''

''*You* were setting ground rules. I was listening.''

''Then shut up and let me get back to them!''

He shrugged. ''You were the one who asked about starlets.''

''You *startled* me into asking!''

''And you don't care a whit?''

''Of course not.''

''Liar.''

She wanted to hit him. She actually fisted her hand before she brought herself back. Once, she thought, she would have launched herself at him, tickling, touching, wriggling all over him until she'd made him pay. Her blood sped up at the memory. She felt the heat of it right beneath her skin.

''I hate you,'' she breathed.

''Same here, but we're going to have to live with it for a while. The ground rules?''

Liv dragged her mind back. ''After breakfast you're on your own, mealwise. I won't ask Kiki to cook for you.''

''Who cooks for you and Victoria Rose?''

''I do. Mostly. Except for the rare occasions when Kiki stays for dinner. I'll claim the kitchen for my own meals from noon to one, and from six to seven o'clock in the evening. But other than that, you can have it. Kiki is cleaning her stuff out of her

Play the
"LAS VEGAS"
GAME

Play the
"LAS VEGAS" Game
and get
3 FREE GIFTS!

FREE GIFTS!

FREE GIFTS!

1. Pull back all 3 tabs on the card at right. Then check the claim chart to see what we have for you — 2 FREE BOOKS and a gift — ALL YOURS! ALL FREE!

2. Send back this card and you'll receive brand-new Silhouette Intimate Moments® novels. These books have a cover price of $4.75 each in the U.S. and $5.75 each in Canada, but they are yours to keep absolutely free.

3. There's no catch. You're under no obligation to buy anything. We charge nothing — ZERO — for your first shipment. And you don't have to make any minimum number of purchases — not even one!

4. The fact is, thousands of readers enjoy receiving their books by mail from the Silhouette Reader Service™. They enjoy the convenience of home delivery...they like getting the best new novels at discount prices, BEFORE they're available in stores...and they love their *Heart to Heart* newsletter featuring author news, horoscopes, recipes, book reviews and much more!

5. We hope that after receiving your free books you'll want to remain a subscriber. But the choice is yours — to continue or cancel, any time at all! So why not take us up on our invitation, with no risk of any kind. You'll be glad you did!

Visit us online at
www.eHarlequin.com

FREE!
No Obligation to Buy!
No Purchase Necessary!

Play the
"LAS VEGAS" Game

PEEL BACK HERE ▶
PEEL BACK HERE ▶
PEEL BACK HERE ▶

YES! I have pulled back the 3 tabs. Please send me all the free Silhouette Intimate Moments® books and the gift for which I qualify. I understand that I am under no obligation to purchase any books, as explained on the back and opposite page.

345 SDL DNX7   245 SDL DNYE

FIRST NAME   LAST NAME

ADDRESS

APT.#   CITY

STATE/PROV.   ZIP/POSTAL CODE   (S-IM-09/02)

7	7	7	**GET 2 FREE BOOKS & A FREE MYSTERY GIFT!**
✤	✤	✤	**GET 2 FREE BOOKS!**
🍒	🍒	🍒	**GET 1 FREE BOOK!**
🔔	🔔	🔔	**TRY AGAIN!**

Offer limited to one per household and not valid to current Silhouette Intimate Moments® subscribers. All orders subject to approval.

◀ DETACH AND MAIL TODAY ▼

The Silhouette Reader Service™ — Here's how it works:

Accepting your 2 free books and gift places you under no obligation to buy anything. You may keep the books and gift and return the shipping statement marked "cancel." If you do not cancel, about a month later we'll send you 6 additional novels and bill you just $3.99 each in the U.S., or $4.74 each in Canada, plus 25¢ shipping & handling per book and applicable taxes if any.* That's the complete price and — compared to cover prices of $4.75 each in the U.S. and $5.75 each in Canada — it's quite a bargain! You may cancel at any time, but if you choose to continue, every month we'll send you 6 more books, which you may either purchase at the discount price or return to us and cancel your subscription.

*Terms and prices subject to change without notice. Sales tax applicable in N.Y. Canadian residents will be charged applicable provincial taxes and GST.

BUSINESS REPLY MAIL
FIRST-CLASS MAIL   PERMIT NO. 717-003   BUFFALO, NY

POSTAGE WILL BE PAID BY ADDRESSEE

SILHOUETTE READER SERVICE
3010 WALDEN AVE
PO BOX 1867
BUFFALO NY 14240-9952

NO POSTAGE
NECESSARY
IF MAILED
IN THE
UNITED STATES

room now. You can sleep there for the duration. It's on the fourth floor. In the attic.''

He frowned. For the first time, he really didn't like what he was hearing. ''Where's Kiki supposed to go?''

''She has an apartment in town. She only stays here occasionally. All my other rooms are reserved well through January.'' And his time would be up on January fourth.

''What if Kiki wants to stay over during the next three months?'' he asked.

''Then she'll sleep on the sofa in my sitting room.''

''Sure. That'll happen.''

Kiki liked her creature comforts. Liv almost smiled again. ''Then *I'll* sleep on the sofa and give her my bed. What do you care?''

''Or I could sleep on your sofa and leave her room alone.'' He grinned.

Warmth rained through her at the very idea of him being that close. It started suddenly at her pulse points and coursed deeper, into central, integral parts of her. ''Over my dead body.''

He read her expression, the awareness there. He took a step closer to her and reached a hand to her cheek before he knew he was going to do it. ''Not so immune to me after all, are you, Livie?'' But then, he'd known that when she'd kissed him back on the roadside.

She smacked his hand away hard. ''Go to hell.''

''I've got a suite reserved there, but I'm not ready for it.''

''That brings me to my last rule.''

He stepped back a little, making himself do it. Damned if he was going to let her get to him again. ''Shoot.''

''Touch me again—like you did on the highway, like you were going to do just now—and I'll break your face.''

''Point taken.''

''Okay then.'' Liv turned away, back toward the inn. Then she stalled. ''Hunter.''

He watched the shift of her shoulders, watched her posture go from militant to stoic to just plain helpless. And it hurt something inside him. ''What?'' he asked gruffly.

''I haven't told her anything about this yet.''

Hunter thought a moment. "You weren't going to tell her without someone pressing a gun to your temple first."

She jerked back to face him. "You're trying to tear her world up six ways to Sunday! I wasn't going to let you until someone made me!"

"I think the judge has done that."

She hugged herself. "Yeah. She has. Just let me talk to her first," she begged, her voice dropping to a whisper. "Don't put on some great big 'Dad' T-shirt and saunter into her room wearing it until I've had the chance."

Did she honestly think he would do that? "Let me know when the coast is clear."

"I won't have to."

He frowned, then he understood. Vicky would let him know. "I'm going in now." She turned away one last time, jerkily. "Sweet dreams."

"Maybe. In another three months."

God, he wanted to hate her, Hunter thought as he watched her walk back to the inn. He wanted to despise the way her hips twitched gently, the way her spine stayed so straight without robbing her of grace. He wanted to hate the dance of that brown-gold-russet hair against her back. He wanted to hate her for what she had done to him eight years ago and what she still would have done now if he hadn't found a crazy judge to force her hand.

But he was smiling bemusedly when Liv disappeared inside and Kiki came out carting a box. She crossed to him and dropped it at his feet.

"I'm going now. Hurt either one of them and I'll remove pieces of your person with a dull knife."

Hunter wisely remained silent. He believed her.

Thirty minutes later Liv found herself wishing for all her life that Kiki had not gone home.

She needed courage. She needed strength. She needed to be rational, not all knotted up inside after talking to Hunter in the moonlight. She had to forget what he had once meant to her and concentrate on Vicky. She needed Kiki to whisper all that sense she was so big on in her ear.

Liv wanted desperately to find the path to being the kind of hero only a mother could be, the kind who would give her soul to the devil for the welfare of her child and do it with grace and aplomb. She *wanted* to be that woman, but faced with walking down the hall to Vicky's room and telling her the truth of the past several days nearly dissolved her to helpless, frustrated tears.

She knotted the belt on her robe, anyway, and stepped out into the third floor hallway. Cocoa, she thought. That would ease the way.

She spent another ten minutes in the kitchen, eight of them given up to hunting the mix down in Kiki's cupboards. She nuked the water and put a tray together, carrying it back upstairs. She knocked and pushed the door open with one hip just in time to see Vicky shove a book under the covers.

"Oops," Vicky said. "Caught."

"Red-handed. But I knew you'd be doing that." Liv went in and put the tray on Vicky's desk.

The little girl pushed her hair back from her forehead. "Then why do you always give me grief about reading after lights-out? Is it a mother thing?"

"Yup. Eight-year-olds should be in bed by nine o'clock, so I pretend to enforce the rule."

Vicky sniffed the air and frowned suspiciously, mother-rules forgotten. "That's chocolate, isn't it? What's with the chocolate?"

Liv carried the cups over to the bed. She wondered where Hunter was. Had he already moved into the room Kiki had vacated? She couldn't do this with him under the same roof, distracting her, she thought desperately.

She had to.

Vicky peered into her cup. "Is this your version of cocoa, or is it Aunt Kiki's with the shaved bittersweet?"

"Dream on." Liv sat on the edge of the bed.

To her credit, Vicky laughed and guzzled, anyway. She was

that kind of kid. "Something's up, right?" She licked foam from her lip.

Liv caught her breath. "Yeah. Big-time."

"You're putting me up for adoption?"

"I thought about it when you were two, but then I changed my mind."

"Good thing. I'm pretty happy here."

Liv's nerves caught together and tangled. It hurt. "Are you?"

"'Course I am. What's not to be happy with? I have you and Aunt Kiki and Bourne. Except he's a grouch most times. I have the horses."

"You have strangers trooping through your home." Liv dragged in breath then spit the words out. "And you haven't really had a dad."

Vicky's eyes shifted oddly. "That's okay. Mandy Singapore has one and he's a worse grouch than Bourne."

Please, God, guide me here, Liv thought. "They're not like that when you don't live with them all the time," she said. "I get grouchy sometimes, but if you only saw me once in a while, I'd be on my best behavior when I was with you."

"Mom, you do okay." Vicky downed the last of her cocoa.

Liv's next prayer was an old one...for a normal eight-year-old. And, as always, she took it back immediately. She wouldn't trade this child for the world.

"Johnny's not my dad and you want to tell me who is," Vicky said finally, helpfully. "Right? Is that where you're going with this?"

Liv's jaw dropped open. It was all the adults Vicky had spent her formative years with, she thought. It had to be. Eight-year-olds didn't talk like this.

Then Liv spit it out. "He's upstairs in Aunt Kiki's room right now."

Liv waited for her daughter's shock. What she saw instead made the air hard to breathe. Vicky wasn't surprised. She knew this child as intimately as she knew her own skin. She knew her eyes, her gestures, her flippant remarks. She knew the way she breathed. And Vicky wasn't surprised.

"Okay, cough it up," Liv said edgily. "How did you figure it out?"

"Who says I did?"

"It's the way you've collapsed on the floor in complete and utter shock."

Vicky didn't giggle. Her gaze shifted again. "I heard you and Aunt Kiki talking about it once. Are you mad?"

Liv's heart chugged. She'd thought she'd always been careful. She hadn't been careful enough. "No. If I hadn't told you, what were you going to do about it?"

"I was going to give you to the end of third grade to come to your senses."

Liv choked.

"Then I guess I would have written him a letter or something."

"Without my knowledge?"

"If I had to." Vicky plucked at a loose thread on her bedspread. "There's one thing I don't understand, though."

Liv braced herself. "What?"

"You always said you loved my dad bunches."

Something squirmed inside her. "Well, I did. I used to."

"Now you don't like him at all. You said so."

"Things change. Grown-ups change."

"So you only *thought* you loved him bunches? Like I thought I liked pickles for maybe a day until I got sick from eating too many of them?"

Liv's stomach was starting to hurt. She couldn't swallow any more chocolate. She got up from the bed to put her cup back on the tray. "Something like that, yes."

"So how come you're letting him stay here?"

I have to. "He wants to get to know you."

"Are you going to fight with him the whole time?"

"I'm going to try very hard not to."

"How long will he stay?"

"A few months. Maybe. Probably."

"That *long?*"

"Unless you want him to go." Then he would have to leave,

Liv thought hopefully. He'd have to. Surely the judge would see that. "This is all up to you, Vicky."

"Well, how can I know that until I talk to him some?" Vicky asked with the lack of guile of youth.

Liv went back to the bed to stroke her hair. "You can't, baby. Of course, you can't."

"Can I go talk to him now?"

Liv's heart stuttered. She glanced at the clock. It was twenty past nine. Past bedtime. And if she said no, what would that make her? "If you want."

Vicky scrambled out of bed. "Just for a minute."

Liv watched her race out of the room. And everything stopped inside her.

She waited a full minute to breathe again. When she did, the air in the room seemed thin and elusive. She understood what terrified her most now, and it nearly buckled her. It made her feel small.

What if Vicky decided she loved Hunter more than her?

Liv went to stand in the hall. She stared down to the end where the attic stairs were. Vicky had already disappeared up them.

She knew she was being a fool. But...what if?

What if—even though she'd been the one to nurse this child and raise her and coddle her and punish her—what if Vicky went for the guy who was only around for the good times? Because Hunter couldn't be anything else. He would come back into their lives with gifts occasionally and happy laughter. Oh, she knew it, Liv thought desperately. And she, *she,* would be the one left to mete out discipline and say no.

"It won't come to that," she whispered aloud. But as she turned back to her own room, she knew it could.

The room was all Kiki, Hunter thought as he shoved jeans into one of the dresser drawers. No matter that she had officially vacated it. The air still stirred from her presence.

The attic was huge, but it had two sloped dormers that made the ceiling cant on both sides. He had to duck if he moved too much to the left or right of center. The bed—a huge four-poster—took up one end of the room beneath the vaulted V of the ceiling. There was some sort of ballet bar attached to one wall near the stair entrance. The other wall was dotted with windows—thin, narrow things that tried to look out on the barn and the garage and fell just short of succeeding.

The bedspread was crimson satin. The curtains were more of the same. The carpet was white plush that made him think he'd better take his shoes off for the next three months before he stepped in here or Kiki would have his head. There were easily fifteen throw pillows on the bed and probably a dozen candles scattered about, and Hunter decided he didn't want to know their particular history.

There were no other personal touches. It was lush, but somehow simple at the same time. Kiki had always been an odd bird. She hadn't taken that much out of here. There'd only been that one small box.

He'd forgotten to ask where the bathroom was, Hunter realized. He scouted the room one more time and found no hidden doorways. Downstairs, then. He would have to share with the guests.

He was pulling a shirt over his head to do just that when a knock came at his door.

Liv. What was she up to? Was she going to fight this to the death after all? Hunter went to the door and hated the fact that something inside him quickened at the idea that she would come back to talk to him one more time. She'd left him. She'd destroyed him. He didn't want to want her again. He flung open the door.

"What?" he growled.

There was no one at eye level. Hunter looked down.

Victoria Rose stood there in a red calico nightgown. He was starting to catch on to the idea that red was her favorite color. Her hair was a black cloud, wild, disheveled. Her small teeth were impossibly white. She crossed her arms over her skinny chest.

"I know now, so you can stop pretending," she announced.

It took Hunter a moment to find his voice. "Did I pretend?"

"Sort of. It's like the time my teacher said I cheated on a

test, but I didn't. I gave Mandy my answers a whole day before. So I did but I didn't.''

''How'd you know what was going to be on the test?'' Hunter found himself asking.

''It was last year. My teacher was old and not too with-it.'' She swept past him into the room. She moved like her mother that way, Hunter thought again, pivoting to watch her—purposefully but with such grace that you hardly realized it. ''It was always real easy to figure out what Mrs. Geary was going to ask on the tests, because it was exactly the same as our homework,'' she explained.

Hunter was mesmerized. ''I get it.''

Vicky flopped down to sit on the crimson bed. ''So, anyway, now that I officially know and all, you can just act normal.''

He wondered about this ''officially'' business. What did that mean?

He went to sit beside her on the bed, but he kept his distance. He was terrified. She was maybe sixty-five pounds—tops—of precocious wonder. She was messy long hair and dark-blue eyes and she was only eight. But for the first time in his life Hunter was intimidated. Because everything he said now mattered. It mattered more than life itself.

''You could get grumpy sometimes,'' she continued. ''Like Mandy Singapore's dad. Who lives with her. So she sees him at his worst.''

''You want to see me at my worst?''

''What I'm saying is, it would be okay.''

He thought of Liv again. ''It might actually happen.''

''Because, you know, I think if you were nice to me all the time, Mom might get freaked out.'' She stood up from the bed again.

''If I was *nice* to you, she would?'' He was dumbfounded.

''Like when I thought Mandy had a new best friend, I got sort of bent out of shape. So I'm just saying maybe don't be too nice to me around Mom. Because she might not let you stay if you do.''

She wasn't eight, he thought. She was eighty. How had she become so wise? ''I'll take that into consideration.''

"Okay, then. I guess I'll see you tomorrow." She went back to the door.

Hunter finally got his wits back a little. "Does your mother know you're here?"

Vicky looked back at him and nodded. "Yeah, but she looked like she swallowed a goose when I asked if it was okay. So I'm going to go back now and not stress her out anymore." She swept one last glance around the room. "Night, Sarah."

Before he could ask who Sarah was, Vicky was gone. And he couldn't think about even one more woman tonight because two of them had already tied him in knots.

Chapter 8

For a week, it seemed to Liv that Hunter kept to his side of her many lines.

She watched Kiki sweep into the kitchen after breakfast on Friday, holding two platters that had been almost completely denuded. It was nine-thirty. Guests—their own as well as tourists from town—were already gathering at the barn for the morning's trail ride.

"He even ate the garnish this time," Kiki muttered.

Liv stepped closer to scowl at the plates. "Has he used the kitchen at all?"

"If he has, he's bringing in his own food and burning the evidence." Kiki stacked the plates on the counter and went back to the dining room for more.

Liv followed her. She didn't care about this. It wasn't her problem. "He doesn't cook," she said, anyway.

"Neither do you, but I don't hold it against you."

Liv barely heard her. Hunter had once existed on anything that could be eaten straight out of a can, she thought. His mother would rarely cook for him once he'd turned eighteen and began to regularly leave the Res. Later, when he'd visited Liv in Flag, they'd been big on fast food because they'd both been rock-bottom broke. She'd refused to whittle away her trust fund on groceries. Sometimes she'd brought home leftovers from the resort kitchen.

But he wasn't broke now.

"He's not eating out—at least not often—because he's almost always here," she fretted.

"So starving him out might work yet. Want me to cut down on the breakfast portions?"

"I'm not trying to starve him out! I just don't want to cross paths with him any more than I have to."

"Of course."

"I'm going to help Bourne saddle the horses," Liv decided abruptly. There was no sense in arguing with Kiki once she'd made her mind up about something.

She went outside. There was a bite to the air. It wasn't near enough to deter the guests from the trails, but Liv couldn't get warm.

She found herself glancing back at the inn repeatedly until she saw Hunter come out the back door and head for the garage. Movie stars, she thought. Pacific Palisades. None of that had changed him. In so many ways he was still the same man. The new polish was only skin-deep.

He still had that same lean grace to him. She'd noticed it often during the course of the week. The leather jacket he wore was top-of-the-line. His boots, his black jeans and turtleneck, all had the look of money, as well. But his gaze prowled as he moved and there was that sense of volatility about him that had once sent her blood skittering with excitement and anticipation with a single glimpse of him.

A moment later the black Monte Carlo moved off down the drive. Where was he going? Liv reminded herself that she didn't care. She and Bourne got the guests mounted and they headed out.

By the time they got back from the trail ride, Liv knew she really was getting sick this time. Her throat was raw, on fire. Her head throbbed, but not with the same nervous ache that had hounded her for weeks now. This was cranial and deep.

This time it really was the flu.

Bourne took one look at her when they had all gathered back at the barn and grabbed her reins from her hand. He was a borderline hypochondriac. "I'll take things from here. Go inside. I don't want your germs."

Liv held fast to her mare. This was something else she had to fix, she thought, another unpleasantry brought about by Hunter's arrival. Bourne had been annoyed with her ever since the trail ride when Hunter had first shown up in Jerome.

"In a minute," she rasped. "We need to talk first."

"Then breathe the other way."

Liv pivoted obediently. "Better?"

"If you say so."

She dragged air into her lungs and it burned going down. "He's Vicky's father," she blurted.

It startled the old man enough that he actually stopped moving and stared at her, right in the eyes, something he rarely did. "Who?"

"Hunter. Hawk-Cole. The owner of the black Monte Carlo. He turned up on the trail ride that day, remember? He's Vicky's father."

"Thought Johnny was her daddy."

"No."

"She know this?" Bourne asked.

"Yes."

"Now or always?"

"Pretty much always," Liv said hollowly.

Bourne thought that over. "She ain't never said nothing to me about it."

"You're always grumping at her. Especially since the sweet-feed incident."

He cracked a grin. One of his incisors was gold. She'd always wondered how he'd afforded that, and why he so rarely smiled to show it off. "She wraps the rest of you 'round her little finger," he said. "I'm just making sure she has a harder sell with me."

"Which is why she goes out of her way to irritate you." Liv

coughed into her hand. This time she let Bourne take the mare, but she followed him up the barn alley.

"Truth to tell, I love that kid to pieces," he said roughly.

Liv managed a smile. "I know."

"Is this a good thing? This business of her daddy being here?"

"For her, maybe."

"Not for you."

"No, Bourne. Not for me."

"You ain't been yourself lately. Now I get it." He unsaddled the mare and threw a blanket over her back.

"I was trying to contain the situation, but then it blew up in my face," Liv admitted hoarsely.

"How come he's here?"

"A judge ordered it."

"Well. Nothing you can do 'bout that. Whiskey, honey and tea," he ordered, changing the subject. "Go inside and get yourself some. It'll help calm that throat of yours some."

He wasn't going to thank her for the confidence, Liv realized. He was too crusty for that. But he was back to his old footing with her.

Liv glanced at her watch. She had two hours until tea. Maybe she would just lie down for a while.

She left the barn and was nearly to her room when Hunter came down the stairs from the attic room. When he saw her, his stride slowed until he stopped completely.

She supposed it was inevitable that they'd bump noses sooner or later. Liv realized that she had stopped, too. She forced herself to move again, as far as her door.

"You look like hell," he said bluntly.

"Thank you."

"You're sick."

"I'll fight it off." She closed her hand around the knob. But for some reason she couldn't open it.

"That's always been your problem. You don't know when to back down."

"Please. Don't fight with me now." She hated the quaver in her voice.

"It's your way or the highway," he said relentlessly.

"Hunter, this isn't necessary. I always knew that if you felt any of my virtues were redeeming, you would have stayed with me."

She was rewarded by a tightening of his jaw. "I thought we agreed that we were going to leave the past out of this."

Liv shook her head weakly. "We agreed that that would be damned near impossible." She thought briefly of what Kiki had said, about them having to link hands again to get through this or they would kill each other. And she knew, too—suddenly and with sick certainty—that they probably wouldn't be able to do that until they hashed out all the old grudges and the hurt.

But not now, she thought desperately. Just not now. "I've got to lie down."

"What else do you have to do for the rest of the day?" he demanded as though she hadn't spoken.

"Tea. But that's not until three o'clock."

He'd noticed the way she made it a point to mingle with her guests then. "I can do that for you."

He watched her drag her spine straight. "No. You cannot."

Hunter frowned. "I can hold my own in polite company."

"Right. I forgot. The California ritz and glitz."

"Why the hell does that bother you so much?"

"Because I knew you when!"

"We've both grown up, Liv. We're not what we were."

No, she thought again, but those kids were still buried inside them...hurt and broken and desperate to drag all the old feelings out for airing. "I always do tea," she said rather than acknowledge his point.

"And I always finish out the season, too. But you've got to know when to throw in the towel."

"You just don't give up, do you? You're a stubborn—"

"Leave name calling out of this and let me do tea."

"I never miss it. It's a matter of personal pride."

His eyes glinted with frustration. "You always were a stubborn—"

"Let's leave name calling out of this," she interrupted quickly.

This time he smiled. Almost.

"And I'm not stubborn," she argued.

"As a mule."

"I only stop in briefly at tea on Fridays, anyway. Fifteen minutes or so, tops."

"Why?"

"Because I have to get over to Mustang Ridge for Vicky's lesson." Then she saw the look on his face and her heart sank.

"All right," he said. "You do tea and I'll do the riding lesson."

Liv opened her mouth to argue. And closed it again. Because that, too, would be flying in the face of the judge's intentions. If he wanted to pick up his daughter at the riding academy, she had to let him.

But she hated it.

Liv pressed her hands to her cheeks. She was feverish. He took her arm and she yanked back from him. "I told you not to touch me!"

"I want to choke you!"

"I didn't say anything!"

"You didn't have to. It's all over your face. *I'm not going to hurt that child!* Damn you, Liv! I'd cut you to the bone in a heartbeat, but not her! I'll pick her up." He stepped around her and moved off down the hall. "End of discussion."

Liv watched him go until the top of his black head disappeared down the stairs. Then she let her spine slide down her door until she sat on the floor. She put her forehead to her updrawn knees and let herself wallow in misery, both physically and the kind that came from broken dreams.

Liv felt no better after a nap. In fact, she realized that it was entirely possible she felt worse.

She swallowed a handful of ibuprofen and forced herself into the shower at two-thirty. By three, she'd changed into a denim jumper and a long-sleeved white turtleneck. She pulled her hair back into a ponytail because she was too woozy to fuss with it. She had high hopes that makeup would erase the drawn, pinched look about her eyes, but she was disappointed.

She glanced at her watch five times before she went downstairs.

She heard the distant rumble of the Monte Carlo leaving the inn at 3:10. She poised for its return, her ears begging for the sound, even as she knew she couldn't possibly expect them back before 4:45.

Ed Stern had finally gone, and this week they had a quartet of elderly women in residence. Agnes was vaguely senile and Katherine Joan felt strongly about people addressing her by her full name. Liv was reasonably sure that the youngest—Isabela— was every day of eighty-three. And Dee was a borderline kleptomaniac. Normally Liv found them amusing, but today every cell in her body hurt. She kept her distance, knowing that at their ages her germs might well be the death of them. She should just say hello and go back upstairs, she thought, but she wasn't sure she could hear Hunter's car from her third-floor room, at least without opening her window, and she couldn't get warm as it was.

By five o'clock, as the ladies were finally departing, he still hadn't brought Vicky home.

Something was wrong, Liv thought fretfully as she watched Dee surreptitiously tuck one of Kiki's plum tarts into her pocket. Maybe Hunter had been driving too fast and they'd cracked up against the cliff side and they were both in the hospital. She pressed her fingers to her temples. *Where were they?*

Liv gathered up the tea service and took it to the kitchen. "I'll clean up today." It would give her an excuse to stay downstairs.

Kiki looked up from something simmering on the stove. "Mother Theresa's shoes are going to be hard ones to fill."

Liv winced and coughed. "Don't talk in riddles today. I'm not up to it."

"My point exactly. I made you my Ama's stew with a twist."

Liv scarcely heard her. She went to the window and looked out. "They should have been back by now."

"Veal cubes instead of mutton," Kiki explained as though she hadn't spoken.

Liv nodded. She hated mutton. It reminded her of the Res,

the one and only place she had ever eaten it—and then she had eaten it often. Even after centuries, it was still a staple of the Navajo diet. "I don't feel like eating."

"You will, assuming they ever get back."

Liv spun on her, and the move left her dizzy. "You think something's wrong, too!"

"I didn't say that."

She looked at the kitchen clock. "It's 5:15. It doesn't take forty-five minutes to come back from Mustang Ridge!" He was running with Vicky. With his financial resources, no one would ever be able to find them, she thought hectically. They could land in Bora Bora or Iceland. They could—

"He's not going to leave the NASCAR circuit," Kiki said as though reading her mind.

"Why not?" Liv countered harshly. "He's left everything else."

Kiki opened her mouth and closed it again. It took her a moment to think of a logical response to that, Liv thought, because it was absolutely true.

"He hasn't done that for a long time," Kiki argued finally.

Liv looked out the window again. "Leopards don't change their spots."

"No. But when they grow old, they do tend to fade a bit."

"Nothing about him has faded." Liv hugged herself. *Come home, come home, come home.*

And then she heard the car.

She was out the back door before she realized that she was giving him an edge. By rushing out, she'd let him know how worried she'd been. He'd exploit it.

He drove into the garage and before Liv could get there, Vicky came tearing out. "I got a new bridle!" She held it high in one hand.

Liv stared at it. Her brain wouldn't work. "I just bought you a new bridle," she said finally. "Not more than two months ago."

"This is the red one."

"You don't need two bridles."

"Mom, would you look? This is the *red* one!" she said again.

Liv felt the pain in her head explode. She remembered the bridle. It had been thirty dollars more than the one she'd bought when Bourne had advised her that the old one was every bit as bad as Vicky had said. She'd been planning on splurging on the red one for her for Christmas.

"Go inside," she said hoarsely.

Vicky frowned. "What's wrong?"

"I need to have a word with your—with Hunter."

"About the bridle?"

"About the sunset! Go inside! Kiki has stew."

"Aunt Kiki cooked tonight? Cool!" She was off like a shot.

Hunter came out of the garage and lowered the door, then he turned around and saw her. Liv didn't let him get in the first word. "How dare you?" She marched toward him.

"What did I do now?"

"You're *buying* her!"

His face went dangerous. She remembered that look. It made his cheekbones seem more stark. It made his eyes go almost black. It was the look that said someone had crossed a line at his expense.

"I'm going to pretend you didn't say that," he said too quietly, stepping around her.

She was beyond caution. She pivoted to shout after him. "Where do you get off buying her things without even talking to me about it first?"

"You weren't in the car when the subject came up." He kept walking.

Liv went after him and skirted around him to poke him in the chest. "Well, here's a parenting lesson, pal. Kids don't need every damned thing they ask for! And there's a word for the ones that get them! *Spoiled!* It means they have a father trying to purchase their affection!"

"What the hell are you afraid of, Livie?"

That she'll love you more than me because you never say no! "That you'll turn her into something despicable before you go!"

"You have so little faith in your own child? In *yourself?*"

"I don't have anything to do with this," she grated. "Stop turning this around."

"If you think I can undo eight years of lessons you've taught her in three months, then yeah, you have a lot to do with it. You're doubting yourself."

"Ha!" Her voice came up another notch. Liv heard it and hated it, knew she was being irrational. She was picking a fight. Or trying to. Trying desperately. "You're admitting that you're going to vanish again when these ninety days are up!"

His own temper finally snapped. Heat flared into his eyes. "I'm not admitting any such thing! I'll return to the circuit! But I'll be back!"

"You'll just flit in and out of her life bearing gifts, is that it? She didn't need that bridle! *And I was going to get it for her for Christmas!*"

His face cleared slowly. "Ah. Stepped on your toes, did I?"

"Yes," she hissed.

"Then I'm sorry."

Liv was shocked enough to take a step back. "You never apologize."

"I do when I'm wrong."

"You're never wrong."

He flashed a grin. "Thanks for that."

"You never *think* you're wrong," Liv amended.

He took in a deep breath and let it out again very slowly. "I keep telling you, I'm not twenty-two anymore."

The comment reminded her too much of what Kiki had said about closure, about the fact that they'd been so young before. Liv hugged herself without answering.

"You need to grow up, too," he said calmly.

She reeled back as though he had slapped her. "I grew up the day I took responsibility for another human life!"

"No offense, Livie, but marrying Guenther was pretty juvenile."

How could he do this to her? How could he stoke her temper into such a fury with only a few well-placed words? She'd spent more than eight long years safe from this kind of emotion, and now it blazed through her all over again as though not a moment had passed since he'd left her. "Don't you dare judge me!"

"Your decision changed my life. I have a right."

"You weren't in my shoes. How can you say what's right or wrong when you've never been in that situation?"

He rubbed his jaw. "I'll tell you what, Livie. If all the rules of life were suddenly changed and *I* had been the one carrying that little girl, I would have told you. And I wouldn't have married someone I didn't love just to glom on to a white picket fence."

It struck ice at the very core of her. "I'm going in now," she said, half turning. "I'm going to have dinner with my daughter."

"Uh…too late." He held up a hand and for the first time she noticed a crumbled, empty fast-food bag in it. "We hit a drive-thru on the way home."

"I *hate* you!"

"Keep telling yourself that, Livie, until you believe it."

"You can't just keep doing these things without consulting me first!" She shouted after him as he went toward the inn again.

His steps slowed, then he turned back. "You're sick. I couldn't imagine how you'd feel like cooking tonight. So I fed her for you. The proper response would have been 'thank you.'"

This time when he turned back to the inn, she let him go. Liv couldn't think of a single thing to say to that.

She'd robbed him of one of the most precious things a man could call his own, Hunter thought four hours later—his child. She would have kept the secret of Victoria Rose from him forever if he hadn't stumbled into them in Delaware against all odds. That still made his gut twist, and he still hated her for it. He blamed her for fighting him when he'd come to Jerome and for forcing them into a court scene that had landed him here. He despised her for watching him every moment of every day he'd spent in her home, expecting him to do something to break his daughter's heart.

And he knew her too well to forget that the last thing Livie Slade would ever do when she was frightened was admit it.

She'd skipped around Guenther and had created for herself what she'd always needed—a safe haven, a civilized home. And now she thought he was somehow going to fracture all that—even as she tossed recriminations at him for not staying around long enough to do it. Yeah, he hated her. And he had never learned to hate her enough.

He thought fleetingly of tracking her down in her rooms, but he wasn't sure there was anything more either one of them could say. His stomach growled, but he didn't feel like driving back into town to find a restaurant. Besides, it was nearly ten o'clock. He wasn't sure if he could find anything open.

Time to raid the kitchen, Hunter thought. He'd put it off all week, mindful of Liv's rules, but enough was enough. Most of her rules were irrational, anyway. And a man had to eat.

He started for the door and out of the corner of his eye saw a light shift. Hunter turned back fast. The far corner, he thought, there under the south eave, the same place he had noticed it before. Though he wasn't exactly sure what he thought he'd seen. Not *someone*. But movement as though someone had been there.

"Damn it," he muttered. Liv was really getting to him. He was seeing things.

He left the room and went downstairs. And found manna from heaven on the kitchen counter.

There was a loaf of bread, an unopened jar of mayonnaise, a knife and a note in Kiki's strong, slashing handwriting:

Spread the bread with the mayo. Look in the deli drawer in the bottom of the smallest refrigerator for cold sliced beef. Layer beef on bread over mayonnaise. Apply salt and pepper—they're on the table. Press bread slices together. PS—If you tell her I did this, I still have that dull knife.

Hunter laughed aloud.

"What's so funny?"

He was genuinely spooked. Maybe it was an after-effect of the weird light in his room, but Hunter came out of his skin and jerked around to find Liv. "What are you doing here?" he demanded.

She crossed her arms over her breasts and lifted a brow. "I

live here. The better question is, what are you doing in my kitchen?''

''You said I could have access to it anytime, except between noon and one, and six and seven o'clock.'' He moved to put his back in front of the sandwich stuff so she wouldn't see it. He never betrayed a friend.

Liv seemed to think about that, then she nodded. ''Fair enough.''

She looked too good standing there in a silky robe, he thought. It was long, ankle length, but it clung. And he wondered how it was that he still knew exactly how she would feel under his hands, how all those dips and curves of hers would mold to his palms through the silk.

It bothered him, so he tried to antagonize her. ''It could be said that you're infringing on *my* kitchen time right now.''

He thought she twitched a little, but then she pulled her temper back. ''Except for the fact that I buy the food. What did *you* buy?''

''You mean besides a red bridle?''

She stiffened visibly. ''Besides that.''

Hunter waved a hand. ''This and that.''

''This and what?''

''Bread. Mayo.''

She nodded. ''Even you should be able to master a sandwich.''

Especially with a note full of directions, he thought.

She moved stiffly into the room and sank down at the table. ''Bourne said that I should try whiskey and tea and honey for my throat. I'm desperate enough now to give it a shot.''

''Feel that bad?''

''Wow, Hunter. You've learned understatement.''

He almost grinned. He almost offered to get it for her. Except he was still trying hard to hate her, and if he moved, she'd see what Kiki had done. ''I'll be out of here in five minutes.''

Liv curled her legs under her on the chair. ''I'll wait, then.''

''You should be in bed. I'll bring you the tea concoction on my way up. I have to go right past your room, anyway.''

She frowned. ''Why? Why are you being so nice to me?''

He thought fast. "Because I never kick when my adversary is down."

She propped her chin in her hand. "You forget that I've known a few of your adversaries."

No, he thought, he'd never forgotten a moment, a breath, a word. And that was what was killing him. "Name one."

Liv rubbed her forehead. "Can't I just have my tea?"

"I said I'd bring it to you."

"Never mind. I'll get it myself." She stood and went to the stove. Hunter pivoted with her to keep his back to the sandwich makings.

His gut grumbled again. They both heard it.

"Lose your taste for fast food, Hunter?" she asked idly, putting the teapot on.

"What's that got to do with anything?"

"You took Vicky for a burger. Didn't you get one for yourself?"

He had. But Vicky had gobbled up half his fries. He hadn't realized a kid could eat like that—complaining all the while about the lack of quality. "It didn't fill me," he said.

She had turned around to face him and was staring at him now. Hunter leaned nonchalantly against the counter.

"Why are you standing there like that?" she asked.

"Like what?"

"Like this." She imitated his stance. "You haven't moved from that spot since I got here."

"Where am I supposed to go?"

She almost grinned. "Don't tempt me like that." Then her eyes narrowed.

And that, he thought, *that* was the exact moment she became suspicious. He saw it in the way her chin came up fast, almost as though she had taken a blow there, and in the way her hands fisted.

"Move," she said.

"Where?"

"Left or right. Doesn't matter to me."

"I'm fine right here, thanks."

"You're hiding something."

He was desperate. He looked down at himself. "Nope. You haven't turned me on in a very long time, Livie." A lie. "And when you used to, I never hid it."

He glanced up again in time to see the heat fly into her face. "You're changing the subject," she accused, "and doing a poor job of it."

She came toward him. Hunter backed up. He thought of reaching behind him and trying to sweep the bread and the mayo and the note into his other hand. Wouldn't work. He'd never catch it all. She stopped within inches of him and reached around him.

He was all out of distractions. So he kissed her again.

He brought both hands up fast and cupped her face. There was no more room for finesse now than there had been the first time he had finally tasted her, a lifetime ago now. He plunged in and took things she'd never consider giving if she had enough time for thought. He swept his tongue past her teeth, invaded and felt something rock inside him as memory leaped up again, craving, needing, like he had never needed anyone before or since.

She had been cold, so cold, Liv thought crazily. And then, suddenly, there was heat. Licking along her nerve endings. She couldn't remember that she had never wanted this to happen again. Every beat of her heart answered his, and every beat pumped more fire through her. She managed to reach up and wrap her fingers around each of his wrists, but she didn't pull his hands from her face. She found herself touching his tongue instead, meeting it with hers, wanting to swallow every essence of him.

"Not in the rules," she said desperately against his mouth.

"Damn your rules. And damn you, Livie, for making me still want you."

He was crazed with it, Hunter thought, with this business of wanting that had never gone away. He turned her hard and fast against the counter, needing to press himself up against her, agonizing for that old feel of how she would fit against him. Her hands came free from his wrists as she gasped, and her arms went around his neck.

Then something crashed and shattered at their feet.

She cried out and jumped forward into him. He closed his arms around her, even knowing it was too late. She started beating against his shoulders with her fists. "Stop this, Hunter! Stop! What *was* that?"

He didn't know, didn't care, but he took a step back and his heel slid in something greasy. Hunter looked down. It was the mayonnaise and what was left of the mayonnaise jar.

"I'm sorry," she said hoarsely, bending down. "We broke your—"

And then, with her sudden movement, Kiki's note fluttered off the counter. It floated down onto her head. Liv trailed off and reached up when she felt it. Her fingers closed around it and she came to her feet again, staring at it. Reading it.

And he saw everything inside her go hard.

She crumpled it in her fist and veered for the trash can, tossing it.

"Liv, I didn't ask her—" He broke off when she hit the kitchen door with both hands, then jerked back to him as it swung wildly behind her.

"Shut up!" she interrupted. Her voice was so hollow it hurt him. "You know what, Hunter? I'm not sure what bothers me most—that she's aiding and abetting you behind my back, or that you kissed me again just to protect her."

Then she was gone.

Hunter stared down at the mayonnaise, wishing his blood would stop raging, feeling five hundred times the fool.

Chapter 9

Liv didn't mention the betrayal to Kiki.

Through the next few days, while she was down with the flu, she told herself that she didn't have the energy for that kind of confrontation. After that she reasoned that Kiki would only talk circles around her, anyway. Finally she decided there was no way to confront her without admitting that Hunter had kissed her again. And that was something Liv only wanted to forget.

The truth was, losing Kiki to Hunter's corner cut her clear to the bone and she couldn't face it head-on. And the kiss stayed with her, anyway, a shadowy, haunting memory that could make her body come suddenly alive whenever it slipped past her defenses.

The first time he had kissed her—on the roadside—had been a reflex born of anger. She'd convinced herself of that. What had this time been? He had been protecting Kiki. Diverting her attention. It was the only thing that made sense.

The alternative—that they still wanted each other so much that they couldn't keep their hands off each other—terrified her.

She'd kissed him back.

Liv forced herself to keep busy so she wouldn't have time to dwell on it. She put a calendar on her sitting room wall and took to crossing each day off as it arrived, another minimilestone to the time when Hunter would leave again. She made a solemn ritual of it every morning before munching cornflakes in the kitchen while Vicky and Hunter gobbled up all the good food with the guests. Then she dragged Vicky off to the school bus.

When she got back she generally went straight to the office and shut herself inside. She worked for an hour until it was time to go to the barn for the trail ride. On Tuesdays Liv went to Mustang Ridge. On Fridays it was Hunter's turn. They fell into the rhythm by unspoken accord.

Vicky brought home no new coveted possessions. On a night when Hunter took her out for dinner, he asked Liv first.

It was all very civilized and manageable. Liv wanted to scream.

Three weeks after the night in the kitchen, she got her chance. She went downstairs to tea and found him there. The guests du jour included a handful of men in their midtwenties, intent on seeing their country on a budget before they settled down. There was also a young couple from St. Louis—Beth and Alex Roberts. Hunter was holding court with the men, lounging against one wall with a delicate china cup in his hand.

He looked ridiculous. And this was *her* turf. Liv's blood boiled.

She stepped up beside him. "What are you doing here?" she demanded in an undertone.

"Well, if it's not our lovely hostess," he drawled loudly enough to include the guests.

Liv backed off, gritting her teeth, and went to pour her own tea. "You're joining us today?" she asked as pleasantly as she could manage.

"Eddie here has convinced me that Kiki's baking is even better than her breakfast offerings."

"And you've sampled those widely enough," Liv said tightly.

"It's my main meal of the day. I've learned to stay clear of the kitchen otherwise. It's scary there."

She felt her face flame. She bracketed her teacup in both

hands to avoid a spill and turned to the men. She forced a bright grin.

"Are you enjoying Jerome, Byron?" she asked one of their group.

"Yeah, it's great." He glanced at her, then looked back at Hunter. "I saw that race. Last lap and Rowland spun you out."

Liv frowned. She turned to Eddie, another of the cross-country travelers, and opened her mouth, but Hunter's voice cut her off before she could say a word.

"It was the only way he could win."

"Yeah, but you popped him on pit road." Eddie laughed. "That was a hell of a retaliatory move."

Hunter grinned. "It cost me ten thousand bucks. NASCAR fined me."

"Fined *you?*" asked Alex Roberts.

Hunter shrugged. "The race was over by then. They said it was uncalled for."

"Except Rowland cost you a first-place finish," Eddie reminded him.

"Rowland needed it more than I did. And he told them his brakes went soft. He got too close to me, couldn't ease back, tapped my rear bumper, and I went into the wall. Purely an accident."

There was a chorus of disbelieving guffaws. Liv cleared her throat loudly. All eyes swiveled her way.

"I want to invite you all on our daily trail ride tomorrow morning," she began. "It's—"

"Are *you* going on it?" Beth Roberts interrupted to ask Hunter, adoration in her eyes.

Liv put her cup down and gave up.

She left the room and headed for the kitchen. Kiki was cleaning up when she got there. She stalked past her and went to the office.

"What's wrong?" Kiki asked. "Why aren't you at tea?"

"They're having a Hunter-fest in there. You might as well join them. You're one of his biggest fans."

"What's that supposed to mean?"

Liv slammed the office door hard.

A moment later she heard a fist rap against it. She launched out of her chair and went back to the door, ready for a fight now. She would finish this off with Kiki once and for all. She'd let it simmer too long. She had a few things to say on the matter, even if she did have to admit to the kiss. Damn it, it *hurt*.

Liv yanked open the door. Hunter stood there instead.

"Get away from me," she warned when she recovered from her surprise. She tried to close the door again.

Hunter stuck one booted foot over the threshold to stop her. "I've given you a month to come to your senses. We're going to have this out now, Liv."

"There's nothing to have out."

"How about the fact that you're a lousy loser? You acted like a disgruntled child back there."

It ignited something inside her. Liv shoved hard against his chest until he took a step back. She squeezed past him into the kitchen again and looked for something to throw at him.

She only barely registered that Kiki was gone.

"You took my Friday afternoons at Mustang Ridge away from me!" she shouted. "Then you took my best friend away from me! Now you want my tea hour, too?"

"You're being an idiot. But you're so wrapped up in resenting my presence here that you can't even see it."

She grabbed a spatula off the counter and heaved it. It only infuriated her more that he caught it cleanly.

"I've been holding my tongue," he said, "thinking you'd get it out of your system and settle down. But that's not working, is it?"

"Your tongue's not the problem," she grated. "It's your very existence that ticks me off."

"What's happened to you, Liv? You used to be gracious in defeat. Give it up. You lost. I'm staying the ninety days."

She felt herself shaking. Then tears burned at her eyes and she was appalled. Liv blinked hard. "I never adapted well to things being forced on me. Never."

He leaned one shoulder against the frame of her office door. "You used to make plans, design rational escape routes. Now you're just being cranky."

The Res. "I was a kid. Being cranky wouldn't have done me any good."

"It's not doing you any good now."

"I've only just gotten started." He grinned fast. It tugged at something near her heart. She closed her eyes, hating it. "If you want to have tea with the guests, then go do it. I'll back off."

He didn't move except to cross his arms over his chest. "You just can't get past the fact that I actually left all those years ago when you told me to, can you? What did you want me to do, Livie? Beg?"

Yes. Things were cracking inside her, the thin, strained civility that had held her together this long. "You're forgetting one thing, Hunter. I *wanted* you to go away. Why would I blame you for it? I was marrying Johnny."

"Someday I'll get to the bottom of why you did that, too."

"He was what I wanted. You weren't."

"But I was what you needed." His voice dropped a notch. He pushed off the door and took a fast step toward her. "You're holding a grudge, Liv. And the only thing that's going to make you happy now is if my daughter hates me, if Kiki hates me, if every tourist who sets foot into this inn hates me. That's what you want. That's the only revenge you'll accept for something you started in the first place by marrying another man when you were pregnant with *my* child."

He was standing too close to her. Liv drove a hand against his chest to back him off.

"I never would have left you, Livie. Never, if you'd just told me the truth."

Something broke inside her.

She threw herself at him. She wanted him to defend himself, to fight back. But he only caught her wrists in his hands and held them as she tried to wrestle free of him again. And that was when they heard the back door slam.

"Stop it, stop it, stop it!"

Vicky's voice ricocheted through the kitchen. She came through the back door from the school bus, into the kitchen like a bullet. She didn't aim for Hunter. She went to her mother.

Hunter let go of Liv abruptly and she stumbled back.

"You *lied!*" Vicky howled.

Oh, God, Liv thought, how much had she heard? "Baby, no—"

"Shut up! You *did!* You said you loved him once but that was a lie because you're hateful now! All you ever do is yell at him!"

It drove into her chest like a blade. "It's grown-up stuff, Vic—"

"Then how come no other grown-up is doing it? Everybody else is nice 'cept you!"

Liv felt the room spin away. "I've got to go," she said hoarsely.

She headed for the back door. She was running. Like a coward. But she felt as though her entire world was coming apart...just as she had feared, every moment of every day since he had come here.

Vicky blamed *her* for the discord in the inn. *Everyone is happy 'cept you!* Liv jolted all over again—painfully, deeply— as she reached her mare's stall. The horse skittered nervously in the enclosed space when she burst in. Liv put a hand to her neck to calm her, and she felt the tears coming on again.

This time she wouldn't be able to stop them.

No one else had been hurt as deeply all those years ago as she had been, she thought desperately. She remembered every crack of her heart the night she'd tried to tell him about the baby. She had a *right* to be bitter, to hold a grudge.

The only thing that's going to make you happy now is if my daughter hates me, if Kiki hates me, if every tourist who sets foot into this inn hates me. She'd been clinging to that all along, she realized. To the idea that it would make him go again. That he wouldn't see the ninety days through.

Yes, she thought, yes, she *had* been trying to starve him out.

The stall door opened abruptly and Hunter looked in on her.

"I sent Vicky to her room," he said flatly. "She had no business talking to you that way. No matter what."

A giddy laugh tried to get past the knot in Liv's throat. "I guess you just blew your Favorite Parent Award."

"Well, there you go then. You've won a round."

The tears came again. Liv twisted her head to the side so he couldn't see them. "Get out of here."

He never listened, she thought. He just kept talking. "Ah, hell, Liv, I did it, too."

She looked at him again sharply. "Did what?"

"I started this just to make you pay for the lie. To rock the complacent little world you'd locked me out of. I wanted everyone to hate you, too, wanted to advertise what a rotten thing you'd done to me all those years ago. But it's not about that anymore."

She knew it wasn't. She'd seen it in his eyes whenever he looked at his child.

"Let's take a ride," he said.

She glared at him. She looked around for something to dry her eyes with, then gave up and just grabbed a handful of the mare's mane and buried her face there.

"I'm not going to ride, after all," she said finally. "I just wanted to get away from you."

"Well, I followed you."

"I hate horses."

"I know. I meant in my car. We'll give Vicky some time to cool down."

She seemed to think about it, then she tilted her chin up. "Okay. But I still hate you. All I'm conceding is that maybe I'm glad you just earned a few demerits from her."

Hunter nodded, satisfied. "That's my girl."

"There has to be *something* I can make," Liv fretted in the kitchen two weeks later.

Kiki blew out her breath and planted her hands on her hips. "We go through this every Thanksgiving. There's not."

"I'll do the mashed potatoes."

"You leave lumps."

"I'll bake a pie."

"Not in my kitchen, you won't. Don't you remember the time you blew up the chocolate layer cake?"

That *had* been memorable, Liv thought, sitting at the kitchen table. It had been for Vicky's sixth birthday. She still wasn't sure what she had done wrong, and Kiki—with all her scientific wisdom—was clueless, too. But she'd put something in the batter that she shouldn't have because it had exploded all over the inside of the oven. It had taken them a week to scrape out all the little brown pieces.

"Why are we arguing about this again?" Kiki asked. "I thought we'd agreed that you'd just stay out of the cooking end of things."

Liv rubbed her forehead. "I need to keep as busy as possible under these current circumstances."

Kiki was quiet for a long time. She came to the table and pulled out a chair for herself. She sat and chewed on her lip. "Where's Hunter?" she asked finally.

"He and Vicky are in my sitting room, watching the race. It's the last one of the season." It was Sunday, and she'd been exiled from her own rooms, Liv thought.

"Well, that's cozy," Kiki commented.

"It would be cozy if I was there, too. But I'm not."

"If he's watching races, then maybe he's starting to chafe."

Liv thought about it and she knew in her heart that it wasn't true. Since they'd taken the drive that afternoon of their last major fight, he'd mellowed. He'd said his piece and he'd dropped it—that was his way. It was behind him now. He just wouldn't tangle with her anymore.

But Vicky's accusations still made her ache. And so did Kiki's complicity.

"Why did you make him that sandwich?" she blurted.

"I didn't. I just gave him the fixings for it." Kiki sat back in her chair. "Is *that* what's been eating you all these weeks?"

Liv lifted one shoulder in a shrug.

"I was finding weird things missing from the kitchen."

"Like what?" Liv was startled. "You said you couldn't find any evidence that he'd been using it."

"Right." Kiki waited.

Liv frowned. "So what was missing?"

"Half a tray of deviled eggs. Six of my cinnamon miniquiches and a dozen oysters."

Liv felt her heart sink. The oysters were the giveaway. "Vicky."

"She was taking him food."

Liv put her head down on the table. "Oh, my God."

"Everything that was missing was high on her hit-list of favorites. And I knew she wasn't starving. Not unless the frozen food companies suddenly went out of business and you'd stopped feeding her. Liv, I had to step in. She was taking it on her own shoulders to make things easier for him so he wouldn't have to go out to eat all the time."

Liv sat up again. "I should have known you'd only do that for Vicky," she said hollowly.

"Is that an apology for doubting me?"

Liv hesitated. "Yeah."

"Then I'll be honest. I also did it because he looks really fine in those black jeans."

Things inside her rushed. Then dove. *The ultimate betrayal.* "You've got your eye on him now?" she squeaked.

"Oh, get real. I just appreciate the male form. Doesn't mean I have to touch it." Kiki stood again. "Anyway, back to Thanksgiving."

Liv was perfectly willing to change the subject. "We could break our rule this year and allow guests." It was the only day of the year they didn't accept them, because it was Liv's most precious holiday. It was the last one she'd spent with her parents and her sister.

The next day her family had all driven off for Sedona to enjoy what was left of the four-day weekend. Liv had stayed behind to go to a symphony Saturday night with her best friend, Julie. She'd never made it to the symphony because her parents' car had gone off a cliff that Friday night in a driving rain. And shortly after that, she had landed on the Res.

There hadn't been Thanksgiving there. Her grandmother didn't honor it. It wasn't a Navajo occasion. No matter that Ama herself had married a German and had loved him dearly. No matter that her daughter had married an Irishman and Ama held no grudges. Liv's grandmother did not celebrate Anglo holidays.

During her years in Flagstaff, Liv had worked every holiday.

But when she had come south to Jerome with Kiki and a tod-dling Vicky in tow, that had changed. It had become *their* day, revered and special, if poignant. No guests. Just the three of them and all the food Kiki could cook.

This year there would be four.

"Kind of late to be getting reservations now," Kiki pointed out.

"We have a waiting list," Liv replied. "If I put it out on the Web site—"

"Liv. Thanksgiving is Thursday. There's not enough time."

"People from town—"

"What are you afraid of?"

She took a deep breath. Why did everyone keep asking her that these days? "That Hunter is going to ruin it," she said baldly.

Kiki thought about that. "He won't. But you might."

It was too close to what her daughter had accused her of two weeks ago. Liv felt her heart cringe. "Dinner will be tense. I don't want that for Vicky."

"You don't want it for *you*. Look, it's not going to be a banner year. There's no getting around that. But Vicky will sail through it. She always does. Let's just make the best of it, and leave the cooking to me."

She wasn't going to win this argument, Liv realized. She stood from the table. "Okay. But if I throw the sweet potato casserole at him, it's your fault."

Kiki nodded. "I'll keep that in mind."

At half past eight on Thanksgiving morning, Liv found Hunter in the dining room when she went to dig the good china out of the breakfront. He stood in the middle of the room, looking around with a baffled expression.

"Where is everybody?" He frowned at the sideboard. "Where's the food?"

"Empty house today." Liv thought of fleeing, of coming back for the china later. But Kiki got testy if it was dusty. And Vicky wanted to watch the Macy's parade in a little while. Her only chance to wash the plates was now.

She sat Indian-style in front of the breakfront and opened the doors. Civility, she reminded herself. "Didn't you notice everyone checking out yesterday?"

Hunter rubbed his jaw. "Yeah. I thought that was odd on a Wednesday. There's *no one?*"

"I close on Thanksgiving."

"It was never an important holiday to you."

Liv looked up at him. It seemed impossible that there was actually something he didn't know about her. There'd been a time when he'd examined every angle of her soul. "It never had a chance to be when we were together."

"So now you send everyone home for the day and revel in it?"

"Yes."

"When will they come back?"

"We have several check-ins tomorrow."

"What about breakfast today?"

She choked on a laugh. "No cinnamon quiches left?"

She watched his face change. He looked almost abashed. "How'd you know about them?"

"Kiki figured it out."

"Do you know about the oysters?" he asked warily.

"She said some were missing."

"That's all?"

Liv nodded slowly, wondering what he was getting at.

"Oh, well. I'm going to run into town for something to eat." He turned away.

"Freeze."

"That might work with an eight-year-old, but not with me." He kept walking.

"What about the oysters, Hunter? I know when you're hiding something."

He stepped through the door and paused. "Is there anything open in town on Thanksgiving?"

"You'll probably find something, but you might be better off throwing yourself on Kiki's mercy. Or maybe Vicky will share her cereal. Like she shared her oysters."

He rubbed his jaw. "Man, I *hate* those things."

Liv started to understand. She pushed to her feet. "What did you do with them?"

"I threw them out."

"You threw out *oysters?* Do you have any idea what they cost me fresh?"

"I'll pay you back," he said quickly.

"I don't want your gobs of money!"

"You've got to get past this money thing, Liv."

"I hate waste!"

"Yeah, well, I hate slime. And oysters are slimy."

"Are you two fighting again?" Vicky demanded, ducking under Hunter's arm to enter the room.

"No!" they shouted in unison.

She backed out again. "Man, you guys sound just like Mandy's mom and dad."

Liv felt her heart fall down into her toes.

"Well," Hunter said finally when Vicky was gone. "That's good, right? It's healthy."

She sat down unsteadily in front of the breakfront again. There'd been a time, she thought helplessly, when she'd wanted to be a parent with him more than she'd wanted air to breathe. "I'd keep those oysters to myself if I were you," she said without answering. "Don't tell Kiki. She does the books."

"Uh, no. That probably wouldn't be wise."

He finally left the dining room. Liv forced herself to breathe—in, out, in, out—until her muscles uncoiled. She gathered up the china.

She didn't see him again until after it was washed, the parade was over and they were gathered in the kitchen. It was another Thanksgiving tradition. They couldn't exclude Kiki, who was up to her elbows in pie crust dough, so they congregated there. Liv was opening a bottle of wine when Hunter ambled in.

"Dad!" Vicky yelped.

The wine slid in Liv's hands as though it had suddenly turned into a greased pig. She groped for it and caught it. She could feel Hunter's eyes on her and she knew they were amused.

"Bet that bottle might cost even more than oysters," he drawled.

Liv closed her eyes briefly. She'd been ready to face him over dinner, but this was too early. And she couldn't send him away. How could she send him off into exile on Thanksgiving? She clutched the bottle against her chest and turned back to the table as he pulled out a chair and sat down.

Kiki moved from the oven, dropping a head of cabbage in front of him. "Don't just sit there. Make yourself useful."

Hunter eyed the cabbage warily. "What am I supposed to do with this?"

"Start shredding for cole slaw." She deposited a steel grater and a bowl on the table. "Just rub it up against the rough side of that thing there. You'll learn to cook yet before I'm through with you."

Liv's jaw dropped open in outrage. "You never let me help!"

"Mom." Vicky sighed. "The last time you tried to do cabbage, you almost took off your finger." She looked at Kiki. "Can I peel the carrots?"

"Go for it."

Vicky whooped with pleasure and jumped up to go to the refrigerator.

Hunter looked at the bottle Liv was still cosseting against her chest. "I'll take some of that."

"Me, too," Vicky said.

"Apple cider, squirt," Kiki said. "Unless you can show me a driver's license."

Hunter started shredding cabbage. "You know, back on the Res you can drive at fifteen."

Vicky ogled him. "For real?"

"Actually, you can do it at eight if you know how because there's no cops around to tell you not to."

"Don't fill her head with that," Liv warned, finally moving again for the corkscrew.

"Cool!" Vicky looked at Liv. "Can we move there?"

"Not in this lifetime," Kiki drawled. "At least not with me."

"How come you don't like it there?" Vicky asked her.

"It's hundreds of thousands of square miles of kitty litter. What's to like?"

"But kids can *drive* there."

"Your father was fibbing."

Liv nearly lost the wine bottle again as she set it down to work on the cork. When had they all gotten so close, so warm? *While I was busy wallowing in the past.* She stabbed the screw point into the cork hard.

"Bet that taught it a lesson," Hunter murmured.

"Shut up."

"No fighting!" Vicky warned, but then all her attention was on Hunter again. "Did you? Fib?"

"Sort of."

"Tell the truth."

"Okay. There's hundreds of thousands of square miles of kitty litter on the Res, and a handful of Navajo Nation cops to patrol the whole thing. Bottom line is they can't be everywhere at once. They can hardly be *anywhere* at once. It's just too big. So it's illegal to drive at eight, but you can probably get away with it, anyway."

"Don't tell her that!" Liv burst out again. "She'll be packing her bags tomorrow! She thinks she's eighteen as it is!"

"No, I don't, Mom." She looked back at Hunter. "Tell me more. Did you guys all know each other there?"

Liv felt Hunter's eyes on her. She turned her back to him to finish with the wine. And the touch of his gaze kept stroking her skin, hot and close. "We were best friends," he said.

There was a beat of silence. Kiki slid smoothly into the seam. "All of us were."

Liv poured the wine and took it to the table. "Just in the beginning," she said. "Then Hunter kept leaving."

"Tell me about the beginning," Vicky said, going to the sink to attack the carrots.

"There were always so many stars there," Liv heard herself say. She glanced at Hunter. "Do you remember that?" Then she flushed and avoided his gaze. "I remember trying to count them."

"How about when we convinced Fat Louie they were falling?" Hunter's voice was vaguely husky.

She nodded and smiled.

Working with the pie dough again, Kiki hooted. "We bought firecrackers in Tuba City."

"Who was Fat Louie?" Vicky asked.

"Big, old bully," Hunter explained. "From the school. He was always telling everyone that he was descended from some shaman."

Liv felt her mouth pull into a wider grin. "We all hated him. He was so obnoxious."

"He tried to kiss me once," Kiki confided.

"Yuck," said Vicky. "Was he really fat?"

"No," Hunter said, "he was just a big dude. We only called him fat to get his goat."

"He had goats?" Vicky asked.

Liv stroked her hair. "No, baby. It's just an expression." She looked around for something else to do.

"No!" Vicky and Kiki said in unison, following her gaze.

"Sit down and drink your wine," Kiki advised. "You're safest there."

"How did you live that last year on your own if you can't cook?" Hunter wondered aloud. "I never knew that about you."

Because that last year on the Res, Liv thought, they'd been wildly, passionately in love. When he'd visited, they'd steeped themselves in each other. Their time together had been so precious. The last thing they'd wanted to do was spend it with her fixing them something to eat.

Before that, her grandmother had always cooked for both of them. Hunter had eaten at her hogan more often than not.

Vicky's voice broke her reverie before her breath could catch at the memories. "Mom! You lived on your own when you were a *kid?*"

Liv sat down and changed the subject fast. What she had done that last year had been vaguely illegal, after all. "Between the three of us, we convinced Fat Louie that his ancestor's medicine was hereditary—unless Spider Woman deemed him unworthy."

"Who's Spider Woman?" asked Vicky.

"A Navajo deity. So we went to Tuba City and we bought up all those firecrackers."

"*I* bought them," Hunter corrected. "You two never had a

dime to your names. At least I had some cash from doing odd jobs.''

That was true, Liv remembered. But, oh, they'd all been so poor. And happy, anyway. ''Okay, Hunter bought the firecrackers,'' she allowed. ''Then we lured Louie to this arroyo one night and told him to meditate to see if Spider Woman would accept him. We hid at the top and started throwing the firecrackers down in there. He thought the stars were falling in on him, that Spider Woman had rejected him.''

Vicky giggled. ''That's mean.''

''No worse than you putting that smelly cheese in Mandy's book bag,'' Kiki observed.

''I only hated her for one day!'' Vicky protested.

''Where'd you get the cheese?'' Hunter asked.

''Kiki's refrigerator.''

''It was Brie,'' Kiki said.

''Is that as expensive as oysters?'' he wondered.

Kiki turned from the counter. ''Will someone please tell me why oysters keep coming up in this conversation?''

''No reason,'' Hunter and Liv said together.

Their eyes caught. And held. Then he lifted one finger to his forehead in a tiny salute. She felt one corner of her mouth catch up in a private smile.

She couldn't believe she had just sided with him on something. Liv felt her bones melt. She felt her heart stop. And then, finally, she knew what she had really been fighting so hard against all along, why she had so desperately needed him to leave before his ninety days were up.

She still loved him. And now that he was back in her life, she wasn't sure she could let him go a second time.

Chapter 10

Vicky polished off a third helping of Kiki's sweet potato casserole and sat back in her chair with a belch so loud it almost echoed. She giggled and Liv found herself falling helplessly into Hunter's answering grin.

"That was just a kid burp," he said. "Pint-size."

Vicky took the bait. "I can do better!"

Liv found her voice again. "Not at *my* Thanksgiving table, you can't."

"Killjoy," Hunter muttered.

No, Liv thought bemusedly, dinner definitely wasn't tense.

"I can do the alphabet!" Vicky announced.

Hunter waved a dismissive hand at her, egging her on. "Big deal. They teach that in kindergarten."

"No, I mean I can *burp* it. I can burp the whole alphabet!"

"Dinner's over," Liv announced, standing up quickly and gathering plates to divert Vicky's attention. It worked.

"What about the pie?" she demanded.

"Well, there you go," Kiki murmured. "You *need* to let out a few more good ones just to make room for it."

And out came *a-b-c.* Liv fled to the kitchen before she could laugh and condone the antics.

She was stacking the dishwasher, working off some room for pie of her own, when Hunter followed her. He leaned one shoulder against the refrigerator and crossed his arms over his chest. Liv didn't quite look at him, but her pulse picked up as his silence drew out.

"She's talented," he said finally.

"In so very many ways," she agreed dryly.

"You've done a good job with her, Livie."

She fumbled with a dish. "But?"

"No buts."

"You're not going to qualify that with criticism?"

"I might not like the fact that you shut me out of her life, but you've done well enough by her on your own."

Liv dried her hands quickly. Her heart was moving too fast. "Is this a cease-fire?"

One corner of his mouth tucked up into half a grin. "You've asked three questions in a row now. Want to give me a statement on what you're thinking instead?"

"I need air," she decided, and headed for the back door.

As soon as she was outside, Liv knew it was a mistake. The night was clear and cold and the sky was littered with more stars than she could remember seeing in a very long time, maybe since their days on the Res. The moon was a thin crescent. It was beautiful, and she didn't dare share a beautiful night with him.

Not now. She felt so vulnerable tonight.

She'd taken a step off the porch when she heard him come out of the inn behind her. She headed to the barn to check the horses. She decided she felt safer with him amid straw and hay than she did beneath stars—though they'd had their moments with both.

"Where did Bourne go today?" His voice came closer behind her than she expected, but then, he had that long stride.

"He's got family in Cottonwood. A sister, I think."

"He doesn't like me."

Liv glanced back at him as she stopped at the grain bin to

scoop out a handful of sweet feed for her mare. "He's just keeping one eye on you to make sure you don't hurt Vicky."

Hunter's black brows climbed. "He knows the story, then?"

"I told him." She went to Daisy's stall and held her palm out. The horse nuzzled up the oats.

She glanced back at him. He'd be angry, she thought. But he only nodded.

"That was the first time I've ever sat down with family at Thanksgiving dinner," he said finally, changing the subject.

She knew his family hadn't celebrated the holiday, either. But along with Kiki, they shared enough memories to start a Navajo clan of their own.

"What do you usually do?" she heard herself ask.

"Sleep."

"You *sleep* through Thanksgiving?"

"The NASCAR season ends the Sunday before," he reminded her. "I usually crawl straight home for some R & R for a week or two."

She didn't have to ask what he did after that. He'd go back to roaming. He was like a shark that way, she thought. He couldn't stay still for long or he would die.

"You're not restless yet," she said suddenly. "You've been stuck here for seven weeks now and you're not prowling."

"Prowling?"

She felt herself flush. "That's what I always used to call it." He waited.

"After you'd been home for a while," she explained. "Sometimes it would start after only a couple of days. You used to go into this zone where you couldn't seem to stop moving."

He grinned slowly. "I think that had more to do with you than with me, Liv. I couldn't keep my hands off you once you seduced me that first time."

Liv choked. "I did *not* seduce you!"

"All right. You challenged me. You backed me into a corner. You stood right there in the middle of the desert and got naked."

This time she felt her face flame. It struck her hard that she still remembered every moment of that day. "I took my shirt off. I was hardly *naked*. At least not until you ripped everything else off me.''

Suddenly his face changed. Something in his eyes flared and his voice lowered a notch. ''I think this is dangerous ground, Livie.''

It was. She could feel things inside her start trembling. She turned away from him quickly so he wouldn't read it in her eyes.

''Tell me why it ended for us.'' His voice was still husky.

Yes, she thought, yes, this was dangerous ground.

''I need to know,'' he said. ''I need the truth this time. You can give me that much, can't you?''

Liv closed her eyes at the vulnerability in his tone. He wasn't a vulnerable man. He was as fierce and strong and wild as the desert itself. If he needed an answer that much, she had to give it to him.

It didn't really matter anymore, after all.

Liv turned around slowly. ''It was because of the baby.''

His eyes glinted. ''You're still going to insist that you were protecting her from me?''

She hugged herself. ''Maybe I was protecting myself from you, too. I tried to tell you!'' she burst out.

His face hardened. ''No, you didn't.''

''I did. The first night you came to the bar, right after I got the promotion to the place.''

''The frou-frou night?'' He scowled.

She nodded jerkily. ''You were on your way to Pritch Spike's place in Anaheim and you surprised me, came through Flag. I started to tell you that night, then you laid it on me that you were going to California.''

He looked confused. ''I was always going somewhere.''

''Exactly.'' She felt her throat close hard.

''I asked you to go with me.'' Hunter shook his head in disbelief. ''Then I stopped by on my way back east again and you were getting married!''

''I wrote to you. I told you not to come back. I had to let you go because you wouldn't stay!''

''I would have if you had told me you were pregnant!''

Liv winced. Their voices were rising steadily. She softened hers deliberately. "I didn't want you to stay with me because of the baby. I wanted you to stay with me because you loved me."

Something like pain slashed across his features. "I thought you were happy with the way things were. You had your dream, I had mine. We were both busy pursuing them."

"Happy?" A thin, pitched laugh escaped her. "I was in love with a man who was never there! You couldn't stay put! You didn't have it in you! You *still* don't!"

"You don't know me anymore, Liv."

She pressed her hands to her cheeks. "You're exactly the same. You'll go again when this is over."

"Not to roam. To go back to work."

"Your work is just one more way of roaming! You're in a different city every weekend!" And it hurt as much now as it had then, she realized wildly. Why, oh, why had she let him get to her again?

She stepped around him and hurried to leave the barn.

"When did Guenther get involved?" he asked.

There was nothing vulnerable in his voice now, Liv thought. It was slashing, cutting. She stopped in the barn door but she didn't look back at him this time. "The next day. The day you left me to go to Anaheim. When you walked out of my life that time, Hunter, it was the straw that broke me. You were running off on some crazy new adventure—as insane as the others, I thought—and I was pregnant. You walked out of my apartment that morning, and things died inside me. The night before, when I tried to tell you, all you could do was talk about racing. I knew then that I was beaten."

"So you picked up with some other guy within *hours?*"

Liv finally turned. "I never 'picked up' with him at all! I tried to go to work that night but I couldn't hold it together. Johnny was the bar manager. He tried to send me home. I couldn't take the time off because I knew I'd need the money for the baby. He asked me what was wrong and I just lost it. I turned into a slobbering, sobbing idiot." She wondered if it was regret she saw flash in his eyes. She didn't dare believe it. "I told him about the baby. Six months later he married me. He said he loved me. He wanted to give my child a real home.'' Liv closed her eyes. ''I needed that, Hunter,'' she whispered. ''I desperately needed to give Vicky everything I had lost myself.''

It broke his heart because her words had the ring of truth to them. Worse, he understood. ''Guenther gave you the mom-dad-kiddie scenario in suburbia. What you had before your family died.''

''Yes.'' Her chin came up. ''He's a good man.''

She heard Hunter growl in response. ''How long were you married?''

The time for lies was so far past, she thought helplessly. ''Three months. Give or take.'' She looked at him again. ''Until right after Vicky was born. I left then because…I couldn't love him.''

His eyes went fierce. ''Love him how?''

Liv only shook her head. She turned again and fled out the door, and this time she didn't let his voice stop her. If she told him that she'd never slept with Johnny, he would know she'd never stopped loving *him.*

This wasn't a cease-fire, she thought crazily, jogging for the porch. It was just a different kind of war.

In the morning, Liv, Vicky and Kiki hashed out their traditional argument about the Phoenix trip.

''I'll be back by nightfall,'' Liv said, guzzling strong coffee. She hadn't slept well last night. Twice she'd thought she'd heard Hunter's footsteps outside her door.

''No need,'' Kiki replied. ''I can spend the night here.''

''Where? Hunter has your room.''

''Change your sheets first and I'll be fine in your bed. But I don't want your cooties.''

Vicky giggled. ''You two *always* do this. Every year.''

It was true. The Friday after every Thanksgiving, Liv and Vicky made a pilgrimage to the city to get a start on Christmas shopping. Kiki stayed behind to watch over the inn, then she took off the following day and Liv ran the show. Kiki always spent weeks cooking in advance for the guests for that day—

safe, simple items that even Liv could warm up in the oven. They never had a full house that weekend, anyway, after their Thanksgiving break.

"What's going on?" Hunter asked, walking into the kitchen. Then he breathed in deeply and frowned. "What's that I smell?"

"Hangtown fry," Kiki said absently. "There's plenty in the dining room. Help yourself."

He glanced at Liv. "If I begged, could I have a bowl of your cornflakes instead?"

Her eyes narrowed. "If you know that I keep a stash of cornflakes, that explains why the box empties so fast."

"Are you accusing me of theft?" He actually managed to look offended.

"Pilfering. And only on the days that Kiki serves seafood."

"You don't like seafood?" Vicky asked. "But—"

"Maybe I'll run into town to the diner," Hunter said quickly.

"Hey! I know! You could come to Phoenix with us!" Vicky cried. "We always stop for brunch halfway there!"

Liv felt her heart dive. "I'm sure he has better things to do."

"You're going to Phoenix?" His voice was careful, Liv thought. "For how long?"

"We'll be back—"

"In the morning," Kiki said.

"Tonight," Liv finished.

"Which is it?" Hunter asked, looking between the two of them.

"Probably tonight." Vicky sighed and sat at the table, her chin in her hand. "Mom usually wins this one."

He relaxed a little. Only then did Liv realize how much he'd stiffened. He's afraid I'll take Vicky away for one precious night of his ninety-day stay, she thought. She'd felt that way about his visits once, too, wringing everything out of every moment with him before he'd go again.

"I want to get a start on Christmas shopping," she said faintly. "It's only a two-hour drive on the Interstate. We're always back by bedtime."

Kiki threw up her hands. "Okay, I give up."

"I don't like leaving you here alone overnight," Liv protested.

"Why not? You're usually on your own overnight. Besides, Hunter's here."

"Not if I decide to take Vicky up on her offer," he said.

Liv's eyes flew to his. She knew hers were wide, maybe even stricken. "You want to come along?"

Vicky jumped to her feet again. "Oh, please! Please! We can all shop together."

She couldn't spend the entire day with him. Things inside Liv staggered at the prospect.

Sometime during the course of the night, she'd decided that the only way she'd get through these last weeks with him was to avoid him as much as possible. There could be no more honest, heartbreaking talks in the barn. She couldn't watch him laughing with Vicky. If she stayed away from him, maybe she could still come out of this with her heart whole.

"Or you and I can shop together," Hunter said to Vicky, "and let your mom go off on her own to buy up every present for you in Phoenix."

Vicky liked that idea. "Yeah!"

"What do you say?" Hunter pinned Liv's gaze with his own.

Liv tried to nod. Her neck felt stiff. She knew one thing—if she was the one to break up this little party, Vicky would never forgive her.

"Sounds fine to me," she said weakly.

"Now you *know* we'll be home tonight," he said to Kiki, but his eyes never left Liv.

She caught his implication. Their days of spending the night together were long behind them. She opened her mouth and closed it again, not knowing if she wanted to thank him or cry.

"I'll go change," she said.

He stopped her at the kitchen door. "Wait. What about the cornflakes? I'll never make it halfway to Phoenix to eat."

"Top cabinet beside the fridge." Liv fled the kitchen.

Twenty minutes later she cursed herself for being an utter fool. She'd changed her clothes four times already, and now she found herself peeling out of a pair of purple Capri slacks and throwing them aside, too. She liked to dress a little jauntily for the city. She got there so rarely. But would Hunter think she was doing it for him?

Who cared?

She did.

She changed into her denim jumper, then took that off, too, because it reminded her of their argument the day he'd bought Vicky the bridle. She turned the television on to check the weather station. It would be sixty degrees in Phoenix today. The Capri slacks, then, she decided. The hell with how it looked. She pulled them back on and found a lightweight white sweater. A blousy lavender jacket to keep her warm until they got down into the valley. A couple of rings. And earrings—the garnets, she decided. Blush, lipstick...and then she was ready.

There was a knock on her outer door and Liv's breath shuddered out of her. She thought it might be Hunter and she hurried to answer.

It was Vicky. "Mom, you're holding up the entire show!"

"I'm coming." She reached behind her to close the door.

Vicky sniffed. "Do you have *perfume* on?"

She caught sight of Hunter at the end of the hall, coming down the stairs from his own room. "Of course I do. This is our dress-up day." Then she said a brief prayer that Vicky would drop the subject.

"But it's your *good* stuff," Vicky insisted.

"I'm all out of the other," Liv said quickly.

"No, you're not. You have—"

"Ready?" Hunter interrupted, joining them.

"Absolutely," Liv said a little too heartily.

Vicky turned away with a private grin and raced for the stairs. "Last one to the car is a rotten egg!"

"That's usually me," Liv said under her breath. She forced herself to move, and Hunter fell into step beside her. He leaned closer and sniffed.

"Nope. Not rotten. Nice, actually."

Had he heard Vicky? She eased away from him, her heart moving oddly in her chest. "I'm doing this under duress, you know."

"Allowing me to join you in Phoenix? Of course, you are."

"It just doesn't seem fair to take Vicky away from you for a whole day when you've only got ninety of them."

"I'll be back after the ninety."

Her heart shifted again, trying to cram its way into her throat. She knew he would. And it would be just like before. He'd rip through town for a few precious days, for a handful of sacred hours, then he'd be gone.

She didn't want to think about it. They got to the garage and she headed for her car.

"We're taking mine," he said, stopping her.

Liv looked at the Monte Carlo and shook her head. "Uh-uh. I'm not getting into that on a road where you're *allowed* to go seventy miles an hour." He'd scared the hell out of her on the cliff the one day she'd ridden with him.

"Ah, Livie, I was just yanking your chain."

"What did you do to her?" Vicky asked.

"I showed off my incomparable talents."

"He took a year off my life." Liv remained stubbornly planted by her driver's side door. "Maybe five."

"Mom's kind of a wimp about some things," Vicky confided.

"I'm sensible," Liv protested.

"Well, we're not." He looked down at Vicky. "What's it going to be, pigtails? Mom's wimpy car or my cool one?"

"Your cool one," she said promptly.

"I'm going to hold this against you," Liv muttered, moving to his car.

"You do that so well."

Her heart seized so suddenly—with anger this time—that it almost took her breath away. But when Liv looked at him again, he was grinning. "Say touché, Livie." Then he put his hand on her back to nudge her into his car.

It was a word game of one-upmanship that they'd played so many times before.

She felt the warmth of his touch through her jacket, through her sweater, and it bloomed from there. That gesture was familiar, too, something he had done a thousand times...too long ago to remember. She *shouldn't* remember. But it felt as though not a moment had passed since then. Her legs were unsteady as she got into the car.

It was going to be a very long day, she thought.

Three hours later, Hunter and Vicky dropped her off in front of the Borgata in Scottsdale. The luxurious minimall, built around a central outdoor courtyard, was a weakness of Liv's. She rarely got in and out of the place without buying something for herself, as well.

She closed the Monte Carlo's door, then she opened it again to peer inside. "Will you two be okay?" she asked nervously.

For a moment, some of the old resentment tightened his jaw. "We'll be back for you in two hours, Livie. Jot down my license plate in case you want to issue an APB."

"It's not that." A month ago she would have been terrified that they wouldn't return. But he'd had ample opportunity to run with his daughter since then, and he'd always come back.

Maybe he'd been lulling her into a false sense of complacency.

Liv shook the insidious thought off. She was so tired of it—of the wariness and the bickering, of the exhausting, never-ending battle to hold her own against him.

"Don't let her talk you into chocolate," she warned. *Don't be Mr. Wonderful Dad.*

"Oh, man," Vicky moaned from the back seat.

"There, you see?" Liv said. "She was already planning on how to finagle you into it. But trust me, you don't need the caffeine-high on your hands."

"That true, pigtails?" Hunter shifted his weight to look at her in the back seat.

"It has no effect on me," Vicky insisted.

"Who are you going to believe?" Liv challenged. "The one who bounces off the walls or the one who catches her?"

His expression relaxed. "Don't worry, Livie. We'll be fine." He put the car into gear. "By the way, what do you want for Christmas?"

Her heart stalled. It literally gave a startled, apoplectic chug and gave out. "We're not going to exchange—"

He didn't let her finish. "Close the door, will you? We have shopping to do. Caffeine-free shopping." He reached across the passenger seat and pulled it shut himself when Liv seemed incapable of doing it. Then he sped off, leaving her standing in the parking lot.

Christmas gifts? Was she supposed to get him a *Christmas gift?*

Liv struggled with it on her way inside. She moved dazedly from store to store and was still empty-handed after an hour. She finally stopped in a café for a cappuccino. *Who's on a caffeine-high now?* Her nerves were already corkscrewed. She placed her order and when it came, she drank deeply.

What was she supposed to do about this?

Maybe she'd been hiding from the fact that he would be with them on Christmas morning, she thought. Maybe she had been deliberately avoiding acknowledging that, even to herself. His ninety days wouldn't be up until the first week of January. What would it do to Vicky if they both sat there stiff as rods on Christmas morning, wearing false grins?

She should get him something, Liv decided, for Vicky's sake. But how would *he* take it? Would he think—God forbid—that she was still in love with him, that she wanted to start up with him all over again?

"Livie?"

She jumped out of her skin at the sound of his voice and jerked around in her little wrought-iron chair. Hunter was standing behind her. He moved to hunker down beside her.

"What are you doing here?" she demanded. "Where's Vicky?"

"Bathroom. Hush up, now. We've only got a minute or two until she comes back."

"How did you find me here?"

"You've always been an exotic coffee nut. It followed."

Something was wrong about this, she thought, something that had her pulse both taking off and trying to stop. "What is it?"

"I think I put my foot in it." He scrubbed a hand over his jaw. "Ah, hell, you're going to kill me. I told her there was a raceway right here in Phoenix."

Liv didn't get it. "So?"

"So there's a side-track there for kids."

Her brain cleared. "No! Oh, no, Hunter, no way. She's a *girl*."

He frowned quickly. "There are female stock car drivers."

"None of them are my daughter!"

He pushed to his feet again. "Yeah. I kind of thought that would be your reaction."

Liv stared at him. "You haven't just done it anyway?"

"Let her drive?" One of his brows shot up. "She'd tell you and you'd kick me out."

"I'm not allowed to do that."

"You could find a way to convince Judge Woodingham that I'd endangered her. You're good like that, when you sink your teeth into something."

She didn't take the bait this time. His explanation was only half true, she realized. He was taking her feelings into consideration on this. And he'd come all the way back to the Borgata to do it.

Liv cleared her throat. "I've always...been afraid."

Hunter watched her face. When she didn't go on immediately, he pulled out the chair opposite her and sat. "Of what?"

"That she would inherit it. Your...your...recklessness."

"Don't look now, Livie, but I think she has."

She knew that, Liv thought. Oh, she knew. "I know you wouldn't let her get hurt, but...I don't want to encourage it. Those...those tendencies she has for speed and danger."

"She doesn't know about the speed yet. I've never taken her over sixty miles per hour."

"The danger then."

"You got her the mechanical bull," he reminded her. "You underestimate yourself, Livie."

She reared back in her seat. "No, I don't. How?"

"You're pretty daring in your own right. She could have gotten it from you. I don't know too many nineteen-year-olds who would have had the courage to set off into parenthood on their own without even looking for support from the father."

Liv recoiled, but there was no accusation in his tone now. "I had to."

"You *thought* you had to," he corrected.

"And I didn't set off on my own. I married Johnny."

"You told me last night that you didn't know you were going to marry him until after you sent me away."

No, she thought, shaken, she hadn't.

Then Vicky's voice rang out across the café as she hurried toward them from the rest rooms. "Okay, guys, can I do it? Please, please, please?"

"No," Hunter and Liv said together.

Vicky skidded to a stop a foot from their table, clearly surprised by the verdict. Liv glanced at Hunter. He might not agree with her, but he would support her in this. She went soft inside.

Vicky worked up a pout that she couldn't quite pull off because her eyes were darting between them. "Are you two ganging up on me?"

"That's about the size of it," Hunter said. "How about some ice cream instead?"

She stuck out her bottom lip. "Now you're bribing me."

"Yep. Is it working?" he asked.

"No. How come? Why can't I drive?" She looked at Liv accusingly. "*You* said no, didn't you? *You* won't let me do it."

Hunter's voice went down that notch into warning. "Watch yourself, Victoria Rose."

Liv watched confusion, then misery cloud her daughter's features at the reprimand. She started to reach a hand out to Vicky to comfort her, then she pulled it back. If Hunter was going to cooperate with her, then she couldn't undermine him.

Vicky's chin pushed out and she looked at her father. "*Victoria Rose!* Mom never calls me that." She's spoiling for a fight, Liv thought.

Hunter glanced at her. "What do you call her when you're ticked off?"

Liv shook her head helplessly. "I just get louder."

"You're talking about me like I'm not even here!" Vicky protested.

"Do you want to join in the conversation?" he asked.

"Yes!"

"Then sit down and have some ice cream."

Vicky looked at Liv. "Is it homemade, do you think, or that store-bought yuck?"

Liv put her head in her hands. "For once—just once—couldn't you please be a normal child?"

"Sit down," Hunter said to Vicky again. "If it's store bought, your mom and I will eat it. You can watch us and feel sorry that you're not more open-minded."

"I have coffee," Liv argued. "I'm fine."

"Drop some vanilla in there." He nodded at her mug. Then he winked at her. "Live dangerously."

Her heart rolled over. "It'll melt."

"Exactly. Monique Shaughnessy drank her espresso like that all the time."

Liv felt the fire of jealousy pour into her blood. "It's cappuccino."

He was grinning at her. "No, Monique definitely liked espresso. I remember that clearly."

"*I'm* having cappuccino!"

"I don't get it," Vicky complained. "What are you guys fighting about now?"

"Your mother is jealous," Hunter drawled.

"That would happen on a cold day in hell," Liv grated.

Hunter signaled the waitress. "Three vanilla ice creams," he said when she approached.

"Maybe I could have a *little* chocolate?" Vicky asked hopefully.

He looked at Liv. "We can always tie her to the roof on the way home."

She fell into his eyes. She felt herself shrug.

"You know, you guys are developing an annoying habit of talking about me when I'm *right here*," Vicky said. "Like I can't even hear you. Duh."

"One small scoop of chocolate," Hunter said to the waitress. The woman scribbled on her note pad. "We also have—"

"Maybe quit while I'm ahead," Vicky told her quickly. Then she looked at Hunter. "Why *can't* I drive?"

He seemed to think about it for a long time as the waitress departed. "Because I said so," he decided finally.

Laughter rolled out of Liv. She had to clap a hand over her mouth to stifle it.

He sounded exactly like a father.

Chapter 11

When she woke up on the morning of Christmas Eve, Liv still hadn't figured out what to do about the Christmas gift problem.

She took her cornflakes down from the cupboard and grimaced at them. She'd been eating them for so many weeks now, trying to avoid Hunter and the dining room, that she wasn't sure she could swallow one more mouthful. But lately he was underfoot every time she turned around, anyway. Now he was talking about Christmas presents. So what sense was there in trying to avoid him?

Because he'd be leaving in just two more weeks, she answered herself. She was almost home free. He'd go before she could do anything utterly self-destructive like allow herself to cherish her time with him all over again. As things stood now, she could still get her stride back when he was gone.

Her stomach floated up into her throat with an airy, weightless sensation at the thought.

They'd probably see him again before February, she realized, pouring the cereal. California wasn't that far away. But his presence would be sporadic once the NASCAR season started up again.

She was standing against the counter, munching dutifully, when he pushed through the kitchen door as though her thoughts had summoned him. He grabbed the cornflakes box from beside her.

"Share," he said. He opened the refrigerator, then turned back again, scowling. "What did you do with the milk?"

Liv forced herself to swallow. "Here on the counter." She stepped aside because it was behind her. "Kiki didn't make oysters this morning."

"No, but there's a nymphomaniac out there. I need to hide."

"In the dining room? Who?"

"Lisa Scalantino."

The blonde, Liv thought. Twenty-something, model looks, body to die for. She was at the inn for a week with her boyfriend. Liv had wondered if Hunter would notice the woman.

She was sexy, delightful—the Monique Shaughnessy type without the star status.

"Oh," she said. It was the best she could manage.

"That's all you've got to say? She just groped my backside!"

Liv's gut cramped. She put her bowl in the sink. "Well, I used to think it was pretty gropable."

He stopped moving with the milk still in his hand.

"Used to," Liv repeated, heading for the door. Why had she just said that?

"Of course."

"I've got to go."

"I thought you said you were skipping the trail ride today because it's Christmas Eve."

"And because Bourne is off until Friday. But I have to go into town."

"I'll go with you," he said quickly.

"Coward. Be strong. Face Lisa like a man." But as she stopped in the door, her heart yearned suddenly and it hurt. She paused again. She wanted to believe that Hunter honestly wasn't attracted to the woman. That his reluctance for Lisa's groping wasn't just for show. She clapped a hand to her chest as she realized that there was still a piece in there that wanted him to be attracted only to her.

She watched him pour milk into his own cereal. "That'd be a fine thing for Vicky to witness," he said. "Some woman groping me under her mother's roof."

Cold swept through her even as Liv felt herself blushing. *That* was the only reason he was staying clear of Lisa. "Right." Her voice was a croak.

"What's wrong with you today, anyway?" he asked suddenly, looking at her again.

What was she supposed to do about a Christmas present? "Nothing."

"You're acting weird."

"I've got a lot on my mind."

In contrast to Thanksgiving, she and Kiki threw open the inn's doors on Christmas. Every guest room was full this week—predominantly because of the open house tomorrow night. Reservations for Christmas were always gobbled up a year—sometimes two—in advance. They threw a "period" party—a mining-ghost-town Christmas. Kiki's buffet would be 1890s. And most people showed up in nineteenth-century costumes. It drew the whole town—tourists and residents alike.

He was still watching her closely. He finally nodded. "I got my costume yesterday. I decided to be Rhett Butler."

Liv frowned. "Rhett was Civil War. Old South."

"Best I could come up with. The costume rental place didn't have much left. They said people reserve the good stuff months in advance."

That was true. Then, suddenly, a light dawned in Liv's brain. "*That's* why Vicky wants to be Scarlet O'Hara." She waited for the old surge of jealousy. When it didn't come, she was as worried as if it had.

"Yeah?" Hunter grinned. "That's cool. What are you going to dress as?"

"Madame Louise."

"Who?"

"She ran the place when it was still a brothel. I do it every year."

"You're going as a *madame?*" He looked flabbergasted.

Then he grinned. Slowly. Wickedly. He pulled a wad of bills out of his jeans pocket. "What's your going rate, doll?"

Heat swept her. "Don't be ridiculous." Liv floundered to get a grip on herself. "Madames didn't sell themselves. They were above all that. Besides, that's Kiki's role."

His grin widened. "Want to try explaining that one while you're at it?"

Liv knew her face was aflame. She was just digging herself in deeper. "I don't want to talk about sex with you."

He took a step closer toward her. "It still does things to you, too, doesn't it? Even after all this time."

She had a flash of his mouth on hers again, so real and immediate it almost buckled her.

"That was always one of the best things between us, Livie," he said. "The sex."

She flattened her hands against the door behind her as though to hold herself up. "Stop it. I don't want to talk about it." She cleared her throat, then she frowned. "Sex was *one* of the best things? What were the others?"

"You were the only friend I ever had. Come to think of it, maybe that's why the sex was so good."

Liv pushed off the door, shaken. "I've really got to go."

She left the kitchen and hightailed it upstairs. But his words chased her. They nipped at her heels while she changed and when she drove into town. *It still does things to you, too, doesn't it? Even after all this time.*

Too? He'd kissed her the first time to grab the upper hand in an argument, she reminded herself desperately. He'd done it the second time to protect Kiki. He hated her after what she'd done to him—he'd never get past that enough to *want* to kiss her. But they'd both fallen into those kisses as though they'd never been apart even a day.

Liv stopped dead in the middle of the florist shop with the thought. She forgot what she was doing there.

She shook herself and recovered enough to pick up her order. She wandered outside and stashed the poinsettias in her trunk and the back seat. Then she moved on to the gift shop to pick up the party favors they would give the guests at the door. She was waiting to pay for them with two people in line in front of her when her gaze fell to the display case she was leaning against. Her breath caught.

It was less than half an inch across. A tie tack, intricate, special. It was an eagle. Liv closed her eyes.

It could well be her answer to the gift problem. Except…

She'd never seen Hunter wear a tie, other than at the court hearing and last year's televised Winston Cup awards. So he *did* do it occasionally. But still, what use would he have for such a thing, really?

It was too personal, she thought. An eagle was what had brought him to the Navajo res where they'd ultimately landed in each other's arms—that ill-fated hunt on Hopi land when he'd antagonized both his alcoholic father and the authorities.

It was what had brought them together.

"Liv, how are you? Hold on, I've got your boxes right here under the counter."

Liv jolted at the salesgirl's voice. She looked around dazedly. The other two customers had paid up and gone. She cleared her throat. "What do I owe you?"

"$364.20."

Liv frowned. "That's all?"

"We're giving them to you at cost this year. It's our contribution to town tradition."

Liv dug in her purse for a business check. "Thanks." The florist had done the same thing. The inn's Christmas gala had really caught on in recent years. There were those who swore it actually brought in tourists—and tourist dollars.

She wrote the store's name on the check, then she paused. "How much is that tie tack?"

"The eagle? Let me check." The girl bent and pulled it out of the case. "$39.95. Do you want this, too?"

"No, I…yes." If Hunter gave her something and she didn't have anything for him, Vicky would be upset, she reasoned.

If he didn't give her anything, she could return it.

If he said anything about the significance of the eagle, she could just lie and say it never occurred to her.

"Yes," Liv said again.

By the time she left the store, she couldn't shake the feeling that she was standing on a cliff much like the one Hunter had once fallen off. Waving her arms. Teetering over an abyss that would destroy her.

Hunter found himself prowling around downstairs for the better part of an hour after she left. He helped Kiki transfer roast goose and Yorkshire pudding in and out of the oven and strung additional garland over all the door frames until the place looked as gaudy as it must have once looked as a brothel. Kiki told him that was the point.

Whenever he heard a car outside, he found himself drawn to the kitchen window. Once he turned back to see Kiki watching him.

"Just keeping an eye out for Lustful Lisa," he explained. "When she gets back, I'm going to have to head upstairs."

"Guests use the front door," Kiki replied.

"Yeah, well, you never know. She's determined."

Kiki snorted.

Hunter finally went upstairs, anyway. He found Vicky in her bedroom and lured her into helping him wrap presents. They finished too soon. He found himself at loose ends again, pacing his attic room. The strange light shifted in the corner as he moved back and forth. He was used to it now. He'd decided it had something to do with the way the sun hit the windows. He was pretty sure it glinted off the brass pieces on the ballet bar on the other side of the room. He wasn't prepared to explain how the phenomenon could happen at night.

Finally, he heard a car behind the inn, not stopping at the apron on the side. He went to the windows, to the one he had somehow managed to leave open despite the fact that it was barely forty degrees outside and the inn's furnace was pumping heat. Kiki with her business books would never know, he told himself.

He hunkered down to peer out the window and watched Liv tuck her still-battered car into the garage.

She got out a moment later and sprang her trunk open. As she unloaded poinsettias, her long golden-brown hair kept falling forward. She raked her hand through it time and time again. She blew out her breath. When everything was unloaded, she went to the middle of the drive, planted her hands on her hips, and shouted toward the inn for Vicky.

Vicky was in the garage. She came up behind Liv, tiptoeing exaggeratedly. Just on her heels, she stopped and yelled, ''Boo!''

Liv jumped high enough to touch the sky.

Hunter laughed aloud. And that was when it hit him.

He loved them. He loved both of them. With his body and his soul and the very air he breathed.

The anger that came next scalded him. It tried to claw his heart right out of his chest. This was the way it should have been. Livie, him, their child—together. This was the way it would have been every day of the past eight years if she hadn't stolen it from him. Then something moved inside his head, a pain that squirmed there. Because it wouldn't have been this way if she had told him eight and a half years ago...and he knew it.

It wouldn't have been like this at all.

There would have been no inn. No sweet scenes in front of the garage—unless it was a stock car bay. The three of them would have moved on and on and on, maybe traveling the circuit, calling hotel rooms and Winnebagos home. Or maybe stopping in this town for a while, then in the next one, in rented digs, as he chased other dreams. Because he knew, suddenly, that if he'd had them with him, by his side, he might not have fallen so completely into racing. He wouldn't have needed anything to anchor him the way NASCAR had finally anchored him, because he would have had his Liv and she'd always done that for him.

If he'd had them, he could have kept roaming.

Something grabbed his heart and twisted. It was entirely possible that he might even have left them and just kept coming home to love them, he realized, to gather them close, before he took another leap into the unknown. Just as she had accused him of.

Hunter stood unsteadily from the window.

She'd been wrong in what she'd done to him. Damn it, Livie

had been so wrong. Not telling him was bad enough, but marrying Guenther was unforgivable. Still, he thought, one of them *had* to have done the unconscionable. If she hadn't done what she'd done, Hunter knew his answering response would have been abysmal as well.

They'd been doomed. And where the hell did that leave them now?

"Hunter!"

Her voice carried up his attic stairs, startling him. He wasn't ready for her right now. He needed time to come to terms with his feelings. Hunter went to the door anyway and opened it.

"What's up?" he called down. The stairs were steep. He could just see her legs from the knees down. Who besides Livie Slade could get away with pink suede boots?

"I need you," she answered.

He ran a hand over his eyes. "I need you, too." Always. It never ended.

"What?" she called back. "I can't hear you!"

"Never mind." He raised his voice, got a grip on himself.

She was waiting for him when he reached the bottom of the steps. "They delivered the Christmas tree," she said. "It's so big. Kiki and I can't get it inside. And they just dumped it on the front porch."

Hunter scowled. "There's already a tree in your sitting room. What do we need another one for?"

She raked her hair back again, harried, beautiful. "The one in my sitting room is ours. This is the one for the parlor, for tomorrow night."

Ours. "Most establishments would just stick an artificial thing in there," he said, his voice unaccountably hoarse.

She looked at him as if he had just uttered a blasphemy. "Which is why they're not the Copper Rose."

She strode off ahead of him to the staircase, tall and elegant. Hunter followed her to wrestle with a tree the size of Arizona, trying not to notice the way she moved.

She'd known him since she was twelve, Liv mused on Christmas morning, and never once had she realized that Hunter was allergic to Christmas trees. Then again, there hadn't been many evergreens in their area of the Res—at least none that she'd ever known him to tangle with.

Vicky was literally shivering with excitement as she knelt beside the tree in Liv's sitting room, waiting for him to join them. Santa's gifts spilled halfway across the floor; family gifts in special blue paper were interspersed. Hunter's tokens were wrapped in black and gold. He'd admitted that a fan had sent him the paper, sparing him the chore of buying it. It matched the colors of his NASCAR car.

Kiki was curled up on the sofa with a cup of coffee, her eyes at half-mast. She wore red long johns, something Liv was reasonably sure only a gorgeous sprite of a woman with a waterfall of black hair could get away with. She'd stayed over last night.

There was a sharp knock on the door and Liv called for Hunter to come in. He did, and his skin was red. Liv was so startled her jaw dropped open.

"What happened to you?" she finally asked.

Kiki pried one eye open. "Those are welts," she said.

"Who cares? Let's open presents!" Vicky pleaded.

"Thank you so much, Victoria Rose, for your moving concern," Hunter drawled as he came into the room.

"How did you get welts?" Liv demanded.

"Since each of them is associated with a scratch, I'd say they came from that abomination of a tree you've got downstairs," Hunter replied. "I must be allergic."

Liv's heart dove. "You can't be Rhett tonight looking like that."

"Now I know where Vicky got her compassion."

"Hold on." Liv shot up from the floor where she'd been sitting beside Vicky. She headed for her bathroom.

"Where are you going?" Vicky wailed after her. *"Santa Claus came!"*

Liv glanced back once over her shoulder. It amazed her that as worldly-wise as her daughter was, she still believed in Santa. Wholeheartedly and with a passion born of innocence. Last season she'd decked a kid who had tried to convince her otherwise.

Liv had been achingly aware for months now that this could

be the last year for the purity of make-believe. She felt a spasm in her chest. She should be at the tree, nurturing that, savoring it. One more glance at Hunter convinced her otherwise. His skin was livid.

"Santa has been around for hundreds of years," Kiki replied, yawning. "He'll come again, squirt, and in the meantime, these presents aren't going anywhere. Chill out and let your mom take care of your dad."

Liv found the aloe she wanted and returned to stand in front of Hunter. "Take your T-shirt off." She was looking up at him when she said it, and she saw his eyes change. They flared, then narrowed. Her heart slammed.

"I beg your pardon? I think that's your role," he added under his breath.

Liv felt both Kiki and Vicky watching them. "Not now," she whispered. "Hunter, we can't talk about that now. It's *Christmas.*"

"You're blushing, Livie. It always amazed me how you could do that. You're tough one moment, a swooning maiden the next."

"*You're* going to swoon if I slug you."

"Give me the aloe, babe. I'll take care of it."

He hadn't called her babe since he'd left her. Liv felt the room tilt. She couldn't breathe. He pried the tube from her clenched fingers.

"I can do it," she squeaked. "You can't reach your back."

"I don't have scratches on my back."

"Oh."

"And if you touch me right now, I'm not sure the result would be something we'd want our daughter to witness."

Liv's gaze dropped helplessly. He was wearing sweats. One glance told her he was already aroused.

She was suddenly so hot her robe felt as though it was clinging to her skin. She turned away dazedly. When he spoke again, his voice seemed to come to her from very far away.

He did still want her. He definitely still wanted her.

"Come on, Kiki," he chided. "Buck up. I know you're in the kitchen every morning by five-thirty. This isn't any earlier.

Or did Liv make you sleep on the sofa last night? Is that why you're so droopy?"

"She gave me the bed," Kiki said. "But then she sat on it all night, talking at me."

"Yeah? So what was the topic of conversation?"

Liv flushed. She'd been recounting the many, many reasons she felt absolutely nothing anymore for Hunter Hawk-Cole.

"I'm getting impatient," Vicky whined.

Liv went quickly to sit beside her on the floor. "Okay. Start tearing. Let's see what you got."

Vicky dove in. Paper flew. Liv caught most of it, wadding it up and jamming it down into a plastic trash bag. She glanced at Hunter once as Vicky opened a beauty kit.

"She doesn't need lipstick," he said, sitting beside Kiki on the sofa. "She's *eight.*"

Vicky rolled her eyes. "Da-a-a-d."

Hunter looked at Liv. "You're seriously going to let her wear that?"

Liv reached for the kit. It wasn't just lipstick. It was gaudy, youthful, make-pretend makeup complete with the chemistry instructions to mix more. "Trust me. She'll be finger painting with it by Tuesday."

"On her face?"

"Maybe the walls."

"Mandy wears lipstick," Vicky said, but she was already ripping paper off the next present.

"Have you met this Mandy's parents?" Hunter demanded of Liv.

"Yes. They're sweethearts."

It was over too fast, Liv thought. It always was. And this year she had that pain in her chest because she wondered if it would ever be this simple again. Would Vicky still believe the next time around? Would business still be thriving? Could they afford all this?

Would Hunter be here?

"There's still more," Vicky said impatiently.

Liv looked around. It was the family stuff. "You know the rules," she reminded her.

"What are the rules?" Hunter asked.

"Vicky takes a bit of a breather now. Kiki and I exchange."

"Can I get into this part?"

"Of course." Liv felt her air trying to fall short again. The tie tack was in her desk drawer. She'd wrapped it.

But she didn't have to take it out and give it to him.

Kiki finally put her coffee mug down. She got up and went to kneel on the floor beside Vicky. "Move, squirt. My turn."

"What did you get me?" Vicky asked.

"Guess you're just going to have to wait and see, won't you?"

Vicky sighed. "It's so hard."

"Patience is a virtue."

"That's not what Dad says."

Hunter sat up straight on the sofa. "When did I ever say that?"

"You said if I saw something I wanted, I should grab it."

He glanced guiltily at Liv. "I didn't actually say that. And I didn't mean Christmas presents. I meant when she was an adult. With life in general."

"Can I grab now, anyway?" Vicky asked.

"No!" Liv and Hunter said in chorus.

Kiki grinned privately.

She handed Liv and Hunter each a package. Then he stood from the sofa and knelt beside the tree, as well. Liv's heart started beating too hard. Now that all the Santa presents were gone, she could count the black-and-gold ones.

There were five.

All for Vicky? No. He handed one to Kiki. He handed one to her.

"The rest are all for me?" Vicky asked him.

"No. They're for the homeless waif we have living in the barn."

"There's no—" Vicky broke off and giggled. "Mine, mine, mine!"

He'd gotten her a gift. It would be a token, Liv told herself desperately. And the tie tack would be too intimate, too...too *something*.

Kiki peeled the gold-and-black wrapping off a box that contained a crimson and fairly provocative satin robe. She threw back her head and laughed. "You are the only man in the world who could get away with giving this to me."

"Yeah, but I still don't want to know what you do with all those pillows and candles upstairs."

Vicky squealed, interrupting them. She'd gotten into one of his packages. *"Heelies!"*

"Hey, pigtails," Hunter said. "You're out of turn. Your mom was supposed to open one next."

"Too late!" she cried, struggling to put the shoes on over her slipper-socks.

"Do I want to know what Heelies are?" Liv asked, staring at them.

"Sneaks! With wheels in them!" Vicky crowed.

"In them?"

"On them," Hunter clarified. "On the soles. They retract so she can walk like a normal human being when speed is not appropriate or authorized."

"You gave her speed?" Liv croaked.

"Livie, how fast can she go in *shoes?*"

He hadn't checked with her this time, Liv thought. But her fingers were wrapped like claws around her own gift, and she found that she didn't care.

"Your turn, Liv," he said.

"Right." She began tearing off the black-and-gold paper.

It was big. Well, reasonably big. Eight inches high by maybe four across. And heavy. Heavier than she might have expected. What did a token weigh?

She opened the box. It was a figurine. It took her a long time to realize that the reason she couldn't see it clearly was because she was crying.

"I don't get why grown-ups do that," Vicky muttered.

"Hush," Liv heard Kiki caution.

It was a mother and daughter kneeling by a white picket fence. Surrounded by daisies. It wasn't a Christmas present. It was understanding.

Liv dragged her eyes off it. She met his. Somewhere in her

throat were words. Somewhere in her heart there was a *thank you*. She couldn't quite get them out.

"Merry Christmas, Livie," he said.

"I...got you something."

"Did you, now?"

She realized suddenly that there was no one else in the room with them. Vicky chattered. Kiki opened another gift. But there were only his eyes, midnight blue. There was only his crooked smile. *What had she done?*

Yes, she'd fallen in love with him all over again, Liv thought.

In the next moment she shook her head unconsciously. No, she thought, no. Because he was right—he *had* changed. This wasn't "all over again." Because this wasn't the way it had been between them before. There had been no issues back then...just sex and fun. He was a different man now.

This was a man who understood picket fences. He might not ever need them, but he acknowledged that she did.

This was a man who had stayed in one place for nearly ninety days. Without prowling.

This was a father who clamped his hand down on top of Vicky's head now when she started to rise to skate off in her Heelies.

"Plant it, pigtails," he said without taking his gaze from Liv. "We're not done here yet. I get to open one of my own."

Vicky sighed and sat down again. Liv cleared her throat. "I...need to get it." She stood, though she was sure her legs wouldn't hold her. She went to her desk and got the little box. When she turned back to him, he was grinning.

"You tucked it aside just in case I didn't get you anything," he guessed accurately.

"Just in case you seriously ticked me off before this moment." Somehow, miraculously, her voice was still there.

Hunter laughed. "Hand it over."

She did. She couldn't sit. She fretted with the last tossed-aside wrappings, but her ears were tuned to the sound of paper being pulled away by his strong fingers. She couldn't look at him. But she felt his silence like a touch.

"It has all its feathers," he said finally.

Her mouth twitched. "I couldn't find a bald one, or a boy with those feathers sticking out of his pocket."

"I don't get it," Vicky said.

Hunter closed his hand over the tie tack. "I do."

This was the part where she was supposed to say it didn't mean anything, Liv thought desperately. Because she needed to keep distance between them. She needed to keep herself safe. She only had to get through two more weeks!

"Thank you, Livie."

"Uh, yes. You're welcome."

"Great cookbook," Kiki said.

Liv pivoted to look at her vacantly. "What?"

Kiki held up Liv's gift to her, a collection of old miners' and wagon train recipes. "This should be a challenge. They didn't know about ions or molecules back then."

"I, uh, thought you might rise to the occasion, anyway."

"Open yours," Kiki said. "Then I'm going to loll in luxury and go back to bed for a little while." They didn't do an early breakfast on Christmas morning. Brunch was hours away yet.

Liv found the gift from Kiki and unwrapped it. And her heart stopped all over again. It was a framed snapshot of the three of them—Liv and Kiki and Hunter—young, fresh-faced, untouched by heartache, taken way back during their days on the Res. Why had Kiki kept this? She wasn't sentimental.

There was such hope in all their eyes, Liv thought. When had it gone? When had they stopped believing that anything was possible?

When things began to hurt.

"Thanks," she whispered.

"Let me see," Hunter said.

She handed it over to him.

He was quiet for a long time. "Yeah," he said. "That's good."

Liv realized that Vicky was staring at all of them, her gaze hitching from Kiki to Hunter to her. Liv wondered what was about to come out of her mouth, and she cringed a little in anticipation of it.

"What?" she finally prompted her daughter.

"I was just thinking," Vicky said. "Didn't Atlanta burn or something? You know, back in the Civil War? Hey, Dad. The red might work. For the party tonight, you can be Rhett coming out of the fire!"

Chapter 12

Hunter's welts had calmed down considerably by midafternoon. No one was more relieved than Vicky, who kept insisting that she didn't want a lobster for a "date."

"When did dating start to cross her mind?" he asked as they saw to last-minute preparations for the party.

"This is the first I've heard of it." Liv glanced at him as she set out the warming plates for the buffet. "Did you finish trimming the parlor tree?"

"Done. I don't want her dating until she's at least nineteen."

Liv went to the parlor, anyway, to check on it. "I was pregnant with her when I was nineteen."

Hunter punched a fist against his heart as he followed her, as though to restart it. "Twenty-one, then."

"Good luck. Once she goes away to college, I kind of figure it's out of our hands." She looked around the parlor. "We need more seating in here," she decided.

"And where would you like me to find it at three o'clock on Christmas afternoon?"

"The same place you found the Yule logs this morning?" she suggested hopefully.

"I got lucky on that one. The guy happened to stop by his store for something and I was there banging on the door when he did. He took pity on me and sold me the logs."

"You probably gave him the look."

"What look?"

"That fierce thing you do when you lower your brows. You probably scared the death out of him. That's why he opened for you."

"Nope. He wanted an autograph."

Her heart stopped for a moment with the reminder of who— and what—he really was these days. And that he would soon be going back to it. "I think we're done in here," she said quickly.

"No cracks about my money this time?" he asked, following her out of the parlor.

"Not as long as you send Vicky to college with it so she can enter into that errant world of dating you can't control."

"Do convents cost anything?"

Liv's mood passed. There was no way she couldn't laugh at that. "Vicky? A nun? Please! I'm going to go get dressed now."

Hunter watched her head up the stairs and entertained some serious visions of what Liv would look like dressed up as a madame. Then he went to the kitchen to see if there was anything he could do to help Kiki.

"Sure," she replied. "You can shuck the oysters."

Hunter cringed inwardly. "Uh...what does that involve?"

"Just open the shells. Leave the oysters on one half. We'll serve them like that."

"Raw? Uncooked slime on a shell?"

She stopped what she was doing to stare at him. "I thought you were so worldly these days. Don't tell me you've never encountered oysters on the half shell."

"I may have encountered them." He frowned. "But I didn't look at them too closely. Hand them over. I'll do it."

Kiki laughed. "Never mind. I was just testing you."

"For what?" he asked warily.

"To find out if you were the one who dumped half a dozen of them in my trash about a month or so back."

Hunter grinned slowly. "You knew all along."

"I knew Vicky sure didn't toss them." Kiki grinned. "Don't worry. I didn't tell Liv."

So, he thought, she didn't know *everything*. It gave him a good, strong feeling of warmth in the center of his chest that Liv had never confided in Kiki about this.

Then Lisa Scalantino sailed into the kitchen.

"*There* you are!" She let it out on a gasping breath and made a beeline for him. Hunter backed up to the window.

"Uh, yeah. Here I am. But the kitchen's not open to guests." He looked pleadingly to Kiki for help, but she was apparently getting even with him for the oysters. She raised a brow, started humming and went back to cooking.

"*You're* a guest." Lisa was closing in on him with that sexy hip-twitching stride.

"No. I'm not."

Lisa paused, confused. "But I thought—"

"I'm one of the family."

She frowned. "In what respect?"

"I'm married to one of the owners."

He got his own revenge. At the stove, Kiki choked in mid-hum.

Hunter left the window, skirting Lisa neatly on his way to the door, satisfied with himself. And that was when it hit him.

He wanted to marry her. He wanted to marry Livie. He wanted them to be a real family. He wanted them to be what he came home to. He just wasn't sure she would agree with him.

But when had he ever been passive? When had he ever sat back and let the things he wanted come to him? He could convince her to see things his way. He knew how.

No judge in the world would hold it against him if he tried to get his woman back, he thought, heading to his own room, even if he ticked her off a little in the process.

"I need boobs," Vicky decided.

Liv's eyes popped wide as they stood side by side in front of the mirror in her bedroom. They'd just finished dressing for the party. Hunter would drop dead, she thought, if he heard *that* comment.

"They'll come soon enough," she answered finally.

"Not soon enough to save this dress," Vicky complained, plucking at the bodice.

"You look adorable." And she did, Liv thought. The miniature ball gown was a takeoff on the green velvet one Scarlet had fashioned out of Tara's drapes in a pinch. The neckline was scooped low and off the shoulders, the sleeves voluminous. The skirt was tiered with ivory lace trim on each layer. It had hoops. Vicky had already done a great deal of damage to Liv's rooms with the hoops. She'd been instructed to stay out of the parlor and the dining room at all costs. Liv had visions of one sweeping turn taking out half the buffet table.

She still blamed Hunter for the Scarlet craze, she thought. She tried to work up irritation but came up empty-handed.

"Mom. Scarlet was *not* adorable," Vicky argued.

"She thought she was."

"She was beautiful."

"So are you."

"Hard to be beautiful when you're boobless."

Liv leaned toward the vanity mirror to apply lipstick. She dropped the tube just in time to grab the Christmas figurine Hunter had given her when Vicky did an abrupt about-face. The hoops lifted and bounced, nearly knocking it over.

"You really like that, don't you?" Vicky asked, looking back. She grinned at the figurine in Liv's hand.

Liv's heart rolled over. "Yes. I do."

"You don't hate him anymore."

Liv felt her eyes fill with tears. *I love him.* "No. I don't."

"Good."

Liv blinked the tears back and looked at her daughter. "Good? That's all you have to say? One monosyllabic word? That's not like you."

Vicky drew herself up to her full four feet six inches. "Well, fiddle-dee-dee."

She twirled again. This time the hoops whacked up harmlessly against the bedroom wall before she swept out of the room. Liv laughed.

She was so happy. Tonight, she thought, just for tonight, she would pretend that it would never end. Wasn't Christmas a time for miracles?

Hunter was already downstairs, in the dining room, looking over the buffet for anything that might involve a half shell, when Liv swept into the room. He nearly dropped his drink. He should have laughed himself hoarse at the sight. Instead, he felt everything gathering tight inside him.

"Well," he murmured. "This is a sight."

Liv did a little pirouette. She wore a black silk sheath that fitted like a second skin and draped to her toes. It had spaghetti straps. He could just make them out beneath the emerald-green, peignoir-type…something…she wore over it. Her breasts were full and lush, a tantalizing glimpse above the low scoop of the sheath's neckline. The green topper was filmy and sheer and trimmed with feathers. Her hair was done up elaborately, curls layered upon curls on top of her head. Emerald earrings—or a reasonable facsimile—dangled nearly to her shoulders.

She finally slid up beside him. "What's your pleasure, pal?"

He acted. He didn't think. He couldn't have thought if his life had depended on it. Holding his Remy high in one hand, he caught her around the shoulders with his free arm and dipped her until she gave a little cry and had no choice but to grab his lapels with both hands. Then he kissed her.

Hunter did it in a way he knew would drive her wild. He had a mission now, after all. And the first part of it involved getting her naked again, in his bed.

He nipped her bottom lip first to make sure she knew what he had in mind. He watched her eyes flare. Was that panic he saw there? Maybe, he thought, but panic wasn't bad. Panic said she wasn't immune. Panic said that his kiss still did things to her—big things.

He closed his mouth over hers, hard and fast. He felt her hands relax on his lapels. Heard the rumble of something, maybe a purr, in her throat. And his head was filled with her—with everything he had ever needed—as he swept his tongue past hers.

Then a voice spoke behind them. "Oh!"

He still wasn't planning to stop, but Liv uncurled her hand from his topcoat and thumped it against his chest. He took his mouth from hers, but he kept his face close and he didn't let her stand up. "Problem?" he murmured.

"We have company."

"I don't care, if you don't. Want to keep going?"

That old, old spark shone in her eyes. "No, that was satisfactory. What do I owe you?"

Hunter felt the laugh come up from his gut. He eased her upright again, onto her feet, and turned to find Lisa Scalantino in the doorway watching them.

"Can we help you with something?" he asked mildly.

"Uh...I just...someone said the food was in here."

Liv moved away from the buffet table just as the doorbell rang. "You're in the right place. Eat, drink, be merry."

Lisa's mouth crooked into a wry grin. "I think you and your husband have the corner on that last part."

"My *what?*"

"We've got guests arriving, darling." Hunter gave her a little nudge toward the door as the doorbell rang again.

Liv tried to turn back to Lisa. "We're not—"

He shoved her a little harder. Liv looked at him wildly as she let him angle her out into the hall this time. "Did you tell her we were married?"

"Not me. Maybe it was Vicky."

Liv thought about that and nodded. Vicky had probably introduced Hunter as her dad. The married part followed...or should have, if Hunter had been any other kind of man. Her heart stretched with yearning.

"Speaking of Vicky," she said, schooling her voice into nonchalance, "you might want to make sure you compliment her on her cleavage."

"On her *what?*"

Liv smiled sweetly as she swept on to the front door to greet the guests who were arriving, leaving him gaping.

It was better than last year, she thought, half an hour later. It was better than any year so far. She lost her efforts at a head count somewhere past two hundred. Given the town's population, she figured she was best off just giving up.

The mayor was there—in fact, the entire city council turned up. Ingrid Small arrived, as well. "Just wanted to see how you were holding up," she said, taking Liv's hand. "It's an open house, right?"

"Uh, right," Liv murmured, staring at her. The attorney was dressed as a miner. "We're doing fine."

Ingrid nodded. "Woodingham's money was on it."

Liv didn't have a chance to ask her what she meant. Another group spilled through the door.

She stayed there for two more hours, greeting people, welcoming them. Her mind returned, over and over, to Hunter's mouth closing over hers. She didn't see him again until he brought her a plate of oysters.

"Tell me please," he said, "how these things constitute 1890s fare?"

Liv slurped one up during a break in the humanity pouring through the door. "They were considered a delicacy. Copper equaled money equaled something ostentatious to spend it on."

He wiggled his brows at her. "I can think of better things."

Her heart slugged. "I'll bet. But Sweet Sarah is probably still in the kitchen."

"By the way, who *is* this Sarah? Vicky mentioned her once, too."

Liv grinned privately. "She's the lady of ill repute Kiki is dressed up as tonight."

Hunter laughed. "Yeah, she came to the dining room once, and six men passed out."

Liv grinned. "That happened last year, too. She's wearing that red teddy-type thing again, right?"

"She is. But *you* look better. Kiss me again, Madame Louise."

Liv eased back against the door. She took a deep breath in, very slowly. "Hunter, what are we doing?"

"Personally, I'm giving up on being stupid. How about you?"

What was stupid? Falling for a man who walked out on her when the wind changed? She opened her mouth to answer, then her jaw fell open entirely when a scream sounded from the kitchen.

She had time to gasp once before she collided with Hunter chest to chest. They both turned back into the inn at the same time. It had been Kiki's voice. They raced for the kitchen.

She couldn't think of anything that could have gone wrong to warrant such a sound from a woman who could walk on coals without flinching.

They'd hired six girls from town to keep the food flowing from the kitchen to the buffet tables. They had waiters from the Connor's dining room circulating with champagne, wine and beer. Had something happened to one of them? Shoulder to shoulder, Liv plowed with Hunter through the kitchen door—and ran in on a geyser.

Liv yelped, too. The water was coming from a place where the sink faucet used to be. It gushed straight up in a mighty spout, hitting the ceiling, raining down again on platters of food. Kiki stood in the middle of it, the faucet piece in her hand, soaked to the skin, her hair plastered to her skull.

"Turn the knob off!" Hunter bellowed, moving in on the sink.

"It *is* off!" Kiki shouted back.

"Then why's the water still coming?"

"If I knew that, I'd be dry!"

Liv watched helplessly as Hunter waded under the spout. He grabbed the hot and cold nozzles and twisted as though he didn't believe Kiki.

Nothing happened.

"The food!" Liv cried.

She and Kiki dove for it together—trays of sliced pheasant and goose, and pastries for the dessert round. They snatched them off the counters and dropped them on the table where the geyser didn't quite reach. Liv was shocked to find that she was only slightly damp when they finished.

Hunter hollered again for a wrench, and Kiki took off in sodden slippers for the mudroom. When she came back with one,

Hunter got down on his knees in the puddles and his upper half disappeared beneath the sink.

Abruptly, with barely a fizzle, the water stopped shooting.

"What *happened?*" Liv gasped.

Kiki made a growling sound and wrung out the hem of her teddy. "I turned on the water tap and the faucet piece blew off."

"Was it loose?"

Kiki glared at her. "Sure it was. And I neglected to get someone in here to fix it so we could have a disaster on our hands tonight."

Liv held up both hands as Hunter crawled out from beneath the sink. He grabbed a kitchen towel to dry his hair. "I had to turn the water off entirely. We won't have a working sink until we can get a plumber in here in the morning."

Liv looked at him helplessly. "Can't you fix it?"

"Babe, I know restrictor plates and carburetors. I know alligators. I know the Army. I don't know plumbing."

Liv sank down at the table in a ripple of black silk and green tulle as her legs gave out. The food was ruined and they had no running water. "This is bad."

He was watching her closely. "Are you throwing in the towel?"

She looked up at him. It was a challenge. "You told me a few weeks ago that I need to learn when to do that."

"This might not be the best time. Besides, I didn't mean it. I was just mad at you because you were pushing yourself to be superwoman when you were sick. Near as I can tell, you're not sick now."

She blessed him for the adrenaline it shot into her blood. "I'll learn the lesson next lifetime." She pushed to her feet. "Save the food," she said to Kiki.

"Are you out of your mind?"

"Dry the damned goose off and nuke it."

"The glaze—"

"People have been out there drinking steadily for two hours now. They won't notice. And in case they do…" She trailed off and looked at Hunter. "The owner of the Connor is out there. Can you charm him?"

"Into what?" But one corner of his mouth kicked up into a grin.

"Hard liquor from his establishment. If I ply people with more than beer and champagne, we might just be able to pull this off."

"You don't have a license for that."

"I'm willing to live dangerously."

He grinned slowly. "Consider the man charmed." He started to move for the door.

"Wait," she said quickly. "I meant *after* you get those clothes off."

His gaze shot back to her. "Kiss got to you that much, did it?"

Something hot slid through her. "I just meant to put your clothes in the dryer. You're soaked."

"You're not. More's the pity."

Liv pressed a hand to her heart and headed back to schmooze the guests until Kiki could catch up with the food and Hunter could do something about the liquor. What were they doing, teasing each other like this? she wondered again.

She didn't know, but she was pretty sure she liked it.

While the grandfather clock in the hallway chimed two in the morning, Liv saw the last inebriated guest into a cab in front of the inn. She came back inside and closed the door behind her, leaning against it, exhausted.

Hunter stood in the hall, watching her.

"Well? What do you think?" she murmured.

He shrugged. "The word overkill comes to mind. When you decide to get people drunk, you don't horse around."

"It worked." Then she felt laughter tickle her throat. It finally seized her, fully, until he grinned back. "You look ridiculous."

The trousers of his Southern-gentleman-rogue costume now only reached midankle. The sleeves didn't quite hit his wrists. It strained over his shoulders. It had, apparently, been only dry-cleanable. The geyser and the dryer had pretty much killed it.

"Come on. I'll help you clean up." He held a hand out to her.

"We can't. We don't have running water."

"We can tidy up."

Liv didn't move. "I just want to sit. I haven't sat since five o'clock."

"If you do, you won't get up again."

"So what?"

"I have plans for you later."

Her heart vaulted. "Hunter…"

"Hmm?" He came toward her.

"We have to talk about this."

"I wonder why." He reached her, took her hands in his own.

His touch was so warm. And somehow rough at the same time. All the things she used to crave. "Because…because…" No reason came to mind. Liv blew her breath out.

"You're shaking," he said quietly.

"Aftermath of adrenaline."

"Right." He touched her mouth with his again, as softly as a whisper this time. "Livie, I'm about talked out on the subject of us. I can't think of too many topics we've missed in the past two and a half months. And I want you."

She squeezed her eyes shut against the need that ripped through her. "You *left* me," she whispered.

"I was hurting, Liv. I was hurting bad."

And she had done that to him. But—oh, God—he had destroyed something in her, too, when he had gone. Was it even possible to go back and fix all that?

She eased back from his kiss, but then she only leaned her forehead against that incredibly strong shoulder. "We were never right for each other in the first place, Hunter. We were always so different…"

"Were we?"

Liv straightened. "I needed that picket fence you gave me this morning. I needed it *then*."

He brought his hand up to cup her cheek. "No, Livie. You only thought you did."

She felt her spine harden. She didn't want to fight with him. She wanted to love him. But the words spilled from her anyway. "You *still* don't understand."

"On the contrary, I finally do. I figured it out watching you tonight. If you had really needed that fence, Livie, you'd have it now. I've never known you to walk away from one single thing you wanted to do."

"I *do* have it!"

"No. This wasn't the kind of Christmas you shared with your parents."

She didn't want to hear this. Things reared up inside her in violent protest. *No, no, stop!* Because she knew what he was going to say, and she knew it would change everything.

"Santa came," she whispered.

"Then our daughter dressed up as Scarlet O'Hara. Minus the breasts."

Her throat clogged.

"I've been watching you all night, Livie. This isn't the life you always said you wanted."

"It's solid," she whispered, "secure."

"But it's not a neat, nuclear family. It's you, your best friend, Vicky…and me. And a lot of strangers."

Something started shuddering deep inside her. How many times had she said that herself? "But no one can take it away from me."

"That's the first true thing you've said yet."

Her temper flared again. "What do you want from me, Hunter? Damn it, what are you angling for here? What do you want me to say?"

"That maybe what you always coveted when we were teen-agers doesn't define you as an adult after all."

She went at him with both hands, pushing off the door, planting them against his chest. Then she forgot that she wanted to push him away and she curled her fists into his jacket, clinging instead. "Stop it," she pleaded aloud this time.

"Uh-uh, Livie. I guess I've got a few things left to say after all. Then I'm going to take you upstairs and I'm going to love you like I should have done before."

Her legs were going to give out. She kept holding on to him to keep herself upright. "That won't solve anything."

"I think it will solve a *lot.*"

"Stop being such a man."

"Tell me that without holding on to me so you don't swoon at the prospect."

She loosened one fist to thump it against his chest. "I hate you."

"Yeah, yeah, yeah. That's getting old, babe."

Nothing had ever changed, she thought helplessly. What she felt now was exactly the same as that day when she had pulled her T-shirt over her head in the middle of the desert. Every limb was filled with air…with expectation. And it shimmered and trembled. Things at the very core of her coiled and tightened until they ached.

"Tell me one thing, Livie. Tell me the truth." His mouth was a breath away from hers again, but he didn't kiss her this time. "Are you happy? Take me—and these last three months—out of it. Were you happy with your life before you went to Delaware?"

Her breath shuddered out of her. "Yes." Except she hadn't had him.

"You're an innkeeper, babe. You tend to the needs of others. You could have chosen any life you wanted after you pushed me away. You sure as hell had the traditional thing going with Guenther. But you left him and this is what you grabbed. Because it's *you.*" He startled her by dragging her against his chest, wrapping his arms around her and holding her tight. "You had the perfect family when you were a kid, and you lost it. But you never did go back to that life because when your world shattered around you, you changed."

"No," she whispered against the taut black of his Rhett jacket.

"You adapted. And you ended up taking all those things you knew about family, giving it to strangers to make them feel at home while they're on the road."

She struggled in his arms until he let her go. "Thank you, Freud."

"Kiki isn't the only brain around here. And even she didn't know what to do with a broken faucet."

"She just panicked." Liv tried to laugh. The reflex got caught in her throat and strangled her. "If you take the picket fence away from me, Hunter, you've taken every reason I sent you away in the first place."

"I know."

It wasn't just her body shaking, Liv thought. It was her heart.

He was right, too right. She'd thrown away love. She'd thrown away something real and tangible with him, something hers for the taking, to grab her version of security. And then she had never ended up keeping it, anyway. Because security—with Johnny, without this man—was nothing. But...

"I hated letting you go all the time!" The words ripped from her. "It *hurt*."

"You should have told me, Liv."

"Would it have made a difference?"

"I don't know, babe. I just don't know. But we're together now." He caught her hand again. "Come upstairs with me."

Liv looked around dazedly. She had responsibilities. She had the life she'd made without him. The parlor was a shambles. And—she noticed for the first time—their daughter was asleep on the divan, a small, peaceful face poking out above burgeoning hoops of green velvet.

Hunter caught her chin in his hand and pulled her face back. "When was the last time you stayed up all night, Livie?"

"The time we camped in Canyon de Chelly to listen for the ghosts of our ancestors."

"Well, then. Let's go upstairs and listen for a few ghosts of our own."

"This could be such a mistake," she whispered.

He moved back another step, her hand still in his, drawing her with him. When she hesitated, he scooped her up in his arms. "Frankly, my dear, I don't give a damn."

Laughter caught in her throat again. "Hunter."

He carried her up the stairs. "Hmm?"

"Rhett was a renegade."

"Yeah. But he loved Scarlet."

Things inside her were dancing. With hope. With dreams. He meant Vicky. Surely he meant Vicky. "Scarlet is asleep downstairs in the parlor."

"Ah, but she doesn't have boobs."

"Yet."

"Don't ruin my mood."

He stopped in front of her door. "Your place or mine?"

She didn't want him in Kiki's bed, Liv thought. She wanted him in the place where she had dreamed about him through so many empty nights. She wanted him in the place where she had cried over him. She wanted him in the place that was her only real, true home—her suite of rooms—because she hadn't needed the whole fence after all.

"Here," she murmured. "Right here."

"That's my girl."

He tried to nudge the door open with his shoulder, but there had been people all over the inn tonight so she had locked it. A giddy laugh filled her throat as she reached down into her bodice for the key. His gaze followed her hand.

"It was the only place I wouldn't lose track of it through all the chaos tonight," she explained.

"You vixen."

"Oh, Rhett. You say the sweetest things."

He plucked it from her fingers. And somehow, still holding her, he got it into the lock.

He moved into the sitting room and kicked the door shut behind him. He started for the bedroom before she gasped. "Wait! Don't forget about Vicky."

Yeah, he thought, yeah, everything was different now, and it made everything seem more right. He settled her on her feet and went to lock the door again in case their daughter woke and took it into her head to pay her mother a midnight visit.

When he looked back, Liv was shrugging out of the green filmy thing with feathers. It wasn't quite the same as dragging a T-shirt over her head in the middle of the desert…but it was close, he thought, damned close.

He went back to her and drove his fingers into her piled curls. A bobby pin flew. A lock sprang free and landed in his hand. He found a few more pins and her hair spilled. Cupping her head, the curls spilling over his hands, he lowered his mouth to hers again.

And she died inside.

Picket fences inside her crumbled. All the walls around her heart gave out. As they had once, they did again...dropping, shattering, because the only thing that had ever really mattered was him. Liv met his tongue with hers, needing something so much more deep than the touch of his mouth to hers. She swallowed everything he was. The magic. The daring. And the broken boy inside that had only ever needed her.

She'd known that, had always known that. She'd only wanted him to know it, too, enough to stay with her.

But he was here now. His hands left her head to slick over her shoulders, down her arms. Their fingers twined at their sides. Their lips cleaved. She pressed herself against him, her breasts to his chest, and listened to his breathing change. It went ragged. She knew that sound. She knew it from long ago.

But when his fingers left hers to gather up the black silk sheath at her hips, something stuttered inside her. She closed her hands over his again. "Hunter. I'm not what I was."

He pulled back and there was something opaque about his eyes. She thought need glazed them, and a thrill shot through her. "You're everything you were," he murmured.

No, she thought desperately, no. She'd been nineteen and pregnant the last time he'd touched her. Now she was easing toward thirty. Her body had pushed another one into this world.

And somehow, he understood. He'd always been able to read her mind.

He kept pulling the sheath up her legs. Over her hips, over her shoulders, over her head. She wore a black strapless bra beneath it, something she wouldn't have bothered with all those years ago. She wore black panties that he hooked one thumb into at her hip. He tugged them down.

"I have scars, too," he said against her mouth. "But none that gave life, Livie. None that gave me all I didn't know I needed."

Her knees gave out. He caught her up in his arms again and buried his face between her breasts as he carried her to the bedroom, somehow tugged her panties over one ankle as he did.

He didn't lay her on the bed. He flowed with her. They landed there together and he rolled and she rolled with him. They had been apart long enough, she thought desperately. Now they needed to be together. Skin to skin. Connected. Somehow she was on top of him. She found the buttons of his shirtfront with one hand.

"You used to make this easier on me," she said against his mouth, struggling with them. There were too many.

"You never dressed me up as a Southern dandy before." But his hand followed hers, popping buttons.

She found the fly on his trousers and tugged it down.

"Why, Scarlet, how brazen you've become." He licked her tongue with his.

"Scarlet's asleep downstairs. I'm Louise. The madame."

"Who can't be bought."

"Except with your promises."

He flipped her over onto her back and caught the front of her bra in his hand, yanking it down until her breasts spilled. "What promise do you want, Louise?"

She wouldn't whimper. "Don't leave me."

"I never wanted to the first time."

It wasn't an answer. It wasn't a promise. But then his mouth closed over her nipple. And everything inside her surged there, to the point where his tongue tweaked her skin.

He left her to shrug out of his shirt and step out of his trousers. And it was agony. When he came back to her, he reached behind her and unhooked her bra. And then it was as it had always been as he settled himself on top of her again, two souls linked by flesh, two hearts pounding together with only skin between them. Just when Liv thought the pain of remembering, of not having, would kill her, he drove into her, deep, without apology or prelude, coming home.

Her breath tore out of her. "I love you," she said.

She listened hard before things shattered inside her, but she didn't think he answered.

Chapter 13

As the holiday week wound down toward New Year's, Liv told herself she was floating on air. And she almost believed it. Everything was perfect. Vicky was happy. Hunter was content as she'd ever known him to be. Even Kiki seemed mellow.

And in eight more days she was going to lose Hunter all over again.

She'd all but pleaded with him not to leave her again in that moment of near desperation when they'd finally made love. He hadn't really answered. She couldn't—wouldn't—ask him again. Her pride was something thorny jamming her throat, refusing to let the words get past.

He spoke to Pritch more and more often on the phone these days. He paced while he did it. She recognized the signs. He was prowling.

As she lay sprawled on top of him, three nights after the party, their skin damp and dewy, he kissed her temple and eased her onto her back so he could sit up. Liv found her fingers trailing down his arm for one last touch before she deliberately pulled her hand back. She curled it into a fist beneath the sheets.

"I'm bone tired tonight, babe," he murmured. "If I stay here one minute longer, I'm afraid I'll fall asleep."

By unspoken accord they'd kept the change in their relationship from Vicky. If she found him in Liv's bed in the morning, she would...expect things. And, Liv was sure, it would devastate her when she eventually realized she wouldn't have a "normal" mom and dad after all.

"I could set the alarm," she offered, then she winced. More begging.

"I don't want to take the chance." He stood from the bed and looked around for the sweatpants she'd ripped off him hours before.

Why wouldn't he stay with her? she wondered desperately. *Because he didn't want her to expect things, either.* Liv rolled over onto her side. She listened to him dress again. He leaned down to kiss her one more time...then he was gone.

She balled her pillow up and clutched it to her chest. It was a long while before Liv realized that she was crying silently.

Hunter ripped his sweatpants off again when he reached his attic room, wadding them up, throwing them angrily against the wall. This was asinine. Sneaking down to her room at night as though he was doing something wrong. Sliding out again before his daughter could realize he was in love with her mother. Why the hell wouldn't Livie let the child know what was going on?

If it was a marriage license she wanted, he was willing to give it to her. But she was still protecting Vicky from him, he thought, his gut seizing. Nothing had really changed at all.

He tried to sleep the last few hours until dawn and did a poor job of it. At five-thirty he gave up and went downstairs to the kitchen for coffee. He got there just as Kiki was turning on the pot. She glanced over her shoulder when she heard the door swish open.

"Well. Look what the cat dragged in."

"Long night."

Kiki wandered over to the walk-in refrigerator and opened it, pulling out trays and piling them on the counters. "It must be exhausting, trying to squeeze the rest of your life into a few remaining days.''

He had his cell phone out and was ready to tap in Pritch's number. Pritch was in North Carolina and would be awake in the East Coast time zone. Instead of doing it, Hunter narrowed his eyes at his friend. ''What's that supposed to mean?''

''You're leaving again.''

''Well, what the hell did you expect?''

''I'm not sure my expectations have anything to do with it. But you should probably be aware that I've kept that dull knife ready for you.''

Hunter felt temper seep into his blood. It felt like acid. ''Maybe you ought to consider using it on your partner.''

That startled her. Kiki stopped kneading dough to stare at him. ''Why would I want to do that? I can't run this place by myself. I don't do people.''

He put the phone down hard on the table. ''Tell me something. How come I always get cast in the role of bad guy in this situation?''

Kiki recovered. ''Because you always leave.''

''I have a job!'' He roared it.

Kiki wasn't intimidated in the least. She bellied up to him, nose to nose. ''Next Thursday? NASCAR's season doesn't start up until February nineteenth!''

''She doesn't want me to stay!''

Kiki's jaw dropped. She snapped it shut again and backed off. ''You're an imbecile.'' But her voice had lost force.

''She won't let us be a family, damn it!'' And until he said it aloud, he didn't realize how much—how really much—that hurt him. It ate at him inside.

Kiki's expression softened. ''She's scared, Hunter.''

''She's holding the same old grudges.''

''Because you haven't given her anything to sweep them away with.''

''You're doing it again. Putting it on me.''

''You're the man. You're supposed to take charge of things. Isn't that what you did when you dragged her off to bed after the party?''

She always saw too damned much, Hunter thought. He didn't bother to deny it. He combed fingers through his hair. "Well, maybe I'm scared, too."

He was so scared, he thought, that when she'd told him she still loved him, he hadn't been able to answer. He was scared spitless that she was going to shove him right the hell out of her life again because she was doing nothing to invite him to stay. Because she might be loving him with her body again, but she was still keeping her soul safe and clear from him.

He looked at Kiki, lost in a brief moment of vulnerability. "What am I supposed to do about this?"

She shook her head helplessly in a rare moment of her own. "Let me think about it."

"Well, think fast," he growled. "The clock's ticking."

"I know," she said quietly. "I know."

The next day Hunter remembered that there really was no way to anticipate Livie Slade. She'd always been able to throw him curve balls, and her routines with the inn were no exception.

They'd been able to steal away for a few brief hours in the early afternoon because Vicky was off playing with Mandy Singapore. He watched from the bed as Liv rose, naked, and stretched. Things inside him heated up all over again.

"Let me get this straight," he said, because he really didn't want to think about what she did to him. "On Thanksgiving you ship everyone out. On Christmas you open up for the whole town. And on New Year's Eve you do…nothing."

"Right." She bent and picked up a pair of lacy panties from the floor. Hunter tried not to watch.

"Why?" he asked.

"We're not that kind of establishment. You've seen the kind of guests we attract. Old biddies, young families." She stepped into the panties and dragged them up her hips.

His tongue hit the roof of his mouth and tried to stay there. There were so many unanswered issues still between them, she had his gut tied in knots…and he still wanted her beyond sense. "There were those traveling Lotharios," he said finally.

Liv felt a grin tug at her mouth. The band of twenties-something men who had been so avid to hear Hunter's racing stories had turned out to be a handful, trying to sneak women into their rooms repeatedly. "Well, they're not here this week. We have a mother with her teenage son, three pairs of newly-weds and a couple celebrating their fiftieth. None of whom would be inclined to trip the light fantastic. The newlyweds will probably hole up in their rooms. They've barely left them for days, anyway."

"We'll do it, then."

Liv stopped dressing and stared at him, surprised. "Do what? Hole up?"

"Actually, I was thinking of tripping the light fantastic."

"You want to do something for New Year's Eve?"

"That's what I'm getting at, yeah. Can you get one of those girls from town to hang out here for a few hours to keep an eye on the place while you're gone? I'll even pay her from my gobs of money."

The money he earned through a career that was going to take him away from her again. Liv pushed the pain down deep inside her. "What about Vicky?"

"I meant all three of us." He pulled air into his chest. "A real family outing."

Yearning swept her. Liv started to shake her head, to tell him no. She didn't want one more precious family night to remember after he took off again. It would hurt too much. She'd never be able to face another New Year's Eve without the memories eating her alive. Thanksgiving and Christmas were going to be bad enough, if he didn't return for more of them.

"We could even drag Kiki along with us," he suggested. "Does she have plans?"

Liv shook her head, trying to clear it. "I don't know. She hasn't mentioned anything about her personal life lately." Liv doubted if she would have heard her if she had. She'd been too caught up in her own.

"So ask her."

"I…okay. Sure." Yes, Liv realized, she *did* want this. One last perfect night. "I've got to go pick up Vicky," she said before her heart could take over her good sense entirely.

"That's my cue." He threw his legs over the side of the bed and stood.

"Um. I suppose."

"Can't have our daughter figuring out that her mom and dad are an item."

Liv felt heartache building in her chest again. "I'm just not sure what that would accomplish, Hunter."

"A sense of family, maybe?"

"Except we're not." The words were out before she could grab them back. She wanted them to be. Oh, God, how she wanted it! But Pritch had called four times today—and those were only the calls she knew about.

"Right." Hunter snapped out the single word as if he was flicking a whip.

Liv winced. "I'm open to discussion if you disagree."

"Livie, when it comes to that child, you have never *once* been open to discussion." He started grabbing up his own clothes.

"That's not true!" She was stung.

She watched him visibly calm himself down again. He wasn't going to rise to the bait. He never did anymore. Not really.

She was almost itching for a good fight. For a shoutfest so she could howl out her misery over him leaving. Again.

"Go pick her up," he said more mildly. "I'll be cleared out of here by the time you get back."

"Right." She thought she spoke, but the word was barely a croak. Liv headed for the door.

Vicky was waiting at the curb when she finally got to the Singapore home fifteen minutes later, and she was bouncing up and down on her heels impatiently.

"What's up?" Liv asked as the little girl spilled into the back seat of the car.

Vicky fastened her seat belt and crossed her arms over her chest. "Nothing."

Something, Liv thought, making a U-turn and heading toward home again. "Did you and Mandy fight again?"

"No." A pause. "She is really just too stupid for words."

"Why? What did she do now?"

"It's what she *said.*"

Liv took a breath and worked on it a little more. "Which was?"

"That if Hunter was really my dad, you'd…like, be sleeping with him or something."

Liv's heart whipped into her throat and almost choked her. "That's not necessarily true. Lots of parents live apart."

"He lives *with* us, Mom, in case you didn't notice."

"Not for much longer." More words she hadn't meant to say. The closer they got to January, Liv thought, the more she fell apart.

Vicky went very still. "What do you mean?"

"He has to race, honey."

"Yeah, but that's just on weekends."

"It takes him all week to get the car ready."

"So he's *leaving* us?"

The pain in her heart was like a mushroom cloud, swelling and lifting to fill all of her, Liv thought helplessly. She hadn't explained this clearly enough in the beginning, she thought. Neither she nor Hunter had. She pulled the car over to the side of the road. "Yes."

"Forever?"

"I'm sure he'll visit whenever he can." He was good at that, she thought bitterly.

Vicky was quiet for a long time. "So Mandy was right."

"No," Liv said vehemently. "Mandy was wrong. Hunter is your dad. His work makes him travel a lot so…so we're not always together."

She watched in the rearview mirror as that stubborn little jaw came up and forward. "He needs to find another job."

Liv felt laughter grip her throat. She couldn't let it out because she knew it would sound crazed. She decided to change the subject. "By the way, do you have a hot date for New Year's Eve?"

The tactic almost worked. "I'm going to smooch up with Rhett again," she muttered. "Might be the last chance I get."

Liv took a deep breath. "Then you'll have to share him with me."

"You're going to *kiss* him?"

"I still love him, baby. I'm going to miss him as much as you do."

Vicky scowled. "This is bad."

"Could be worse. He could never have come back at all." And she knew then that that *would* have been worse, because there had been a hole in her life from the moment he had walked away. Even filling it partially again was better than having it gape.

Vicky thought about that and nodded. "So where are we going on New Year's?"

"I don't know yet. I need to see if Mandy's sister can watch over the inn." Denise Singapore was seventeen, frantically saving money for Radcliffe next fall, and had been one of the girls she'd hired to serve at the party.

"Just as long as it's not *Mandy,*" Vicky said.

"She's a little young for the job."

"I'm never going to speak to her again."

"Two days this time?"

"Maybe three. Does Aunt Kiki have any really good, smelly cheese?"

"You'll have to ask her." Liv pulled back into traffic.

When they got back to the inn, she called Denise and got an okay from her to work that night. Then she left the office and cornered Kiki in the kitchen.

"Do you have plans for New Year's Eve?" she asked her.

Kiki was busy putting together the last of the goodies for tea. "Yep. With my cat."

"When did you get a cat?" Liv was startled.

"Spinsters have them. It seemed only fitting."

"Have you sworn off the male race again?"

"You might have noticed if you weren't so besotted in love." She shoved a tray of tarts into the oven.

"I'm not in love."

"Sorry. My mistake. That rosy glow to your cheeks must have thrown me off." She closed the oven door and turned back to her. "Either that, or the agony in your eyes."

Liv felt her air catch and a headache instantly bloom. "Kiki,

I don't want to talk about this." She'd done enough of that with Vicky this afternoon to last her a lifetime, she thought.

"You're going to send him away again, aren't you?"

"*Send him away?*" Liv choked. "When have you ever known that man to stay put long enough for anyone to have such an opportunity?"

"You managed it once."

"That was different."

"How?"

Liv floundered. "I was pregnant."

"And now the result of that pregnancy is out in the barn harassing Bourne." Kiki shook her head. "That one won't fly. Keep trying."

"I had to give her a life!"

"Which you've done. Go on."

"*He doesn't want to stay with me now anymore than he did then!*" Liv shouted, and felt her face flame. She covered her cheeks with her hands and sat down quickly at the table.

Kiki came to stand beside her. "He didn't want to leave then, Liv," she said quietly. "And I'm not sure he wants to now."

"Then why is he making so many plans to go? He talks to Pritch a dozen times a day!"

"He thinks you want him to."

Liv stared at her. "No. Did he tell you that?"

Kiki turned away abruptly. "Tell you what. I'll be damned if *I'm* going to kiss *you* to protect *him.*"

Liv found a strangled laugh hit her throat. She'd finally told Kiki about that. "That's okay. I don't want you to." She stood shakily.

Kiki watched her go, almost satisfied. But what each of them wanted was only part of the dilemma. As the man had said, he had a job to go to. And that simple fact was going to break Liv's heart in two this time.

For the first time in her life, Kiki faced a problem she admitted she might not be able to solve.

Liv watched Hunter escort Vicky into the Connor at half past six on New Year's Eve. He had made dinner reservations for seven o'clock, so they'd have a drink first in the Spirit Room. Vicky was primed for being included in such a grown-up night, Liv thought, things inside her softening. She'd bought her a new dress for the occasion—red, of course, a whisper-soft velvet A-line with long, demure sleeves. She wore white hose and black patent-leather flats and pigtails—she'd been partial to the style since Hunter had given her the nickname.

How would Vicky cope when he was gone?

"You're doing it again," Kiki murmured from beside her.

Liv glanced at her. It was a measure of her love for her friend that Liv would even consider being seen in public with her. When Kiki was dolled up, Kiki was devastatingly beautiful. Tonight she wore an austere black pantsuit with huge gold buttons on the jacket. The jacket flared just a little at her hips and cut low at the top, showing a hint of cleavage. It was chic and sleek. She needed no other adornment. Her hair was an onyx waterfall, her features just chiseled enough to be perfect.

"What do you mean?" Liv murmured.

"You're foisting your own worries off onto your daughter again," Kiki said.

Liv hung back a little to finish this before they joined Hunter and Vicky. "No, I'm not. Why would you say that?"

"You're wondering how she's going to react when he goes. It was all over your face while you watched them."

Liv flushed. "Your IQ is one of my least favorite things about you."

"Live with it. I'm just telling you that when he goes next week, she'll adapt. They'll probably talk on the phone every day. She'll write to him and send him things she did in school. She'll wait with bated breath until he returns again. You, on the other hand, will curse the ground he walks on because he can't be a traditional dad anymore than you can be a traditional mom."

Liv felt her stomach cramp. "This isn't the time for this."

"You brought it up."

"No, I didn't!" She blew out her breath. "So where does this leave us?"

"Untraditional and loving it?" Kiki stepped forward again.

Then she looked back. "Liv, don't be stupid and narrow-minded twice in the same lifetime."

Liv froze. She wanted to swear at her, but Kiki was already headed for their table.

Hunter had ordered champagne and a ginger ale for Vicky by the time Liv recovered and joined them. He lifted his flute in a toast. "To a whole new world."

Vicky gulped ginger ale. "What does that mean?"

He tugged one of her pigtails. "That I wasn't with you last New Year's."

"So where were you?"

Liv didn't want to know.

"Monte Carlo. With Monique Shaughnessy." Then he winked at Liv, telling her it was a lie.

She didn't want to care.

They were seated on time, and Vicky picked apart the menu. Liv shrugged at Hunter apologetically. "Blame Kiki. She's spoiled her from the time she was born. Jarred baby food never passed her lips."

Hunter raised a brow at Kiki. "You're kidding, right?"

"No godchild of mine is going to eat any vegetable I didn't strain myself." Kiki put her menu aside. "I'm going to give Frisco a chance to earn his stripes with the sea bass."

"Who's Frisco?" Hunter asked.

Liv rolled her eyes and shook her head. "Don't go there," she warned.

"The devil incarnate," Kiki said.

"He's the chef here," Vicky explained. "And Aunt Kiki hates him. He doesn't know an ion from his patootie."

"His entry beat her berry cobbler at the fair last Fourth of July," Liv said, sotto voce.

Kiki glared at her.

Hunter winced. "Ouch. He must be good."

Kiki ground her teeth together. "He cheated."

Frisco Carre came out of the kitchen a few minutes later when he learned his adversary was dining at the Connor. Kiki abruptly shoved back her chair and went off to the kitchen with him.

"Well, that's interesting," Hunter murmured.

In the end, Kiki had no valid complaint with her sea bass. She claimed it was because she had contributed to its creation. They laughed, they talked, and the evening passed in a blur. Liv was sorry. With a sinking sensation she watched Hunter take the check. She'd decided that she wanted this night, this one last special night, to last forever.

"Let's go, squirt," Kiki said, standing to dangle Hunter's keys from her fingertips.

Liv frowned. "Why do you have them?"

"Because you're not invited where we're going," Kiki replied.

Liv felt her forehead pull into a frown. "Where's that?"

"To my apartment for a girls' sleepover."

Liv didn't know who to narrow her eyes at—Kiki or Hunter. Or Vicky. "What's up and who's behind this?"

Hunter looked mystified. "Not me. I gave her my keys to take Vicky home so we could go back to the bar and dance a bit. That ends my involvement."

She believed him, Liv thought. "Then how are we supposed to get home?"

"Stay here," Kiki suggested, standing. "You might as well. I'll have the squirt all night."

Vicky was practically twitching, she was so beside herself. "We surprised them, Aunt Kiki! We really did!"

"Told you so," Kiki replied. "Come on, let's get your coat."

"Wait, wait," Liv protested. She looked at Vicky. "You need a toothbrush. Clean underwear."

Kiki held up a purse that Liv had earlier considered to be very oversize for her outfit. "It's taken care of." She looked between them, her gaze shifting. "Fix this, you two. I've about lost patience with heart-to-heart talks in my kitchen."

Liv frowned. "What did she mean by that?" she asked when Kiki and Vicky were gone.

Hunter stood as well. "Beats me. What do you think the odds are that we can still get a room here overnight and not have to worry about walking home?"

"Slim to none. Unless Kiki thought of that, too."

Kiki had. Twenty minutes later Hunter slid the room key into his trouser pocket.

"She's up to something," Liv murmured, dazed.

"Obviously."

"I don't have a toothbrush or clean underwear, either."

"I've known you too long to hold it against you."

She found herself staring at the tack—the copper eagle—on his tie. "Are we going upstairs now?" she asked hopefully. They had only a few days left together. She wanted to spend every second of them touching him, loving him, hoarding the memories so she would have something to cling to when he was gone.

But Hunter shook his head. "No, Livie. We're going to the bar. We're going to dance and sing Auld Lang Syne and we're going to trip the light fantastic. It's New Year's." His voice was husky.

Hers was a croak. "Oh. Okay. If you insist."

"*Then* we'll go upstairs."

It was delicious, she thought an hour later, swaying in his arms to the music. It was everything she'd dreamed of all those years ago. If she could have closed her eyes back then and made a wish the morning he'd left her—the morning after telling her about Pritch and Anaheim—she would have prayed that nine New Year's Eves later, they'd be dancing in each other's arms, sharing a child between them who was as bright as the sun. That Kiki would still be on the fringes of their lives, manipulating, analyzing, cooking with ions.

She didn't want it to end.

"Resolution time," Hunter said as the song ended.

Liv looked quickly at her watch. It was ten minutes before midnight. She felt dazed. She didn't know where the time had gone. "I never make them anymore."

"Because you always break them?" His hand found hers and he guided her back to their table.

She couldn't help thinking how different this night was from the first time she had met him here, more than three months ago. "Because I *always* keep them."

He laughed. The sound was rich and warm and touched her skin. "We're not so different, babe."

Something shuddered deep inside her. "I think we reached that conclusion Christmas night after the party."

He pulled her chair out for her, and she slid into it. Then he sat, as well, and leaned close to her. She saw something in his eyes, Liv thought. Some struggle. Some pain. She thought she saw fear, but this was a man who once dove headfirst off a cliff to catch an eagle.

"What?" she whispered.

"I love you, Livie Slade."

She didn't know where the tears came from. One moment, her eyes were fine. The next, they were ablaze. *He was going to stay.* She swallowed once, twice, trying to find her voice. And she gave it back, with all her soul. "I never stopped loving you, Hunter. Not one minute of one day you were gone."

He touched his forehead to hers. She thought she could die in that moment and have no regrets. Then he spoke again and reality rained through her.

"I called Montague today."

She couldn't think. The name rang a bell, a distant bell, but she couldn't quite put it into context with what they had just been talking about. Then she remembered. His lawyer. "Why?"

"I dropped the custody thing. I don't want to take her away from you."

This was good, she thought hectically. It was everything she'd wanted three long months ago. And things inside her went as cold as stone. "Thank you. I...that's good."

"You'll let me see her again." It wasn't a question.

Liv tried on a shaky smile. "Of course. If I didn't, she'd murder me in my sleep."

Hunter nodded. "I need to drive back to California on Tuesday. But I can be here again by Friday. Okay?"

He seemed to be waiting for something, but she didn't know what it was. "Yes. Yes, of course."

He straightened away from her and let out a heavy breath. "Good."

Liv fought frantically to make her brain work. Why was disappointment such an icy feeling? It chilled her from the inside out. "You can see Vicky whenever you're here. I won't—I can't—she loves you," she finished feebly. And why did *that* make pain flash over his face?

"Peace?" he asked shortly.

"Yes. Peace."

From somewhere distant, the crowd was chanting down numbers. Ten-nine-eight... Liv rallied. "Happy New Year, Hunter."

He grabbed her and dragged her to her feet. "I wanted to be upstairs right now. Inside you."

"Too late." Her words were breathy and barely out of her mouth before he wrapped his arms around her.

"Then I'll have to settle for this."

And she would settle, too, Liv thought. Because the alternative was to go back to living without him entirely. *I love you, Livie Slade.* She clung to that as she met his mouth. She tasted all the heat of him, that sizzling intent that was Hunter Hawk-Cole alone. This was as good as it was ever going to get, she thought helplessly. It was too late to turn back time. But...as always...he would return to her.

Now. Again. Here and there. She remembered how she had always felt before, years before, until she'd decided she couldn't live with it anymore. *They had tonight.* That sentiment had always gotten her through.

"Let's go upstairs," she whispered against his mouth.

It wasn't until he chuckled that she realized they were already halfway across the bar to the exit. She didn't remember riding up in the elevator, either.

They hurried down the hall. When they reached their room, he backed her up against the door. He was crazed, he thought. He had never wanted her more than he did right here, right now.

His fingers found the blue silk fabric at her hips and dug into it while he drowned in her mouth. There was a pounding in his head, in his groin, counterpoints keeping tempo. Yes, they had peace now, but he didn't want peace. He wanted more.

He framed her face in his hands even as she caught his hips, holding him against her. Then she groaned and tore her mouth from his. She tilted her head back, giving him her throat, and he feasted there. He tasted her strength and all her heartbreaks on her skin. He wanted to steep himself in the first because maybe that would make him strong, too. And he wanted to heal the rest.

She drove her hand into his pocket. "Key," she rasped. "Hunter…we're in public."

"Yeah." There was no one else in the hall, but he dug for the key, as well. Found it. Jabbed it into the lock. Pushed the door open. They spilled inside.

When he turned to lock it again and looked back, she was wrestling her dress over her head. He'd wanted to do that for her, and couldn't complain. He went at her fast, gathering her up in his arms, angling them both back toward the bed. They fell there, her fingers frantic at his belt.

"This is how we always wanted it to be, right?" he said against her throat, his mouth sliding lower. "You have the life you want, I have mine."

"We got our dreams." She finally freed his belt, went for his zipper.

"We're happy." His hands covered her breasts, molding them, then, impatient, he tugged one cup of her bra down to nuzzle there as well. "The way only we can be."

"This is perfect," she whispered, pushing his trousers down his hips.

"We'll meet in the middle." He finally reached behind her to unclasp her bra. His mouth fell to one nipple. The other. Not enough. Not nearly enough. He dragged himself away from her to stand and step out of his pants, to wrestle out of his shirt. He was only sane, safe, whole, when he was inside her.

When he leaned back over her, she closed her hand around his hardness. "Mine. Whenever you come back to me."

"Every moment I can."

She pushed him down on his back and straddled him. "Please," she whispered. "Please mean that. Every moment."

"Every moment."

She sank down on top of him, taking him in. And it was as it had always been, lifetimes ago. And now that they had found each other again, it was as though the rest of her spirit had come home. He filled her, gently at first, then urgently as they started to move together. And when the crest came, she sobbed his name. She collapsed on top of him and heard him say her name, as well, like a prayer.

And neither of them could understand, as their hearts slowed, why they still felt hollow.

Chapter 14

Liv found herself back in Ingrid Small's office three days later.

"Coffee?" the woman asked. "Or arsenic?"

Liv grinned wanly and folded herself into one of the chairs. "None of the above. Not this time." Her stomach was roiling. She figured coffee might come right back up. "I still don't understand why this is necessary."

"Because Woodingham runs a tight ship. If you don't mind, I'm going to drink without you." Ingrid got up and went to the coffeepot. "Great party, by the way."

Liv's mind spiraled back to Christmas, and she returned the compliment. "Great costume. I was surprised to see you."

"I thought I'd stop by and check the carpet for bloodstains."

Liv managed to laugh. "Everything really did turn out fine. But..."

Ingrid took her coffee back to her desk and waited expectantly, her brows lifted.

"You said something that night that I didn't understand," Liv continued. "That the judge was banking on it?"

"Ah. That." Ingrid sipped and sat back, crossing her legs. "Well, it was clear three months ago that the two of you were either going to kill each other or turn into a family. I just think she was gambling on the latter.''

It was more or less what Kiki had said. Liv felt a spasm in the area of her heart. Kiki had also said that when they parted this time, it would be forever.

"One way or the other," Ingrid continued, "Woodingham knew her job would be over. You'd either resolve this between the two of you—which you have—or one of you would have been tried for murder. And that would have been on the criminal docket, not in her courtroom."

"She's wily," Liv said halfheartedly. Then she frowned. "Why didn't you tell me any of this back then?"

"I did. Sort of. I warned you she was unorthodox. Anyway, she wants to make sure things are nice and tidy before she lets you guys off the hook from having to appear in front of her again on Monday."

"She wants a...what did you call it?"

"A Consent Order. It just memorializes everything you and Mr. Hawk-Cole agreed to between yourselves. In effect, there has to be some final paper filed to close out Hunter's petition. Most judges would have settled for a Stipulation of Dismissal. Woodingham wants your agreement drawn in blood. She doesn't want to see you in her courtroom again."

Liv wasn't eager to ever cross paths with the judge again, either. "I can live with that."

"Okay, then. Montague drew up the order and had it hand delivered to me this morning. I've read it over for any loopholes, and there aren't any. It's safe for you to sign. After that, I'll drop it off in Woodingham's chambers tomorrow morning when I'm in court." She slid the paper across her desk toward Liv.

Liv took it with shaking hands. This was *good*, she told herself again. It was the best Vicky could hope for. It was the only way this could be resolved. Hunter couldn't stay planted, and a child needed a steady, solid home. So she would raise Vicky in Jerome and he would come back to visit...whenever.

She read the terms of the order.

It said that visitation would be worked out amicably between the two of them when Hunter could make it back to Arizona.

He agreed to give her a two-day heads-up sign so she could effectively clear Vicky's schedule—or, in the event that she couldn't, she could let him know before he made the trip. She agreed to let Vicky spend at least a month traveling with him on the NASCAR circuit in the summer. They both knew Liv would be going along.

He'd spend his off-season with them again. At least, Liv thought, feeling dead inside, until another Monique Shaughnessy came along...or until he got itchy with the routine.

She'd declined child support. She couldn't stomach taking the money he earned from the career that kept him away from them. On that issue, she'd flat-out refused to compromise. So Hunter was setting up three separate funds for Vicky—one for college, the other for use when she got out of college. The third was a household fund for red bridles.

Liv signed her name on the bottom line and pushed it back to Ingrid. "That's it?"

"That's it," Ingrid agreed. "You know, I'm relieved. For a while, there, I really believed we'd end up in appellate court over this."

Liv let out her breath. "It wouldn't have solved anything. When Hunter wants something...he wants something."

"He's one hell of a man," Ingrid said honestly. "I'm looking forward to seeing him race again, especially after he blew off the end of last season. I know that surprised both Montague and me."

Had it surprised her? Liv wondered. No, not deep down, she realized now. He'd wanted something, she thought again, and he'd always known he would go back to the cars later.

She stood a little unsteadily. "Thanks for all your help."

Ingrid stood, as well, to shake her hand. "Take this in the spirit it's intended, but I hope we don't meet again, unless it's at another of your parties. That really was a fun, fantastic night."

"Thank you."

The lawyer frowned. "I've got to admit, though, that I had a hell of a hangover that next morning. And I really didn't drink much."

Liv bit her lip. Hunter had admitted later that he'd even added whiskey to the eggnog, just to be on the safe side with the kitchen disaster. "Sorry about that."

Ingrid shrugged. "Everyone needs to kick up their heels now and again. I had fun. I'll be there again next year for sure."

But Liv wondered if Hunter would be around to spike the eggnog. Ingrid might just be disappointed.

She made it back in plenty of time to see him off, even with a side trip to Mustang Ridge to collect Vicky from her riding lesson. He'd wanted to leave by five o'clock, Liv knew. He'd drive all night and hit Pacific Palisades well before dawn. Half of her wanted him to spend the night—*one more night.* The other half knew that having him leave her bed before dawn and hit the highway would kill her.

By unspoken accord they'd agreed that having him go right before dinner was best.

When Vicky and Liv entered the kitchen, Kiki was just rattled enough that Liv forgot her own pain and stared at her in pure surprise. "What's wrong?" she asked. She looked wildly at the sink. No geysers this time.

"Don't you *ever* do that to me again!" Kiki burst out.

"Do what?"

"I'm going to go find Dad," Vicky said, and ran off. Liv's heart cramped. *One last time.*

"Don't ever leave me to do tea by myself!" Kiki almost shouted.

Liv frowned. "I had to. I had to sign that thing before Hunter could leave, and it was the only opening Ingrid had. You've done tea before, albeit rarely."

"Well, I don't like it." Kiki began banging baking trays into the sink. "Besides, you've *always* done tea. It's your thing. You always used to find a way never to miss it. Now every time I turn around, you're running off."

Yes, Liv thought. Somehow, lately, other things had become more important. "I still don't understand why you're so upset. Did someone take offense to your photon theory?"

"Yes," Kiki ground out from between clenched teeth.

Liv couldn't believe it. They had a very mild group of guests this week. "Who?"

"Frisco Carre."

She felt her brows climb. "Frisco-the-chef-from-the-Connor?"

"He said he was checking out the competition. Just sailed right in as smug as you please."

"Well." Liv couldn't think of one single thing to say to that.

"And he made *suggestions*."

"What kind of suggestions?"

"A little butter between the phyllo of the tarts."

Liv almost grinned. "How dare he."

"That's what *I* said."

"What's going on down here?" Hunter asked, coming into the kitchen. "I could hear you banging all the way up in my attic room, Kiki."

Kiki was in an exceptionally foul mood. "*My* attic room, buddy. And now it's time to adios, amigo. Next time around, you can damned well share her bed." She thrust a thumb at Liv. "I'm not coughing up my space."

"They don't do that," Vicky said, sailing into the room behind Hunter. "They're a mom and dad not together anymore."

The room pitched into silence.

Liv couldn't look at Hunter. She knew—she *knew*—her agony would be in her eyes. She couldn't look at Kiki because she knew Kiki would rue every word that had just come out of her mouth in temper, words that Vicky had overheard. She couldn't look at Vicky—because Vicky was right.

"Hey, pigtails," Hunter said finally. "What's up?"

"I brought your suitcase down." She turned to pull it through the door. It was almost as big as she was. Liv watched her bend over to slide it across the floor. She stopped at Hunter's feet.

"Throwing me out?" Hunter asked. His voice sounded odd, Liv thought. Tight.

"I'm a minor," she reminded him. "I've got no say in this." She crossed her arms over her chest. Her bottom lip was sticking out.

Liv wasn't sure she could identify the sound that came from Hunter's throat in response.

All she knew was that in the next moment, he was on his knees and Vicky was in his arms. And her own heart was cracking. She could feel it happening, in an ever-widening rift. Liv pressed a hand there against the pain.

"I told you how we're going to do this, pigtails," he said, his voice husky. "And why we have to."

She yanked free of him. "How much stupid money do you *need?*"

Liv watched him open his mouth and close it again. When he held his arms out to her again, Vicky burrowed back in.

"I'm just going to go home tomorrow to take care of some business. Then tomorrow night I'll fly to North Carolina and see Mr. Spikes. I'm only going to stay there for a day or two. Then I'll be back here on Friday. You and your mom are going to drive down to Phoenix and pick me up at the airport."

"What about your car?" Vicky sniffed.

"My car?" He looked at Liv, as though for guidance, she thought. She shrugged.

"Where's that going to be?" Vicky persisted.

"In the garage at my house in California."

"I like that car."

"I like it, too, pigtails."

"Can't you just leave it here?"

Hunter looked mystified. "Why?"

Then Liv understood. Vicky wanted to hold on to a piece of him. She herself had done it too many times to count.

"Well, if you have it," Vicky thought aloud, "then you could just drive straight back here from North Carolina. So maybe don't leave it in California."

Hunter rallied. "That would take at least two days, pigtails, even as fast as I drive. If I fly instead, that's two days I could be spending with you and your mom."

She thought about that. "You've got a point."

Hunter squeezed her tight one more time and stood. His eyes found Liv's. "I think on that note, I'd better go."

She nodded jerkily. Yes, she thought, oh, yes, please, before someone cried. "I'll walk you out."

She was vaguely aware of Kiki catching up Vicky before their daughter could follow them. She thought she heard her say something about talking to the guy in the parlor and telling him that his patootie was for the birds.

They went out to the garage. "She's going to…miss you," Liv said. Her voice cracked. "So much."

He swore, a dark sound under his breath. "This is what you were protecting her from."

Her eyes flew to his. "Yes."

"I didn't see it back then…I didn't know."

She believed that. Liv knew in her soul that he would never do a thing to hurt his daughter. If he had foreseen how painful this was going to be, he would have…well, at least he would have handled their war some other way. He wouldn't have moved in here.

"Livie, I still couldn't have turned away from the chance to know her," he said, as though reading her mind.

She understood that, too. "Hunter, just go. This is killing me."

"Ah, babe."

He held his arms out to her. She wanted to be like Vicky. She wanted to be able to melt right into them. She backed up jerkily instead. "See you Friday."

Pain creased his strong features, if only briefly. "I'll call you with the flight number as soon as I have it."

"Right." Liv fled back to the inn. Without a goodbye kiss. Without a lingering touch. She knew either one would shatter her.

She'd forgotten the agony. Or maybe she hadn't. Maybe it had never been this bad before. Because for the first time since she'd been fifteen years old, for the first time since he had graduated from high school, this time…*this time*…they'd spent every day together. This time he'd been every breath she'd drawn.

Liv wondered how she was ever going to live through this.

Six weeks later she knew the answer. She wouldn't. She just existed.

* * *

They had everything they wanted, Hunter reminded himself six weeks later as he sped down the track at Daytona.

She was the track from hell. She had killed men, and she would kill again. It was his dream to conquer her, something he had never done before. He'd finished second here last year. He had the lead now, 1.7 seconds over the driver behind him, with six laps to go.

This lady, this track from hell, *was his.*

"Kirby's on the apron," his spotter squawked in his ear. "You'll want to go high on turn three to avoid him."

"Can't do it," Hunter snapped. "Rowlands is on my tail. It'll cost me two-tenths if I go high, and he'll gain on me."

There was dead silence. Then the man pointed out the obvious. "He's going to have to go high, too, Hawk."

Of course he was, Hunter thought. Where the hell was his head? The same place it had been for nearly four hours now, for nearly five hundred miles. He was wondering if Vicky was watching and if his daughter knew he had the lead.

He wondered if Liv was beside her on the sofa in her sitting room, watching with her. He had talked to them last night. He called them every day. They had promised they would tune in for the race.

Counting down the last laps, that was all that mattered to him.

Vicky held nothing back so—if they really were watching—she'd be screaming him on. Liv would be...well, she'd be praying, he decided. That he would win, that he would come out of this alive. How did he know suddenly that she'd watched, she'd prayed, through every race of his whole career? It was a certainty in his gut, and it came from the look in her eyes months ago when he had first buried himself inside her again. That look had said she'd been with him through every race, through every year. It said that love—real love, true love—was something huge and never ending, something you couldn't turn off like a light switch, something that rode you and consumed you through season after season, month after month, decade after decade, whether you liked it or not, whether you were together or not.

His spotter shouted into his headset.

Hunter realized that he was coming up hard on Kirby. He veered around him, putting the man a lap down. Nothing but black track ahead of him now. Dinny Mason in the number six car was going into the far turn, but Dinny—not allowing for the now defunct Kirby—was actually the last man at the end of the line.

Five laps to go.

The crowd was going wild. Black and gold flags blurred in the corners of Hunter's vision. Their Hawk was back and he was returning in fine style. He was giving them what they wanted.

But it wasn't enough. What *he* wanted was to come out of this alive to go back to Arizona.

In seven years of racing, he had never once given any consideration to his life before, he realized, or to the end thereof. He'd never thought about dying. Because he'd never had anything to live for.

Hunter downshifted into the curve. Came out of it, slammed his foot hard onto the accelerator again. And flew. Four laps later he sailed by the green flag for the last time. The next time he came by this way, it would be the black-and-white checkered. The last lap.

He glanced at the nonexistent passenger seat again. Liv was there again.

"Faster and faster, Hunter?" she asked. "What are you trying to catch?"

"I'm not trying to catch. I'm trying to quench."

"Tell me what."

"Anger. The fury that came from being pushed place to place by people who didn't want me."

"We want you. We never pushed you away. But you're still going faster."

He was. According to his crew chief, who passed the news on over his headphones, Hunter had just drawn out his lead over Rowlands to 2.3 seconds.

"What's the finish line?" Livie asked him.

"You. It was always you."

"Then come home. You have pigtails who needs you."

"Do you need me, Livie?"

She didn't answer. Because, Hunter knew, he'd destroyed her heart again when he'd gone away this time. And maybe this time he'd hurt her more than she could stand.

Her voice was always strained whenever he talked to her on the phone. Vicky had said Liv was crabby.

Your work is just one more way of roaming.

And still, even knowing that, she'd let him go again, Hunter thought. Knowing what it would do to her, to Vicky, she'd let him go. And she waited for him to come home.

Home. Yeah, he thought, yeah, the inn had become home. It was the place where she always welcomed him back with open arms, in spite of the pain. It was the back kitchen door his daughter scampered through, holding no grudges for the time he had been gone.

He had everything he wanted, but he had nothing at all. Not when he was away from there. From them.

His car roared past the checkered flag. The fans were on their feet. He heard them chanting his name. And he knew where he was going now, knew what was at the finish line.

He downshifted. They'd want him to do a few donuts on his way to Victory Lane. He'd give them what they wanted.

How much stupid money do you need?

I never stopped loving you, Hunter. Not one minute of one day you were gone.

He yanked the car around, drove onto the infield. Tore it up with his tires, going in tight circles. Then he stopped the car right there.

The crowd went silent. This wasn't the way it was supposed to go. He was supposed to drive into Victory Lane. Talk to the newscasters. Climb up onto the roof of his car, wave a champagne bottle. Maybe open it and let it spew on the heads of his crew. Shout, jump up and down, carry on with happiness.

Hunter thought maybe he ought to do the roof-of-the-car thing after all.

He pulled himself through the window there in the infield. The crowd was chanting his name. They figured he was breaking custom just because he was back. They didn't know he was leaving them again.

He climbed up on top of the car. Raised his arms in victory. Waited for the camera crews to zoom in on him there. Looked into one of the cameras.

"I'm coming home," he told her, and prayed like hell she really was watching. "To stay."

Vicky was doing somersaults down the center of Liv's sitting room. But she went still when Hunter stopped his car in the infield. "He says only hot dogs do that! Only hot dogs stop out there and do all that spinning stuff."

Liv was staring at his mouth. Trying to read his words. "He never won Daytona before," she murmured absently.

"Is this what he meant about monkeys on his back?"

"Mmm. Maybe. Probably."

"Hey, what's he saying?"

Liv stood unsteadily. Her heart was going crazy in her chest. "He says come to the airport."

She shouldn't have brought Vicky, Liv thought five hours later, cooling her heels at the gate. She couldn't be sure he'd said what she thought he'd said, and there had been too many moments of hope before. Moments that had passed and withered.

If he didn't do this, if he didn't come, it would destroy their child, just as it had destroyed her back in the days when she had been little more than a child herself.

If he didn't come...

The flight from Daytona was landing. They watched it hit the runway.

"Mom, are you *sure?*" Vicky asked again.

Of course she wasn't.

It was half past eight on a Sunday night—but whether he showed up or he didn't, Liv had already given up on the idea of sending Vicky to school tomorrow. There would either be a reunion...or there would be heartbreak.

Maybe he just wasn't on this flight. That was a possibility. This flight had left Florida at ten past five, Eastern Time. He might not have been able to make it.

There was another flight coming in from Daytona at four in the morning. They'd have to wait for that one, too, if he wasn't on this one. She'd have to be sure.

Had he meant tonight? Now? Immediately? Yes, she thought, because when Hunter wanted something…he wanted something. He would either be here tonight…or he really wasn't coming back to stay at all.

She watched through the window as the arriving plane taxied up to the gate. She couldn't breathe. Passengers began spilling through. Then she heard Vicky's cry and she saw him.

"Dad!"

Vicky ran. Leaped. He caught her in the air. And held her. And then, over her shoulder, he found Liv's eyes.

He didn't say anything. He waited. His gaze was a question. *Okay?*

Liv nodded. Then she finally let herself cry.

She started to run for him, but he was already carrying Vicky in her direction. They collided. Somehow he found another free arm to hold her, too.

He'd known she'd be here, Hunter thought. She was the only one who'd ever noticed when he was gone.

"Don't cry," he said against her hair.

"Mom, this is *good!*" Vicky squealed. She was already wriggling for Hunter to let her down.

"Yes," Liv croaked. She framed his face in her hands. "I can't believe you did this. You really did this." Was this for real? She was afraid to believe.

"Ah, God, Livie, I can't do it—the whole circuit—without you."

Her heart stuttered. "So you just came back to get us? So we can travel with you?" He'd offered her that before, eight and a half years ago, and she'd had to say no then, too. Because she still couldn't spend Vicky's childhood dragging her around the country.

"Sometimes," he said vaguely. "Maybe. Hey, pigtails, where are you going?" She was sliding off.

"You know," Vicky said, looking back, "I always heard airport food was awful, but I'm thinking, why not give it a try?

Do you smell those sausage and peppers? I think it's coming from over there.'' She pointed.

"Not now!" Liv and Hunter chided together.

Vicky held her hands up in a truce and sat down.

Liv gave up on her pride. She clung to his shirtfront. "Please. Don't tell me this is just a visit between races. You said…" She trailed off. She couldn't bear to repeat the words she'd seen on television.

"I have gobs of money, Liv."

Her lip curled.

"More than I need."

She snarled.

"I was thinking I could stay in NASCAR if I own a race team and still be home, at least more often than not. With you."

She was shaking inside. "I'm not enough." Then she thought of another protest. "You're doing it for Vicky." Why was she arguing with him? Because she had to be sure.

"I'm doing it because the two of you are my finish line. Livie." He pressed his forehead to hers, as he had on New Year's Eve. "We're never going to be normal."

A laugh choked her throat. "I hear a but in there somewhere."

"This time you do," he agreed. He waited a beat. "But…we can give it half a shot."

She watched him bemusedly. "What do you mean?"

"I should have done this eight years ago." Then, to her amazement, he went down on one knee. In the middle of the airport. "Livie Slade, will you marry me?"

She sank to her knees with him, her hands diving into his glorious hair, her heart gallivanting. "Here? Now?"

"Do they have preachers at airports?"

Her heart exploded. "I don't think so. But we might want to find one soon. There's something I have to tell you."

Epilogue

The NASCAR awards ceremony had never seen anything quite like Vicky Hawk-Cole. She sailed up to the podium in her red velvet dress and pigtails with red ribbons. Then she took the trophy and did a perfect imitation of her father. She lifted it high and tucked her chin and said, laconically, "Thanks."

The audience applauded bemusedly and exchanged looks. The emcee lowered the microphone for her a little.

"My dad isn't here tonight," she said into it. "That's because he and my mom are at the hospital having a baby. Like this very minute, I think. So you get me instead."

There was a startled silence. Then, in the front row, Pritch Spikes threw back his head and laughed.

The man he'd mentored, had brought along from a fishing-boat hand and gave a ride to nine years ago, had been startling people and besting him all season. Hawk had bailed on him early in the season to start a rival NASCAR ownership out of the blue. That team had done better than Pritch's. But Hunter had also driven for Pritch three times out of loyalty—on long weekends when Vicky had a break from school. He'd won all three of those races.

Now, tonight, he was collecting trophies...by proxy.

"I get to be here tonight to take this award on behalf of my dad because my Aunt Kiki came with me," Vicky said. "And Bourne, even though he says cities give him hives. But my dad had them once, and I happen to know they go down with aloe, so I think Bourne will be fine."

Someone in the mystified crowd hooted with laughter.

"My dad says he's really sorry about not finishing out the season for you as a driver. But, you know, this particular award is for the owner of the very best team. So even though Ricky Rowlands did the actual driving for him this year, my dad says he just keeps on winning because he's the guts behind the operation."

In the audience, Rowlands looked a little nonplused.

"Here's the deal, I think. I thought a lot about this and finally figured it out. My dad only liked to drive fast because nobody cared if he crashed or not. He says he kept looking for something that ended up being behind him the whole time. Now he's got me and my mom and this new baby so we can't have him driving into walls, and he says that's okay with him. But he promises he'll take the wheel of his own car every once in a while because he doesn't trust anyone else to win at places like Daytona and Talledega. But in the meantime, he says to tell you that he happened to look over his shoulder and he finally found where he belonged.

"Thank you." She stepped back from the microphone and curtsied, red velvet, pigtails, and all.

* * * * *

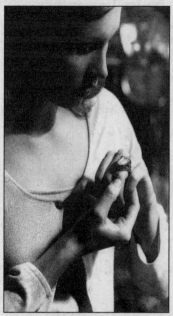

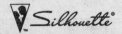

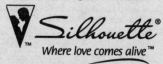

Silhouette®

COMING NEXT MONTH

#1177 THE PRINCESS'S BODYGUARD—Beverly Barton
The Protectors
Rather than be forced to marry, Princess Adele of Orlantha ran away, determined to prove that her betrothed was a traitor. With her life in danger, she sought the help of Matt O'Brien, the security specialist sent to bring her home. To save her country, Adele proposed a marriage of convenience to Matt—fueled by a very inconvenient attraction....

#1178 SARAH'S KNIGHT—Mary McBride
Romancing the Crown
Sir Dominic Chiara, M.D., couldn't cure his only son, Leo. Without explanation, Leo quit speaking, and child psychologist Sarah Hunter was called to help. Dominic couldn't keep from falling for the spirited beauty, as together they found the root of Leo's problem and learned that he held the key to a royal murder—and their romance.

#1179 CROSSING THE LINE—Candace Irvin
When their chopper went down behind enemy lines, U.S. Army pilot Eve Paris and Special Forces captain Rick Bishop worked together to escape. Their attraction was intense, but back home, their relationship crashed. Then, to save her career, Eve and Rick had to return to the crash site, but would they be able to salvage their love?

#1180 ALL A MAN CAN DO—Virginia Kantra
Trouble in Eden
Straitlaced detective Jarek Denko gave up the rough Chicago streets to be a small-town police chief and make a home for his daughter. Falling for wild reporter Tess DeLucca wasn't part of the plan. But the attraction was immediate—and then a criminal made Tess his next target. Now she and Jarek needed each other more than ever....

#1181 THE COP NEXT DOOR—Jenna Mills
After her father's death, Victoria Blake learned he had changed their identities and fled their original home. Seeking the truth, she traveled to steamy Bon Terre, Louisiana. What she found was sexy sheriff Ian Montague. Victoria wasn't sure what she feared most: losing her life to her father's enemies, or losing her heart to the secretive sheriff.

#1182 HER GALAHAD—Melissa James
When Tessa Earldon married David Oliveri, the love of her life, she knew her family disapproved, but she never imagined they would falsify charges to have him imprisoned. After years of forced separation, Tessa found David again. But before they could start their new life, they had to clear David's name and find the baby they thought they had lost.

SIMCNM0902